I0666190

The Wolf Chronicles II

First Edition

Published by The Nazca Plains Corporation
Las Vegas, Nevada
2008

ISBN: 978-1-934625-82-8

Published by

The Nazca Plains Corporation ®
4640 Paradise Rd, Suite 141
Las Vegas NV 89109-8000

PUBLISHER'S NOTE
The Wolf Chronicles II is a work of fiction created wholly by *Alan Weyant's* imagination.
All characters are fictional and any resemblance to any persons living or deceased is
purely by accident. No portion of this book reflects any real person or events.

Cover Photo, Evgeny Kan
Art Director, Blake Stephens

Dedication

Dedicated to the memory of my older brother, Lloyd Weyant, who died of AIDS in 1985. As a gay man living in New York City in the 1980's, he helped pave the way for me in coming to terms with my own sexuality. Thank You.

The Wolf Chronicles II

First Edition

Alan Weyant

Table of Contents

Chapter 1

The Sling

Wolf lay in the sling suspended in a corner of my dungeon. His muscled physique was stretched in a wide spread-eagled position with his booted feet held apart by leather stirrups fastened to the support chains on the lower end of the sling. His arms were also bound, but by thick leather restraints locked around his wrists to the upper chains.

I stood gazing down at my 24 year old half Apache Indian, half Mexican-American slave boy, admiring the look of his sculpted body and his handsome, chiseled face. His golden bronze skin gleamed with a coating of sweat in the warmth of my dungeon, showing off the definition of his solid muscles that had been honed by months of intense, hard core bodybuilding. The color of his skin contrasted with the black leather of his chaps, boots, and slave collar, along with the raven black of Wolf's thick mane of hair that was hanging down almost to the floor. His chest rose and fell with his breathing as he silently awaited whatever I chose to do to his helpless body. His fat, eight inch cock was already fully erect, the veins running the length of the shaft throbbing slightly as it arced up and over his washboard abs.

I reached out and began to gently squeeze and twist his thick, pumped nipples. His brown tits stood out from his chest, surrounded by the reddish scar tissue of his nipple brandings. Wolf sighed with pleasure at my light touch. He loved having his nipples worked and tortured as hard as I could torture them, but he also enjoyed light, pleasurable nipple play as well. His sighs turned into moans as I slowly began to work the thick tits harder and harder. His muscles began to flex and strain throughout his entire torso as the intensity of the sensations slowly built in his erect nipples before spreading into his thick, sculpted pecs.

I continued teasing his tits for just a few moments before I released them and

1

stepped to the shelf containing my toys. Picking up a rubber ball gag, I strode over next to my bound slave's head.

"Open up, boy." I growled.

Wolf immediately opened his mouth wide, allowing me to stuff the gag in, filling his mouth. I buckled the straps on the gag around his head, preventing him from pushing the ball out of his mouth.

I grinned wickedly down into my slave's deep brown eyes. "That'll keep the neighbors from hearing you scream, boy."

Wolf knew I was joking. The nearest neighbors were fully a quarter mile away, and my dungeon was totally sound proofed anyway.

He grunted into the gag as I started to work on his nipples again. This time however, I started twisting and squeezing them harder than before. Wolf's body began to squirm, writhing on the sling as the level of pain increased in his nipples, every muscle in his now sweat-soaked physique flexing and bulging. The veins started to pop out across his rock hard pecs and on his thick arms as he struggled and strained against his restraints. The tendons and cords stood out on his neck as he grunted and groaned into the gag. His eyes were wide open as he watched my hands straining as I tortured his nipples.

I rolled, stretched, and twisted his tits as hard as I could with my fingers until my hands began to get sore from the strain of torturing the thick knobs of tender flesh. Wolf moaned into the gag when I went to the shelves holding my toys and retrieved some of Wolf's favorite torture devices, a pair of alligator nipple clamps with sharpened metal teeth. I attached the clamps to his thick, pumped nips, causing him to moan again, this time in his unique combination of pleasure and pain. I knew from the pleading, almost desperate, look in his eyes that he was ready for some extreme torture by now.

I walked around the sling until I was between Wolf's spread legs. I slowly started to stroke his exposed asshole with my fingers. Wolf growled deeply in his throat when I started to slowly insert one finger into his hot hole.

I looked into his eyes and asked him; "You want it, don't you, boy? You want this hole stretched and fucked, right, boy?"

Wolf nodded his head vigorously, wordlessly begging me to torture him and violate his ass. I gave him another wicked smile.

"Well, you're going to have to wait just a little bit longer, boy!" I told him.

Wolf whimpered in anguished frustration. I loved to tease and torment Wolf by telling him what I was going to do to torture him, but then making him wait for the pleasure pain that he loved so much.

It was a variation on the old "first degree, second degree and third degree" of torture and punishment that had been used for hundreds of years. The first degree of torture was to tell the victim what you were going to do to him. The second degree was to show someone else enduring the torture the victim was going to have to endure. The third degree was to actually torture the victim. I really loved giving Wolf the third degree, literally!

I moved the small table to a position between his legs, setting up my collection of dildos and other ass toys. Wolf moaned again into his gag at the sight. He knew from experience that he would have to take most, if not all of the various sized dildos up his hole before I would fuck him myself.

He laid his head back on the support at the end of the sling, his eyes closed, as I lubed up one of my smaller dildos and slowly, teasingly, inserted it into his tight hole. Wolf almost purred with pleasure around the gag as the latex shaft slowly disappeared inside him.

Wolf started grunting and growling deeply in his throat in rhythm with the dildo sliding in and out of his ass as I started to slowly fuck him with my toy. His thick chest rose and fell faster and faster while his washboard six-pack abs rippled as his breathing increased along with the speed of my dildo fucking.

I pumped the dildo in and out of Wolf's ass until he was moaning constantly, his solid torso glistening with sweat. Pulling the dildo from his ass, I exchanged it for one a full four inches longer and two inches thicker.

Wolf moaned louder as the bigger shaft impaled him, stretching his hole wider.

I pumped this dildo in and out of his ass for several minutes, Wolf moaning the entire time, before I slowly pulled it out.

I gave him a evil grin as I told him; "Now for something totally different, boy!"

Wolf groaned into the gag when I held up a set of gut balls, a string of eight hard rubber balls on a leather thong. I lubed up the first ball and slowly worked it into Wolf's hole. He writhed and strained his muscles as the ball stretched his sphincter. It took about five minutes or so, but I eventually had all eight of the balls up Wolf's ass! He was gasping for air at the feeling of the balls totally filling his gut. I stroked my hands over the rock hard washboard of his abs, feeling the muscles flex with each labored breath, then ran my hands over his glistening ribcage, feeling each rib bulging under his skin as he gasped for air around the gag.

He really began to shriek into his gag as I grasped the end of the thong sticking out of his asshole and began to slowly pull the balls out, one at a time. His entire body heaved and twisted as each ball popped out of him.

By the time the fourth ball slipped out of Wolf's guts, his throbbing cock began to twitch and pulsate. When the sixth ball slid out, Wolf arched his back and shot a huge load of cum, covering his washboard abs, and spraying up onto his chest, howling into the gag the entire time!

I leered down at him, firmly pulling the last two balls out of him, while at the same time pulling on the chain between the nipple clamps, stretching his tits with the clamps. Wolf was almost frantic in his struggles against the restraints holding him spread-eagled.

I grinned wickedly down at my panting, gasping slave. "You don't think we're done, do you boy? Just because you couldn't control yourself doesn't mean that I have to cut my fun short! I might just have to add another couple of hours to your torture because you came without permission, boy! Would you like that, slave?"

He looked up at me with a look of total trust in his eyes, vigorously nodding his head.

"Good, because we're just getting started, boy." I snarled down at him.

I picked up the next size dildo, slowly sliding it into my slave's stretched, but still willing hole. We continued like this, using progressively longer and thicker dildos until Wolf's ass was holding a monstrous latex cock, a full fifteen inches long, as thick as my forearm! I could actually see the muscles of Wolf's washboard abs bulge as the thick head of the huge dildo slid in and out of his gut.

Wolf was whining and moaning around the gag filling his mouth, his entire body writhing with a combination of pain and lust. He started to howl into the gag as I started to pull on the chain between the nipple clamps again with one hand, while I drove the huge dildo deeply into his ass with the other. I tortured my slave's ass and nipples for a few more minutes before I slowly pulled the dildo out of his ass. Wolf sighed with pleasure at the feel of the thick, mushroomed head of the inhumanly large cock slipping out of his ass.

I smiled down at my helpless slave, spread-eagled in the sling. "I know what you want, boy. You've earned it."

He watched intently as I began to spread lube on my right hand and arm. Wolf was about to get his first fist-fucking in several months. I felt that he was now ready for it. Also, it was a reward for his dedication to our bodybuilding workouts. We were both preparing for a contest in late February, several months from now.

One of the things I loved about my boy was the fact that whenever he was getting fisted, or taking an exceptionally large dildo in his ass, he did it without the use of poppers or any other drugs. My most unbreakable rule, the one that would get any slave, even Wolf, booted out my front door faster than anything else, was no drugs of any kind!

I knew from painful and horrific personal experience what damage drugs could do, so none were allowed. Wolf had agreed with my rule from the first day we had met.

Wolf sighed as I slid three fingers into his already stretched ass. They slid easily into him. The dildos had opened up his ass, and Wolf had remarkable muscle control as well. I could dildo fuck him, or even fist fuck him, then slip my cock into him minutes later, and it would feel like fucking an almost virgin ass.

I worked the three fingers in and out of him for just a few moments before adding a fourth finger. Wolf moaned with pleasure as I slid into him up to the widest part of my hand, just under my thumb.

In a few more minutes I asked him, "Are you ready for it, boy?"

He nodded vigorously, his eyes full of lust and desire, then closed his eyes and waited.

I curled my thumb inside my other four fingers and slowly began working my hand into Wolf's ass. He groaned and grunted as I slid my curled hand deeper and deeper into him, until with one final push, my entire hand slipped past his sphincter and into his gut.

Wolf's muscles writhed and strained against his restraints at the feel of my fingers slowly spreading open inside him. He moaned as I slowly worked my fingers to stimulate his prostate, his cock rock hard across his abs. His dick was streaming with pre-cum, leaving a small pool on his belly.

Wolf's eyes flew open wide and he howled into his gag as I pulled on the chain between his tit clamps while driving my fist another two inches deeper into him.

"That's it boy, that's what you wanted, isn't it?" I taunted him while torturing his nipples and stretching his ass at the same time.

He nodded his head and grunted an "Uh-mum" into his gag.

"You want more, slave? You want it deeper, boy?"

He nodded and grunted again.

"O.K. Get ready then, boy. Your ass is mine!" I hissed menacingly at him.

I started slowly but deliberately working my hand deeper and deeper into my slave's body. It took a while, but eventually I was into Wolf's ass all the way to my elbow, his stretched sphincter muscle gripping my forearm. Wolf had already shot one load of cum across his solid abs, but his cock showed no signs of softening. All the time I was working my arm into him, I was also stretching and pulling on his tortured nipples. Wolf was gasping for air at the mixture of sensations, the unfamiliar feeling of my arm filling his gut combined the sharp pain of the clamps biting into and stretching his tits. He was writhing in pain, while at the same time moaning with pleasure. I knew he was ecstatic with the pain in his nipples and his gut, and the knowledge that he had surrendered his body totally to my control.

I kept my hand buried in his ass for about ten minutes or so minutes before the feel of his gut wrapped tightly around my hand started to cause my fingers to cramp.

"O.K. boy, I'm coming out." I told him.

Wolf moaned in ecstasy at the feel of my arm withdrawing from his gut. He then growled into the gag as the widest part of my hand popped out of his hole.

I wiped my hand and arm off on a towel and immediately stepped around to the end of the sling, standing over Wolf's head. I unfastened the head support from the chains at the end of the sling, allowing Wolf's head to lower backwards towards the floor. I unbuckled the gag from around his head and, pulling the rubber ball from his mouth, immediately drove my thick, swollen cock deeply into his throat.

I growled in my throat at the feel of his hot mouth working on the sensitive head of my nine inch cock. Wolf was an expert cocksucker, and knew how to stimulate me better than anyone else who had ever sucked my dick, even when he had to suck my cock upside down!

His tongue slid up and down the length of my cock, tracing the veins bulging on my hard shaft. Wolf groaned and whined around the dick filling his mouth as I pulled on the chain between his tender nipples, stretching them away from his solid pecs.

Every muscle in his glistening, sculpted torso flexed and writhed before my eyes as I relentlessly fucked his mouth and tortured his nipples. The sweat was running down my own hard body, partly from the heat of the dungeon, and partly from the exertions of slamming my cock deeply into the sucking mouth of my torture slave!

It only took about four or five minutes before I felt the familiar tightening sensation in my balls.

"Get ready, boy!" I gasped, even as I increased the speed of the mouth fucking and the nipple torture of my slave. Within another thirty seconds or so, I howled as I shot a huge load of cum deeply into Wolf's mouth as I pulled on the chain between his tits harder then before. He moaned even as his throat muscles worked, swallowing every drop of my load. Wolf loved to drink as much of my sperm as I could feed him.

Finally, I pulled my softening cock from Wolf's hot, sucking mouth. His head flopped back as his chest rose and fell, gasping for air. I bent down over my boy and took the head of his still hard dick into my mouth. Wolf was so turned on that he came for the second time this torture session, this time in my mouth, howling as I sucked his cum from his cock while stretching his tits.

His orgasm spent, Wolf softly moaned "Oh God, thank you, Sir."

As I gently removed the clamps from his sore nipples, he moaned and writhed on the sling. I loved to watch Wolf's ripped, sculpted physique struggling against his restraints as I inflicted whatever form of torment I was in the mood for on his body. Wolf was a true masochist. He enjoyed levels of pain that other men couldn't have endured. As I had told him from the first day that we ever met, I would torture him to his limits, and sometimes far beyond them. It was the only way to expand his limits of endurance.

Finally, I started to release my slave from his bondage in the sling. When he was totally free of the restraints, he slowly stood up in front of me, and then without a word being spoken, knelt down and began to lick my boots clean, as was his duty as my slave.

I watched him clean both of my polished boots. When he was finished, I told him, "Up, boy."

As Wolf stood up in front of me, I wrapped my arms around him and pulled his hot, sweat slick body against mine. "How's your ass, boy?" I asked him with a leering smile on my face.

"Oh God, it feels like a railroad tunnel, Sir! I haven't been stretched like that for a while, Sir. Thank you!" Wolf moaned into my chest as I held him tightly.

"You do know that this means that you'll have to do an extra hard workout the next time we do legs, boy. No one ever won a bodybuilding contest with a floppy ass!"

Wolf looked up at me for just a second or two before he started to giggle. His laughter built, until he was howling. I began to chuckle at his display of mirth. I knew it was a form of release of some of the excess endorphins my slave always had whenever I tortured him. He would either cry his feelings out, or he would laugh them out. Either way, the release was cathartic for both of us after a hard scene.

I held my hard-bodied slave until his laughing jag quieted and he was breathing normally again. He looked up into my eyes, tears from his laughter still running down his cheeks.

"After an ass-plowing like that, I feel ready to go work out right now!" He said to me.

"I don't think the guys at the gym would like having you show up this late in the evening, considering the fact that they closed about an hour ago, boy!" I chided him teasingly. "Besides, we need to work on what we're gonna wear to the Halloween party tomorrow night. Danny had some suggestions, and I think I've decided how we're going to dress, if it's all right with you."

Wolf smiled at me and said; "You know that I'll love whatever you and Danny have come up with. After all, he's the uniform expert, and you know I love a man in uniform!" Wolf waggled his eyebrows in a leering manner, looking for all the world like a manic Groucho Marx!

I laughed at his antics, hugging him close to my chest.

"You're a nut. You know that?" I said, before I kissed him.

I loved the fact that my sexy slave-boy/lover had a wonderfully wacky sense of humor, something he had proved to me many times in the sixteen months or so that we had been together. Wolf's fun loving nature had seen him through some trying times in his life, including a rape by an older cousin, the death of his parents, and the rejection of his gay life by almost all of his childhood friends.

It also seemed to help him endure the rigorous and excruciatingly painful tortures that I submitted him to on a regular basis. Of course, the fact that he was a natural slave and a true masochist helped, as well!

I counted myself among the luckiest leather masters in all of the city, if not the country to have such a gorgeous, muscular and sexy man totally in love with me. Since the day we had first met, Wolf had been the perfect slave and lover.

"Well, the idea that Danny and I came up with should fit right in with the theme of this year's party, 'Captives and Captors'. I don't think anyone else in the city could pull it off as well as we could. Of course, no one else in the city has such a handsome Indian slave, either." I smiled at Wolf. "I hope you don't mind going to the biggest leather man's costume party in the state almost butt naked, boy."

Wolf grinned up at me and said; "Mind? Are you kidding, Sir? I'd love it!"

I laughed. "I told Danny that you'd say something like that. He totally agrees with me that you're about the biggest exhibitionist in town!"

Wolf kissed me and said; "Maybe so, but what else could I do when I'm with the hottest master around?"

I put a mock thoughtful expression on my face and said; "Well, you're right about that, of course. You are with the hottest master in town."

Wolf looked into my eyes and broke up laughing again.

When he had finally calmed down I told him; "Enough of that, boy. Let's get undressed and relax a bit."

After Wolf had stripped off his chaps and boots, and then did the same for me, we walked into the next room of my dungeon area and went into the sauna in the corner by the outside door. The heat hit me almost like a physical blow, but it felt good. We sat on one of the benches in the dimly lit sauna, just absorbing the heat. After about five minutes or so, we were both drenched with sweat. I turned on the bench I was on and, with a groan, lay out flat, stretching my arms out before putting my hands under my head. I closed my eyes and just relaxed, feeling the tension and aches flow out of my muscles. We had both been doing heavy workouts in the gym in training for the upcoming citywide bodybuilding contest we had entered.

I could feel the sweat flowing down the sides of my torso. After a few minutes, I became aware of another sensation. I opened my eyes a crack, and saw Wolf sitting on the bench one level down from where I was laying. He had started to gently stroke a finger across my flat, hard, six-pack abs. I knew Wolf loved to worship my muscles, and he was turned on by a hot sweaty muscular body almost as much as I was, which was one of the reasons we both loved using the sauna as much as we did.

His gentle fingering of my body continued for a few minutes, until I heard him shifting position on his bench, followed by the almost electric feeling of his mouth surrounding my right nipple, accompanied by the soft feel of his hair brushing across my body. I moaned with pleasure as he started to suck on my tit. His hot mouth felt even hotter than the air in the sauna, even though I knew that was impossible.

He sucked on my nipple for a few minutes, then began to lick my pecs. Wolf shifted his position again, climbing up onto the bench I was stretched out on to first straddle me, and then to gently lay down flat on top of me.

I moaned softly with pleasure at the feel of his hot, sweat-slick muscles sliding across my torso. My hands began to knead the solid surface of his broad, rippling back.

Wolf slid up on top of me until he was gazing straight down into my eyes.

He gave me a smile, then softly said; "God, I love you sir."

His mouth clamped down on mine in a passionate, almost fierce kiss. Wolf's hands slipped up to grasp my head as he pressed his mouth even harder against mine. Our tongues intertwined as the kiss continued for what felt like an eternity. My arms tightened around Wolf's sculpted body, feeling every muscle and sinew that I could reach.

When Wolf finally broke the kiss and pulled back to gaze into my eyes again, I couldn't tell if the streams of moisture running down his face was sweat or tears. Wolf slid slowly down my torso, kissing and licking my heated skin as he moved. He buried his face in my left armpit and licked at the sweat pooling there. When he had cleaned out as much of the sweat as he could, he immediately did the same with my right pit. When his pit licking was done, Wolf went to work on my nipples with both his mouth and his hands. He sucked on my tits and pulled and twisted my nipple rings just enough to make me groan with pleasure.

Slowly, almost teasingly, he worshipped every muscle on my sweat drenched torso, licking me from armpits to the base of my balls. Finally, I had to reluctantly tell him to stop, as I was beginning to get really overheated in the sweltering sauna.

Somewhat groggily we walked to the small bathroom in the dungeon and indulged in a warm shower to slowly cool down from the intense heat. I loved the feel of Wolf's strong hands washing my body with my favorite liquid soap. I then did the same for him, enjoying the sensations of my hands feeling and caressing every inch of his sculpted body. I used Wolf's favorite herbal shampoo to thoroughly wash his mane of thick, jet black hair that hung down almost midway down his back, and flowed down past his nipples in the front. I had loved Wolf's hair ever since the very first moment I had ever seen him in the San Francisco Eagle one hot summer afternoon.

His hair, combined with his sculpted, Amerindian/Latino features, made Wolf the single sexiest man I had ever seen in my 32 years. Finding out that he was as attracted to me as I was to him made our relationship all the more special. The fact that he was also a natural masochist with the highest pain threshold I had ever encountered was just icing on the cake!

When I was done with his hair I said; "O.K. boy, time to get out of here and go cool off for a bit before we have dinner."

We climbed the stairs up into the main floor of our home. I went over to the couch in the living room and took my favorite place in the corner. Wolf immediately sat down between my spread legs and leaned back against my chest. I wrapped my arms around his torso and held him tightly. We sat for a few minutes before I said "I know your birthday is coming up in November. Any thoughts as to what you want for a present?"

Wolf turned and smiled shyly. "What else could I need? I've got a great home, good friends and I'm living with the hottest and sexiest man I could ever want!"

"Flatterer!" I said with a grin. "You know what they say. Flattery will get you anywhere, but groveling will get you anything!"

Wolf giggled. "I've never heard the second part of that anywhere. You just made that up!"

I feigned a look of indignation. "Are you doubting my infinite wisdom in such matters, boy? How dare you, you miscreant!" I gave Wolf an imperious, haughty look.

He stared back at me for a few seconds before he started to laugh. I think he recognized the look of barely concealed mirth in my eyes. I held my expression for just a few seconds more before I gave in to the silliness of our conversation as well, and started to laugh myself. Wolf's laughter built as I started to tickle his ribs while my arms held him tightly. Our laughter built and built. Every time I would work my fingers into Wolf's armpits or down the sides of his torso a fresh gale of laughter would be torn from him as he twisted and wriggled in my grasp, which in turn caused me to laugh harder myself.

Finally after long minutes of continuous laughing, I let Wolf go. I could barely catch my breath and Wolf was gasping for air as tears coursed down his cheeks. He turned to me, his chest heaving, and kissing me deeply one again, said; "God, I love you, Sir."

I pulled him to me again and whispered into his ear as I hugged him; "Wow, something else I can use to torture you. Just imagine being tied to the bed or spread out on the cross while being tickle tortured. Sounds like fun to me, boy."

Wolf chuckled and said, "Well, I like the being tied on the cross part. Not too sure about the tickling part, though."

He pulled back and I saw the gleam of mischief in his eyes.

"You might have to convince me of that part, Sir."

I pushed him away in mock displeasure and stood up, towering over him.

"Well, if that's your attitude, slave, I guess I better start convincing you right now! On your feet, boy."

Wolf stood up in front of me. I spun him around and grabbed his right wrist and bent his arm painfully up behind his back. I heard him gasp with pain, then sigh with pleasure. Frog marching him up the stairs, I pushed him into my bedroom and down on my king size bed.

As I turned down the lights from the dimmer at the headboard, I whispered; "How much convincing do you think it's gonna take, boy?"

He gazed up into my eyes and softly said; "I don't know, master. Maybe we had better start now."

As I lay down on top of my slave, I growled; "I've got all night, boy. And if that's not enough, I've got the rest of my life."

I looked down into his soft brown eyes as he whispered; "I'll be here for the rest of my life too, Sir. I'm not going anywhere."

"Damn right you're not going anywhere, boy. You remember that I own you, body and soul, Carlos Greywolf!" I growled at him, using his full name.

I kissed Wolf hard as I felt the heat of my passion begin to rise once again. I wasn't a particularly religious or spiritual person, but Wolf helped to fulfill a need in my life, that no one else ever had come close to fulfilling, even Mike, the man who had trained me up in leather. Perhaps he was my spirit guide to a better life, or maybe he was just my karmic mate, but whatever it was, I couldn't see my life going on without Wolf there with me.

Wolf and I made love to each other for an hour or so, exploring every inch of each others sculpted physiques with our hands and our tongues, before we finally made it back downstairs for a light dinner.

As Wolf was cleaning up after we had eaten, I sat and watched him working. I had rarely just watched my lover doing everyday chores, therefore I had missed out on the joy of seeing him just working around the house. Even while wearing a pair of baggy gym shorts, his body was like a finely honed machine, flowing from one task to another without a wasted move. Watching him do the dishes and clean up the kitchen just gave me a deeper appreciation of just how lucky I was to have this exceptional person in my life. Right then and there I knew how I was going to surprise him this upcoming Christmas. This would be a holiday he wouldn't soon forget!

Chapter 2

Sweat

The next morning I finished my usual morning work on my computer, taking care of any messages or problems with the software business in Indiana I had inherited on the death of my father and mother. We had breakfast before I told Wolf that it was time that we were headed into San Francisco to see Danny. I had talked to him a couple of nights before, and he was expecting us. Since it was a Saturday, he would be at home and not at work at the car dealership where he was the sales manager. As we drove into the city in my Magnum wagon, my everyday car, I told Wolf I wanted him to go into full slave mode for our visit with Danny.

Wolf smiled and said; "Whatever you want me to do, Sir."

I grinned back at him and answered; "Of course you'll do whatever I want you to do. After all, you are a slave, right boy?"

Wolf chuckled and nodded his agreement. "Oh yes, my imperial majesty. Whatever you say, your highness!" He ducked, grinning widely as I tried to give him a dope-slap on the back of the head for being such a smart-ass.

Wolf knew he could get away with that behavior as long as it was just the two of us. He knew not to act up like that in public.

Danny Hendrickson was my best friend in the city. A hard core leatherman, he was also one of the nicest and funniest people that I had ever known. We had a friendship going back quite a few years. Danny was a handsome, lanky but muscular strawberry blonde with a ripped physique and a shock of reddish blonde hair.

When we arrived at Danny's house, I waited for Wolf to get out and open my door, as was one of his duties. Danny was awaiting us at his door. I gave him a big hug once we were inside, and Wolf dropped to his knees and paid proper respect to Danny's boots, as a good slave should do to any master.

I asked Danny; "How's Eddie's retraining coming along? I haven't seen him out with you for a while." Eddie Wong was Danny's 25 year old Chinese-American slave boy. He was enduring a period of forced training after publicly misbehaving in the bar and forgetting some of his slave rules of conduct.

Danny sighed and said, "Well, it's been tougher than I thought it would have to be. Eddie's really sorry he screwed up, but I really do need to punish him. The only problem is that I feel like I'm beating a puppy! He's trying so hard that it's tough for me to be so hard on him. Maybe he's ready to be forgiven."

I told him with a huge grin; " Aah, you're just a wuss. If you're having that hard of a time working him over, maybe you just need to see if he'll behave for a while. Try cutting him some slack and see what happens. Meanwhile, how about showing us what you came up with for the party?"

Danny brightened and said; "I think you guys will really like what I found. I picked up another collection of uniforms from a sale on the Internet. One of the uniforms is the wrong size for me, but I think it'll fit you perfectly, Eric. Come on in and let's see."

We followed Danny into the spare bedroom where he stored his extensive collection of uniforms from many eras of history, and many countries.

My particular fetishes were long haired men, nipple torture, muscles and sweat, while Danny's were uniforms and period clothing. He had one of the largest collections that I had ever seen. Danny was happy wearing leather for a scene, but put him into a uniform, and the transformation was astonishing. He could change his personality to match whatever era and nationality of uniform he was wearing. It was just amazing to see, and sometimes really funny, as well.

I loved being able to find a bit of humor in a scene, contrary to the attitude of a lot of leathermen, who seemed to take themselves much too seriously. Luckily, Wolf shared my feelings about finding something to lighten the mood of a scene as well. Sometimes I would add to Wolf's suffering in a scene by forbidding him to laugh or make any sound during a session of torture, even though I would make a comment or a quip to him or to any observers. It was sometimes a real hoot to watch him desperately trying to keep from laughing even as he was being tortured.

Danny rooted around for just a few moments before coming out of one of the storage closets with a clothes hanger covered with a cleaners bag. He handed me the hangar and a pair of highly polished tall boots.

"Here you go. Try this on for size, and I'll see what extras it needs to finish it off. While you're doing that, I'll try to find what I have for Wolf to wear as well."

I started to undress as Danny dug into a dresser drawer and started to pull out bits of clothes and hand them to Wolf. When I was undressed, I uncovered the clothes on the hangar. I pulled out the pants and slipped them on. They were a pair of dark blue trousers with a bright yellow stripe down the side of each of the legs. Next was a black undershirt and then a blue jumper type top that matched the pants. I then pulled on the boots which fit me perfectly. The outfit was completed with a black leather belt for the pants, a bandanna around my throat, doeskin leather gloves, and a white western style hat, fastened up on one side.

Danny walked around appraising the look of the uniform, before giving me a smile and a thumbs up. When I stepped in front of the full length mirror to look at myself, I couldn't help but whistle appreciatively at the look of the uniform.

Danny said; "That's an authentic replica of an 1880's seventh cavalry uniform. It came from a movie studio auction of clothes and props from some old westerns that was on line. I thought that it would fit you when I saw it. I knew it was a bit too big for me."

While I was dressing, Wolf had stripped down and was now wearing just a soft leather loincloth supported by a woven leather belt worn low around his waist that seemed to accentuate his washboard ab muscles. He also had on a pair of fringed suede moccasin style boots that came almost up to his knees. The light doeskin color of the loincloth and boots complimented his golden bronze skin tone perfectly.

I smiled appreciatively. "Wow! With a few accessories, you're going to be the perfect Indian captive. What do you think of the idea of being my prisoner, boy?"

Wolf grinned at me and said in a mock Indian voice; "Ugh! Me think you one hot stud solider! You tie me up, me follow you anywhere!"

I rolled my eyes and cuffed him playfully along side the head as I chuckled at his antics.

Danny laughed as well, knowing about Wolf's irrepressible sense of humor. I really meant what I had said about Wolf's looks. He was really sexy looking in just the loincloth and boots. For some reason, the exposed sides of his sculpted thighs seemed to emphasize the mass and the shape of the muscles, making them seem even more perfectly developed. The fact that he was so close to being naked without being totally exposed was somehow sexier than if he was nude. I guess the titillation factor was at work, and the fact that you couldn't see everything was very erotic.

Danny smiled at both of us and said; "I'm glad that everything fit so well. I really can't see anyone else being any hotter than you two."

I told him; "Well, I guess we'll just have to wait and see who's at the party tonight."

Danny then said; "I need to go and check on Eddie. Do you want to see how he's coming along?"

"Sure, let's change and then we'll go."

After Wolf and I had changed back into our street clothes Danny led us downstairs and out to the rear of his house where his play space was located in a converted mother-in-law apartment connected to the back of the house. We stepped inside after Danny unlocked the door, and saw Eddie. He was standing in a small bondage cage that was only about one foot on a side and about seven feet high His arms were stretched straight over his head, the wrists held by a pair of heavy iron shackles fastened to the top of the cage on the outside. Every muscle in his lean torso rippled with his slightest movement, and each of his ribs was visible under his taut, tattooed skin. The cage was so small it was pressing against his body on all four sides. Eddie's head was covered by a tightly laced leather hood, with only small air holes for him to breathe. Other than the hood and a collar, Eddie was totally stripped. There were a pair of clamps clipped on his nipples, and a weight hung from his balls. He gave no indication that he was aware that there was anyone else in the room.

Danny said quietly; "I modified the hood a bit. It has a small pair of ear bud speakers in it, so he can't hear anything except for whatever music I put on the mp3 player. I found some slave training music on line that not only has music, but also includes some subliminal commands to enforce his training. I'm not sure if they really work, but I figured that it couldn't hurt!"

Eddie's chest slowly rose and fell in time with his breathing. Other than that, he was totally unable to move a muscle.

I asked Danny; "How long has he been like that?"

He replied; "This time about three hours or so. I've had him in there for as much as twelve hours at a time. Without the clamps or weights, of course."

Wolf was watching Eddie intently. I turned and asked him; "Well, what do you think. Want to try it sometime, boy? I bet you could fit in there if we squeezed a bit."

Wolf just smiled slightly and said; "Anytime you want, Sir. Or should I say, Sirs!"

I just gave him an enigmatic smile and winked at Danny. We turned and walked back into the main house, Danny locking the door to his dungeon behind him.

"So, I guess I'll see you guys at the party. I'm looking forward to see what you do to finish Wolf's outfit."

I said; "I think you'll like it. Are you gonna bring Eddie?"

Danny shook his head. "He really wants to go, but I think I need to continue his training. It'll be a punishment for him to be left here alone, just thinking about what he did. I hate to do it to him, but he did bring it on himself."

I shook my head in sympathy and told him; "Well, you do what you think is best. I bet he'll think twice before he ever screws up like that again!"

I gave Danny a hug, then Wolf did the same.

After we had left Danny's house, I told Wolf we had a few more errands to run before we headed back over the bridge towards home. We visited a few shops in the city to pick up a few finishing touches for our outfits for the party, then headed to the gym we visited in town. Today was the day in our workout rotation to do our back and shoulder workout.

We drove to the gym, just off of Folsom St. and went in. Wolf carried the gym bag with our workout clothes. I greeted a few friends in the gym before we went into the locker room to change.

I said to Wolf; "Are you ready for a heavy-duty workout, boy? We both really have to begin to ramp up the intensity if we're going to be ready to compete in a few months."

Wolf answered; "As long as you're there to push me, Sir, I'll do the best that I can."

I gave him a quick hug and said; "Let's go show the rest of these gym rats what a real workout is!"

We walked out onto the main workout floor and spent a few minutes just stretching and doing some light aerobics to warm up. We headed for the freeweight area and began our series of back and shoulder exercises, using progressively heavier and heavier weights. I enjoyed working out with Wolf more than any other workout partner that I had ever had. He seemed to know instinctively what I wanted him to do at any time in our workouts. The fact that he was almost as strong as me helped when he had to spot me when I was doing exercises with an extremely heavy weight.

I noticed as usual that we attracted a lot of attention, mostly because of the intensity of our workout, but also because the gym allowed working out shirtless. Wolf and I were just wearing gym shorts and sneakers. A lot of the guys watched us working out, then watched as we practiced some basic posing in a corner of the gym that had mirrors set up in such a way that you could see almost your entire body in the multiple reflections. I had been trying to coach Wolf in some basic techniques for posing in a contest, but I was struggling to remember them, since it had been several years since I had last competed. Nonetheless, Wolf seemed to be a natural and he looked incredibly hot and sexy posing, his entire physique gleaming with sweat and rippling with muscle.

We even started to playfully compete with each other with hot and sexy poses in front of the mirrors. I would do a pose like a full double lat pose, which showed off the full width of my upper body, and Wolf would just moan with barely disguised lust. Then he would do a different pose, showing off another part of his amazing physique, and I would have the same reaction to his chiseled body!

I was somewhat bigger than Wolf, being a good seven inches taller and about forty pounds heavier, but Wolf was just a bit more cut and ripped. I was going to compete as a heavyweight, while Wolf was going into the middleweight class.

I had almost forgotten what a turn-on it was to pose nearly nude, muscles straining and flexing in front of a group of guys that were hot and horny, lusting for my body. I had to be honest with myself and admit that it was a real ego boost. Luckily, Wolf was really good at keeping me grounded with a humorous comment or two that kept me from turning back into an arrogant, self absorbed jerk. I had seen too many of them over the years at various gyms, and had even become one of them myself, much to my eventual shame. I was proud of my muscles, and I was proud of Wolf's as well, but now I tried to be low key about our accomplishments.

Our workout lasted almost three hours, at the end of which, we were both dog tired, and drenched with sweat, but with a great pump in our back and shoulder muscles. We headed back into the locker room to strip down, then headed for the steam room with just towels around our waists. The steam felt really good as we both just leaned back and let the heat work deeply into our muscles. After a few minutes, the door opened and in came a couple of young, muscular African-American guys that had been working out at the same time as Wolf and I. They sat across from us, but I noticed that they exchanged furtive glances with each other upon seeing us in the steam room.

We all sat silently for a few minutes more before one of the other guys said; "We saw you two working out. You were really going at it. Of course, I guess that's how both of you got so good looking. You're both really built."

I smiled and thanked him for the compliment. We all started chatting then. They introduced themselves as Jamal and Ricardo.

Jamal was about 6' tall, and amazingly well built. He couldn't have had much more than 4 or 5 percent body fat. The most striking thing about his appearance however was the fact that his body was totally hairless, from his head all the way down to his feet, with the exception of a neatly trimmed mustache and goatee, which added to his exotic look.

Ricardo was just as well built, and even more ripped. The thing I noticed about him that excited me the most, however, was the fact that he had his hair cornrowed and woven into tight braids that hung down to his thick shoulders.

They were in town for a few days, visiting from Los Angeles. We took turns answering their questions about things like our contest training, how long we had been together, and so forth. The more we talked, the closer they shifted to where Wolf and I were sitting.

Finally, Jamal said; "I hope you don't think I'm being too forward, but I'd really like to see what your biceps feel like. You really have great arms."

I smiled, said; "Not a problem," and did a full double biceps pose. Jamal whistled softly as he reached out and stroked his fingers over my arms, tracing the veins that coursed over my biceps and forearms.

"Wow, that's fucking amazing. They feel like rocks." He breathed.

"Wolf, show Ricardo your arms, boy." Wolf grinned at him and did an identical double arm shot. Ricardo felt Wolf's arms, just like Jamal was stroking mine.

I noticed that the towels around their waists were beginning to bulge as their cocks got harder and harder. Within moments the heads of two of the biggest, thickest and most perfectly formed ebony dicks I had ever seen were sticking out of the towels. Both of the cocks had to be a good ten inches long and at least seven inches around. I doubted I could have gotten much more than the head of either of the massive shafts into my mouth!

After just a few more minutes, I said; "Do you want to feel another muscle that's just as hard?" Jamal just nodded his head as I guided his hand across my chest and abs, down to my erect cock.

He moaned softly as he started to stroke my shaft. I saw that Ricardo was doing the same to Wolf's fat eight inches as well.

I leaned back against the wall of the steam room, sweat streaming down my chest as Jamal undid my towel, bent down and began to suck my dick. Ricardo watched his lover for just a moment or two before he turned and started to suck on Wolf's cock. Wolf moaned softly and leaned back next to me.

We sat side by side as the two hot men sucked our cocks, while their hands explored our hard muscles. I enjoyed watching while Wolf got a good blowjob, since I knew how much he enjoyed giving them. There was also something really erotic about having a stranger suck my cock in a semi-public place. Of course since the gym was a gay gym, this was certainly not the first time that someone's cock had been sucked in the steam room. Hell, this wasn't even the first time my cock had been sucked in the steam room!

Wolf started to moan in the way that meant that he was close to cumming. His chest began to rise and fall faster and faster, until with a gasp and a low moan, he shot his load into Ricardo's mouth. He swallowed as fast as he could, even while continuing to suck Wolf's dick, to get every drop of his sperm. Ricardo's hands were stroking and feeling Wolf's hard torso as he sucked off my boy.

Jamal had stopped sucking my cock to watch his lover take my slave's load, but now he turned back to my cock and began to suck it even harder, even while his hands tracked up and down my solid body, feeling my muscles. Within a minute, I gasped and filled his mouth with a huge load of cum. Jamal choked momentarily before managing to swallow my load. After he had drained my dick dry, he finally sat back, saying; "Oh, fuck, that was great! Thank you, Eric"

Ricardo added; "Yeah, thank you too, Wolf. That really was great. I haven't sucked a cock that hot in a while!"

Jamal said; "Both of you are really hot guys. I know you're gonna do great in your bodybuilding contest. What a pair of studs!"

I said; "Thanks. You're both pretty hot yourselves. Do you need someone to take care of those hard-ons of yours, or what?"

Jamal and Ricardo both started to answer at the same time before they both stopped and laughed. Finally Ricardo said; "Thanks, but do you mind if we take care of them ourselves?'

"Not at all. We'd love to see how you handle a cock that size!" I told them.

They both smiled at each other, then Ricardo lay back on the bench he was sitting on. Jamal lay down on top of him, head to toe, and they started to lick and suck each other's cockheads at the same time in a perfect sixty nine position. Within a very few minutes, both of them shot their loads of sperm into each other's mouths at almost the exact same time. I guess practice makes perfect. Of course, if I was able to work on a hot, sculpted ebony body, shining with sweat, and suck on a thick black cock almost a foot long I'd shoot my load pretty quickly, too!

When they were done they sat up across from us again. Both of them were smiling widely.

I chuckled and said; "I guess I'd be grinning if I got to suck on a hot black cock all the time."

Ricardo laughed and said; "That's great. We've both said how hot it is to be able to suck on a hard white dick sometimes. Especially when it's attached to a big blonde muscleman like you, Eric."

I looked at them both for a moment before bursting into laughter. Within seconds, all four of us were laughing. Any traces of embarrassment I might have felt were totally wiped out in our mutual humor.

"I'm sorry, that probably didn't come out quite right." I said when I was able to talk again. "I don't really care about what color someone is. I just think a hot man is a hot man!"

Jamal chuckled. "We both feel the same way. Don't think any more about it. We knew what you meant. Besides, look who you have for a lover." He turned and smiled at Wolf.

"How many really hot Native American men do you see everyday? He's a stud!"

Wolf just smiled his thanks.

Finally I said; "I think it's time we got out of here. It's beginning to get really hot. In more ways than one, if you know what I mean. Besides, we really have to head back home to get ready to go out tonight."

We exited the steam room and showered before getting dressed. I invited Jamal and Ricardo to come up to Sausalito and visit the house if they had time before they had to head back downstate. They both promised that they'd try to make the time.

Wolf and I headed back home to rest up a bit before the party tonight. The event didn't start until 10:00, so we had a few hours to relax. Of course, Wolf didn't know what some of the proper preparation of his for look tonight would entail!

We got back home, unloaded the assorted packages from the car, and both zonked out for a couple of hours. A good nap felt great after a hard workout, not to mention the sex in the steam room.

Finally, it came time to start to get ready. Wolf looked slightly confused when I told him it was time, as we had at least an hour before we had to leave the house in time to get to the party. I just grinned and told him to go down into the dungeon.

"What good is a captive Indian walking around almost naked, if he doesn't have a few marks to show that he is a captive?" I asked Wolf while shackling him in a standing spread-eagle position.

He just smiled and said, "You're right, of course, Sir."

Wolf moaned with pleasure and pain as I started to warm his back up with my lightweight flogger. I worked him until his skin was a glowing red, then switched to my single tail whip.

I told him "This is really gonna hurt, but it will give you the best marks, boy." Wolf silently nodded his head, steeling himself for the sharp, burning agony of the whip. His entire body strained against his restraints at the whip slashed across his broad back and shoulder muscles. I only whipped him for a minute or so, just enough to make some good stripes that wouldn't fade for a couple of days.

I stepped up and looked deeply into his eyes. "Do you want any more, or do you think that's enough, boy? Your choice."

He smiled wanly at me through his pain and said, "I think I'll need some on the front, don't you, Sir?"

O.K. boy, if that's what you want." I switched back to the flogger and, pushing his hair back, warmed up his solid pecs and washboard abs. Wolf moaned with pleasure again when I picked up the whip.

"Put your head back, boy. I don't want any chance of hitting your face." I told him.

Wolf let his head flop back as I started to whip his torso. After the third or fourth hit, he began gasping and then shrieking with pain at each hit.

Finally I decided the pattern of welts criss-crossing his muscled body was just enough to be really effective. I put down the whip and stepped back up to my gasping slave. As usual whenever he was tortured, his cock was totally hard and throbbing. I just couldn't let this hard-on go to waste. I dropped to my knees and sucked his dick into my mouth.

Wolf moaned with pleasure as I started deep-throating his swollen shaft. My hands stroked up and down his sweaty body, feeling his helpless muscles. I reached up and began to twist his nipples, causing him to groan deeply in his throat. After just a few more minutes, Wolf growled and shot a thick load of sperm into my mouth.

This time, however, I didn't swallow his load, but held it in my mouth until the semen finished shooting from his cockhead. I stood up and held Wolf's head tightly between my hands. I pressed my mouth against his mouth before opening my lips, allowing his load of cum to drip into his mouth. Wolf growled in his throat again before sticking his tongue deeply into my mouth to lick out his own sperm and swallow it.

When he had totally cleaned his own load out of my mouth, I broke the kiss and stepped back from him.

Wolf gasped, "Thank you, Sir. Thank you!"

I grinned down into his eyes and told him, "Now, we need to start getting ready."

I unshackled my slave and held him tightly for a few minutes before heading upstairs to dress for the costume party. As I changed into the uniform from Danny, Wolf started to work on his hair. He told me he wanted to try something different with it tonight. He parted it straight down the middle from front to rear, then started to separate each side into four thick strands. Each side was then woven into an intricate braid, hanging down on each side of his head from just above and behind each ear. Then Wolf attached some feathers to each braid with small leather thongs, so that they hung down his back. Next, he pulled on a leather beaded headband we had bought earlier today in a small native goods shop in the city. Wolf then slipped into the loincloth and boots we had gotten from Danny. He finished the outfit with a bone and leather choker around his throat, in place of his usual slave collar and a leather armband fastened around his right arm above the thick bicep.

Wolf said; "I used to have an outfit sort of like this when I was a kid, and I was in a ceremonial dance group back on the reservation."

When he stepped in front of the mirror to finish his outfit, all I could do was whistle in awe. He was awesome! There was something about his look that was even more erotic to me then Wolf usually was. It was impossible to say exactly what it was about him that I found so exciting.

"Holy shit, that's incredible!" I breathed when I could talk. "My God, you're hot!"

His nearly naked body gleamed in the light of the bedroom, the welts from his whipping standing out in stark contrast to the golden brown of his skin. Wolf's thick, pumped nipples were surrounded with the reddish marks of his brandings, which I had given him a little more than a month before. Every muscle rippled under his skin with his slightest movement. He turned, smiling at me before dropping to his knees and beginning to lick my highly polished, knee high boots.

"I said it before, and I'll say it again. You one hot trooper. Tie me up, me follow you anywhere!" Wolf said when he had finished with my boots.

I told him to stand up, then I hugged him tightly to me and kissed him deeply.

"Come on stud, let's go show everyone else at the party what the two best looking men in the city can do together!"

Wolf flashed a wicked grin and grunted in his Hollywood Indian voice "You betcha, solider. Me want to say hello to rest of F-Troop anyhow!"; referring to the old TV show.

I whacked him on the back of the head and gave him one of my mock glares, snapping

"O.K. Chief Thunderbutt, into the car, you smart ass."

Wolf laughed and kissed me again quickly before I picked up the last accessories for our outfits, plus a pair of topcoats to keep out the late October chill. We headed out the door and into the city.

Chapter 3

The party

We drove down across the Golden Gate Bridge into the city, and into the warehouse district near Folsom St. The leatherman's costume party was being held in an old warehouse that had been converted into a private sex club. There were apparently a lot of people already inside, going by the number of cars in the parking lot.

We parked and headed in. Once we had checked our topcoats at the check room, I put the finishing touches on our costumes. I tied Wolf's wrists together behind his back with a short length of rope, then looped a longer length around his neck, in the fashion of a lasso. Finally, I coiled up the whip I had used to give Wolf his welts and fastened it to one side of the gun belt that was a part of my uniform, opposite to the replica pistol and holster Danny had included.

When we were ready to go into the main room of the club, I pulled Wolf to me, giving him a deep kiss. Our tongues intertwined for as long as I held the kiss. Finally I pulled back from my sexy, bound slave boy.

"Ready to put on a show for everyone, boy?" I asked him.

Wolf gave me a huge grin and said "Yes, Sir. Let's go have some fun."

I led Wolf into the main room of the sex club. There were at least 150 other guys and some women there already. I felt a tug on the rope I was holding and looked back to see Wolf pretending to struggle at the other end of the rope. I caught his eye and gave him a wink. He winked back, then began to struggle harder, causing the muscles in his entire torso to ripple and bulge.

I pulled on the rope, loudly exclaiming "Damn redskin, get your ass in here!"

Wolf strained at the rope, but finally had to follow me as the loop around his throat tightened. We walked across the room, Wolf stopping and struggling the entire way, each pause ending when I would yank on the lasso, almost literally dragging him across the room by his neck. By the time we had made it to the bar, almost everyone in the room was watching us. Which, of course, was the whole idea!

I loved the fact that on the way across we heard comments like *"Damn, would I love to have someone who looks like that on the end of a leash!"* and *"Man, look at the muscles on that hot little Indian!"* I had to admit that I almost laughed out loud, though, when I heard one guy say *"Holy Shit! Those whip marks are real!"*

By the time I had pulled Wolf across the room, his body was glistening with sweat from his exertions. The room was actually warm and a bit stuffy from the number of people crowed into it even though the outside temperature was in the low fifties.

I stepped up to the bar and pulled on the rope, tugging Wolf up next to me. Then I yanked down on the rope, forcing him down onto his knees. Our eyes met briefly and he gave me a quick smile, as if to say "I'm having fun, lets keep it up."

I nodded slightly and forced him all the way down until his forehead was pressed against my right boot. I put my left foot on the back of his head, totally immobilizing him. He could only kneel there on the floor, his back painfully bent over.

I stood this way until the bartender worked his way over to me. I ordered a soft drink and just started to watch the crowd. It only took a few minutes before some of the other party goers started to come up and chat about my hot Indian captive. I removed my foot from the back of Wolf's head, allowing him to straighten up on his knees.

I looked down at Wolf, kneeling in front of me, his hands tied together behind his back, and gave him a grin. He winked at me, then began to struggle against his bonds again. Some of the other guys around us said things like "You need some help with that Indian, trooper?" and "He looks like he needs more discipline. If you need any help torturing him, let me know."

I grinned at them and said "If I need any help, I'll let you know. I'm gonna give him one more chance to behave, but if he doesn't, I hear there's a really good torture chamber here we can use. I bet I can break him!"

I looked down at the struggling, straining Wolf and said "What do you think, injun?"

Wolf looked up and growled in his Hollywood Indian voice; "White eyes never break me. Grey Wolf stronger than you ever think!" He then snarled something to me in a language I didn't understand. I had to assume it was Apache, since I knew Wolf was fluent in Apache and Spanish, as well as English.

My eyes flew open wide at what sounded like a direct challenge, and some of the other guys gave a collective gasp and chuckle at his open defiance. Of course, I knew what Wolf was doing. He was playing the defiant Indian part to the hilt. I pulled him to his feet using the rope around his neck and growled "We'll see about that, redskin! I love it when my captives claim that they're strong. It just means that I get to torture them longer before they break!"

I turned to the other guys around us at the bar and said "I guess I've got to show this injun who is the boss around here. I'll see you later."

With that, I led Wolf into the crowd. We worked our way around the party, stopping every so often to chat with friends of ours in the crowd. A lot of them complimented Wolf and I on our outfits. One of my friends from the leather club said that he'd never seen Wolf looking as sexy as he did tonight. I had to agree with him on that! His sleek black braids hung down his back, contrasting with the bronze of his glistening skin that was rippling with muscle with every movement of his body. I could see guys turning and looking and making comments wherever we went in the multi room complex where the party was being held.

For his part, Wolf seemed to really enjoy playing the part of the defiant captive. I knew that he was a natural ham and a real exhibitionist, so he was having fun.

One of the people who stopped to talk with us turned out to be one of the organizers of the party. He told me that he was working his way through the crowd, selecting couples who really exhibited the spirit of the theme of the party, and he asked us if we would like to be included in the group of guys who were going to be chosen by the crowd for some of the prizes for best costume, best slave, best master, best couple, and so forth. I told him that we would be honored. He smiled and said "Just between you and me, I personally think that you have the hottest and sexiest boy in here tonight! We'll just have to wait and see what the rest of the crowd thinks."

I thanked him again, then led my boy off into the crowd. We mingled for a while, greeting friends of ours from the area, and garnering quite a few compliments on both my uniform and on my hot, muscular captive.

Of course, I was enjoying looking at some of the other hot men and boys at the party as well. I guess the last time I had been in a group of so many good looking, hard muscled leathermen was during the last Folsom St. fair that Wolf and I had attended during pride week celebrations.

After a while, Wolf leaned in to me and whispered "Sir, I think I need to use a rest room."

I looked around until I spotted the signs for the bathrooms and led my boy over.

When we entered there was a bit of a surprise waiting inside. In one of the stalls there was a bottom boy sitting on the floor, stripped down to a pair of boots and a collar. On his head he was wearing a full head harness. Attached to the harness with a short brace was a large plastic funnel about eight inches across. Running from the bottom of the funnel was a flexible tube that led into the boy's mouth. The boy also had a pair of tight nipple clamps on his chest. His arms were spread out along the handrail of the stall and were wrapped in chains, totally securing him, while his legs were held apart by a spreader bar fastened between his ankles.

There were a couple of guys in front of us waiting their turn to piss into the funnel. Whenever anyone did piss in the funnel, the boy had no choice but to swallow. To add to his humiliation, his master had also attached a small tube to one side of the funnel with a clip. The other end of the tube was attached to a catheter sticking out of the head of the boy's cock. Every so often a stream of piss would shoot out of the tube, forcing the boy to drink his own piss time and time again.

The two guys in front of us pulled out their cocks and let loose two streams of hot piss. The slave on the floor began swallowing as fast as he could. I could see the muscles working in his throat as he drank.

When they were done, we stepped up to the bound, helpless piss slave. I reached around Wolf's body and pulled the loincloth out of the front of the belt holding it around his hips. I grasped his warm, semi-hard cock and aimed it at the funnel. Wolf gave a soft sigh as a stream of hot golden piss started to flow from his dick. I could hear the slave moan softly as he started to drink my lover's urine.

When Wolf was done, I slipped his loincloth back into place and told him to stand to one side while I relieved myself.

As we were leaving the bathroom, I asked Wolf "I wonder how long he's been there, and how long his master is gonna leave him?"

Wolf smiled at me and whispered; "Not exactly my cup of tea, so to speak, but hey, whatever turns you on!"

I looked at him with a small smile and softly told him "Speaking of things that turn you on…"

I surprised Wolf by loudly shouting at him "Damn redskin. What the hell do you think you're doing?" while giving the rope around his neck a yank. Wolf staggered slightly and shot me a look before he smiled slightly in the way that meant he knew what I was doing. He immediately began to struggle mightily against the rope binding his wrists together behind his back, and to pull and twist as if to escape from me. The thick muscles in his shoulders and upper arms bulged and flexed as he strained against the rope tied around his wrists, but to no avail. I hadn't faked his bondage. Wolf's wrists were really tied tightly together. It would take quite a while of struggling to get himself free.

Guys turned to watch as I nearly dragged my struggling boy into the room at the club where the bondage and torture equipment was located.

Wolf started snarling "No, white eyes. You not break me. Not care what you do. Grey Wolf never talk!"

I smiled grimly and said loudly "We'll see about that, injun."

Some of the other guys in the torture chamber turned to watch as I forced Wolf up against a whipping post that stood close to one wall. A couple of them stepped up and asked if I needed any help.

I told them "Sure, just hold his arms so he can't get away while I tie him to the post."

Two or three guys grabbed Wolf's arms and pinned them tightly while I untied his wrists. I then told the guys holding him to lift Wolf's arms up so I could slip the restraints on the cross bar of the whipping post around his wrists and buckle them tightly. I noticed to my amusement that a couple of the guys holding Wolf were feeling his muscles while he struggled, stroking his chest and abs, as well as his back.

His muscles writhed under his bronze skin as Wolf struggled and strained. He was snarling and yelling something in Apache again. I don't know if he was actually swearing at me, or reciting Mother Goose stories, but it sounded impressive as hell!

I gave him a quick wink as he continued his harangue. I caught the faint glimpse of a grin, and his eyes crinkled with mirth. God, what a ham! He was totally enjoying himself, I was sure.

I grabbed Wolf by the throat and gave it a mock squeeze. His voice trailed off as he feigned choking.

"All right injun, let's see just how tough you really are." I told him forcefully.

Stepping back, I took off my hat and gloves, unbuttoned the shirt of the uniform and stripped it off. Next I peeled off the black undershirt, leaving me stripped to the waist. I smiled a bit as I heard a murmur go through the crowd, and heard comments like *"My God, look at the muscles on him. I thought the Indian was hot, but holy shit, look at that soldier!"* and *"I'd let him whip me anytime he wanted to!"*

Everyone watching stepped back as I pulled the whip out of my belt and started to spin it above my head. Wolf was standing with his broad back facing me with his arms held wide spread over his head. The muscles in his V-tapered back and shoulders flexed and his ribs rippled under his shiny, sweat-streaked skin with every breath as he waited for me to start to whip him again. Finally, I adjusted the path of the whip and let it snap into my boy's stretched torso. The whip curled across Wolf's back and halfway around his ribcage with a vicious sounding *CRACK!!* He howled in pain and screamed out something in Apache as I started to whip him again and again, leaving fresh welts on his body.

What no one in the crowd knew was that I wasn't working Wolf anywhere as hard as I could, and indeed had on many occasions. I also was using the whip in a way that would make a lot of noise without hitting my slave as hard as it sounded like it was. His howling and writhing as I whipped him was mostly just for show, although there was some pain as well. I whipped Wolf for only about five minutes or so before I stepped up to my now limp, sweaty slave and lifted up his head. His head had dropped down with his chin resting on his chest. I looked into Wolf's eyes briefly before he gave me a wink to let me know that he was really all right, and that he was enjoying showing off.

I loudly snarled "Damn injun. Are you ready to behave now, or do you want more?"

Wolf weakly moaned "Grey Wolf obeys you. White Eyes not whip me anymore."

I turned and sneered to the crowd watching "Typical injun. Talks big, but really can't take a good whipping. But, you have to agree, he sure marks up nice. Good looking welts on that back, don't you think?"

Several guys watching us smiled and nodded agreement. I turned back to Wolf and released him from the whipping post. He immediately knelt in front of me and began to lick my boots in a posture of total supplication.

I heard a familiar voice behind me say "I knew I'd find you guys in here. Had to work the savage over, didn't you?"

I turned and was greeted by the sight of Danny walking through the crowd with a huge grin on his face. He was wearing what looked like a World War II vintage U.S. army uniform, and to my surprise, Eddie, his Asian-American slave boy was following him. Eddie was dressed in the tattered remnants of a Japanese military fatigue uniform, his hands cuffed behind him. Surprisingly, his hair was still shaved into a Mohawk style cut. Eddie had endured having his head shaved in my dungeon as part of his punishment for publicly embarrassing his master.

When they walked up to where I was standing with Wolf down licking my boots, Eddie immediately dropped to his knees and knelt in front of me. Danny said "He has something he wants to tell you, Master Eric."

I looked down at the boy kneeling before me and told him "Go ahead, slave. You have permission to speak."

Eddie softly said "Sir. This boy wants to humbly apologize for his misbehavior the last time you saw him in the Eagle, Sir. This boy was totally wrong in what he did, and he begs your forgiveness. This boy also wishes to thank you for helping his master punish him and showing him the error of his ways, Sir."

I looked down coldly at him and said "Look at me, boy."

Eddie looked up from the floor and I stared into his eyes as I told him "Your behavior was close to inexcusable, boy. You embarrassed your master in public, and created a scene. That was totally wrong, as you said. But, since your master seems ready to forgive you, I will do the same. But just remember, boy; If you ever do anything like that again, your master and I can punish you in a way that will make the last time seem like playtime! Is that understood, boy?"

Eddie nodded his head, then looked back down at the floor and said "Yes, Sir. This boy understands, Sir."

I winked at Danny, telling Eddie "O.K. then boy, get to work on the other boot that the injun isn't cleaning!"

Eddie smiled briefly before bending down and going to work on my left boot, as Wolf was working on my right boot. Danny stepped up and wrapped his arms around my sweaty, bare back and gave me a deep kiss.

As we were hugging, I whispered "I thought you weren't gonna bring him out tonight."

Danny softly said "I wasn't, but he's tried so hard to make up for his fuckup that I just couldn't leave him home tonight."

I grinned and snickered; "Aww, you're just a softie, that's all."

Danny gave me a wink and a soft chuckle before he released me and stepped back. He looked down and told Eddie to stand up. As the boy rose to his feet, I told Wolf to stand up as well.

Danny and Eddie both smiled at the sight of my hot, muscular and nearly naked slave standing in front of them, his bronzed body shining with a thin glaze of sweat from his whipping.

"Damn, he's really hot" said Danny. "I thought the loincloth and boots would work on him, but I didn't think he would look that good. The braids and feathers in the hair really finish off the look."

Wolf nodded his thanks and smiled at the compliment, as I was putting on the undershirt and then the uniform shirt. Just after I had pulled myself together, we heard an announcement on the sound system in the club asking for all the couples who had been invited to take place in the costume judging to come to the stage in the main room of the club.

"Well, that's us. We'll see you guys a bit later." I told them.

I tied Wolf's hands back together behind him, then looped the longer rope around his neck and led my boy up to the stage. There were about eight other couples on the stage, waiting. Some of the guys were in just regular leathers, but some, like Wolf and myself, were in costumes befitting the theme of the party.

The M.C. announced that the prizes were going to be voted on by applause from the crowd, then he laid out the various categories to be voted on.

The first couple of prizes were for best leather topman and best leather bottom boy. Then came a prize for best leather couple. The guys who won were awarded various small humorous gag gifts as well as some nice engraved plaques.

Next came the voting for best captive boy in costume. Wolf was competing against three other boys. One was in a shredded tank top and jeans and other gang-type clothing, being led around by his master in a police uniform. The next one was in army fatigue pants and boots, with a master in a German S.S. uniform. The last boy was dressed in a torn peasant type shirt and tights. His top had an interesting stylized barbarian type outfit.

The first three boys were each presented to the crowd by their respective masters, being forced to kneel, or lick boots, or whatever their tops thought was appropriate to have the boys do.

Finally it was time for me to show Wolf off to the crowd. I stepped in front of him and yanked on the rope looped around his throat to drag him forward to the front of the stage.

I snarled "On your knees, redskin!"

Wolf could only kneel in front of everyone at the party, the tight rope around his throat making it hard for him to breathe, while I pulled the fake pistol from the holster on my belt. When he saw the gun, Wolf began to struggle against his bonds, making the muscles of his upper arms and broad shoulders and pecs bulge and ripple. I heard a murmur from the crowd as I took the very realistic looking gun and cocked the hammer back.

"Open your mouth, injun." I growled to Wolf. He looked up at me with an exaggerated expression of fear on his face, whimpering loudly before saying something in Apache.

"I'm not telling you again, savage. Open up!" I snarled at my boy, slapping his face with a sound like a rifle shot.

Slowly Wolf's mouth opened. When he had opened it enough, I stuck the barrel of the pistol in his mouth and told him "Suck it, injun."

I knew this was going to be hard for Wolf to do as a result of the rape he had suffered at the age of fifteen. After being gang-raped, an older cousin had threatened him exactly the same way with a real gun! However, I had asked Wolf if he was up to doing it before we came to the party, and he had told me he thought that he could do it. He thought it might act as a catharsis and help rid himself of the trauma of his rape.

The crowd started to applaud as Wolf began to suck on the barrel of the gun as if it was a hot cock. The muscles on his body rippled and flexed as he worked the barrel of the fake gun deeper into his mouth. Some of the guys in the front of the crowd began to whistle as they could see that Wolf was actually getting a hard on from sucking the gun!

Finally I pulled the gun out of his mouth and told him loudly "That's enough for now, you damn redskin. Later tonight I've got something else for you to suck back at the fort!"

Wolf looked down at the floor and growled out another line in Apache.

The applause was thunderous.

The M.C. stepped back up to the mike and said "Well, I guess it's pretty obvious who wins the award for hottest boy."

The crowd applauded as the announcer handed me the plaque and also a gift wrapped bag of small doggie chew toys labeled 'To keep captive boys from getting bored'.

I laughed at the tag on the toys, as did Wolf when I showed it to him.

The next award, for most unique outfits, went to a couple dressed as medieval looking barbarians, complete with swords, shields and some really sexy looking leather outfits. They looked like they had stepped directly from the set of the old Hercules or Xenia television series. Luckily, the two guys both had the bodies to go with the outfits.

The last award was for hottest topman in a costume that wasn't leather. I was surprised when the announcer asked me to be one of the contestants. I had honestly figured that more guys were looking at Wolf than at me. The uniform I had on wasn't very revealing, and it sure wasn't form fitting at all. The only thing I thought that would help was that this uniform was unique. I hadn't seen anyone else wearing an old style cavalry uniform. I thought that either of the two other guys who were competing with me stood a much better chance of winning.

That was before we stepped to the front of the stage for the judging, and someone in the crowd yelled out "Take off your shirts!"

We all laughed a bit, but then one of the guys actually did start to strip out of his shirt.

Right then I decided to go for it, and began to unbutton the uniform shirt. The crowd began to cheer and whistle as the other guys stripped to the waist, then waited for me to do the same. I peeled off the uniform shirt, then slowly took off the black undershirt.

There was a low moan from the crowd when I straightened back up and put the cavalry soldier's hat back on. The moan changed into whistles and hollers when

I began to flex my pecs and abs. Even the two other guys on stage began to applaud when I lifted up my arms and did a double bicep pose, then finished with a 'most muscular' crab pose that made my pecs stand out.

The M.C. grabbed the mike and said "Damn, how would anyone compete with that? He's got all the bases covered. High boots and a wide belt for the leathermen, cavalry pants for the uniform guys, a western look for the cowboys, and a body to die for, for everyone else!" Everyone laughed at his comments, even the other guys on stage. I just laughed along with everyone else, even though I did feel good about the attention. I hadn't felt that kind of a rush since the last time I won a bodybuilding contest, several years ago.

I accepted the plaque for hottest top, as well as the obligatory gag prize. It was a bag marked 'To help you with your paddling skills'. Inside was one of the cheap wooden paddles with a rubber ball attached by a long rubber band.

Everyone laughed when I showed them the prize, but a couple of the guys in the crowd actually applauded when I started to work the paddle and got about thirty seconds of bounce out of the ball before I missed.

The announcer finally had everyone on stage come forward in one group for a last round of applause from the crowd before we all went back to mingling with the rest of the partygoers. I led Wolf down into the crowd, where Danny and Eddie were waiting. We both got hugs from both of them.

I asked Danny how long he was going to hang around the party before he was planning on leaving. He told me that he was going to be there with Eddie for just a few more minutes because he was planning on meeting a couple of other guys for a session in his dungeon with Eddie and the other slave.

I leered at Eddie as I told Danny "Just remember. Show him no mercy!"

Eddie moaned softly when Danny said "I hadn't planned on it."

Wolf and I walked through the crowd back towards the bar so we could get a couple of drinks while we decided how much longer we wanted to stay.

I was surprised when I heard my name called out, and, turning to see who was calling, saw Jamal and Ricardo, the two hot black men we had met at the gym earlier.

We stopped and waited as they worked their way thru the crowd to where Wolf and I were waiting.

"I'm a little surprised to see you guys here tonight." I told them. "I didn't think you knew about the party."

Jamal smiled. "We were invited by the friends we came to visit to come along with them. Of course, now they've gone off with some other guys, so we're just hanging around the party before we head back to our hotel."

Ricardo said "Congratulations on winning the costume prizes. I totally agree with the crowd. You two are the hottest guys here."

I said "Looking at you two, I'm not so sure about that!"

Both of them were shirtless, just wearing tight denims and boots. Their muscular black bodies flexed and rippled with every movement. I looked at Wolf and gave him a quick wink. He smiled as if he knew what I had in mind, which he probably did!

"I was just about to take Wolf back home and torture him for several hours as a reward for being a good slave tonight. You guys want to come along and help? Or, If you prefer, I could tie up either one of you, or both, and work you over as well!"

They looked at each other and grinned widely at that.

"Man, I've been thinking about that ever since we talked to you earlier today at the gym" Ricardo exclaimed. "I like the feel of good tight bondage and even some torture. Jamal's never been into being tied up and tortured as much as I enjoy it. I've tried to talk him into it, but it never seems to do any good. I don't know if I'm in the same league as Wolf, but I'd like to try and see what I can endure."

I chuckled ; "Well, some guys just don't know what they're missing!"

I stroked my fingers down Ricardo's solid, sculpted pecs, flicking my fingers over his hard, chocolate brown nipples. I smiled evilly at the prospect of having a hard-bodied black bodybuilder with long braids of hair stretched out in my dungeon, waiting for me to torture him.

"You guys want to head out? We're ready whenever you want." I said.

Jamal answered eagerly, "Sure. I can't wait to help you work over Wolf."

I laughed. "Only if I get to work on Ricardo!"

He grinned. "Deal!"

The four of us headed for the front door, only stopping to retrieve our coats from the checkroom. With Jamal and Ricardo following us in their car, we headed back across the bridge for home, and a night of fun with two hot black bodybuilders, neither one of us knowing what this particular night had in store for us.

Chapter 4

Ebony

We drove back up to Sausalito with Jamal and Ricardo following in their car. On the way, Wolf and I discussed what might happen during the night. I told him that he had my permission to do whatever he wanted, as long as it was within our house rules for slave behavior. He smiled and leaned against me as I was driving.

"You know I love you and I love serving you and having sex with you, Sir," he said, "But I have to admit I'm kind of excited at the thought of maybe having two huge black cocks in me at the same time."

I gave him an exaggerated, eyebrow raising stare. "Oh really. So now having my cock in your mouth or ass isn't enough for you. Now you need two strange dicks to satisfy you! I'm totally crushed!" I turned my head away from his gaze briefly, feigning a hurt expression.

He looked at me for just a moment with a shocked, crestfallen look in his eyes before I stuck out my tongue and said "Nyah. Gotcha!"

Wolf immediately started giggling as he realized that I was pulling his leg. He reached out and swatted me playfully across the back of my head.

"You're totally crazy, you know that?" He chuckled.

"Of course. I'd have to be to put up with you. But, how else can I keep you on your toes, boy?" I smiled back. "Except for hanging you in the dungeon so you really ARE on your toes, that is. Which, by the way, is a great position for a smart-assed slave!"

Wolf moaned lustfully. "Oh, that sounds hot, Sir. But only if you whip me at the same time, Sir."

I leered at him. "Behave tonight and I might just do it, boy. But, you have to satisfy both of our guests and me as well."

Wolf grinned at me and said "I'll do my best, Sir."

I turned and gave him a quick peck on the cheek, saying "You always do, boy. You always do. By the way, exactly what were you saying at the party tonight? You know I don't speak Apache."

Wolf grinned and smirked mischievously; "It's probably better that way. You really don't want to know, Sir."

I glared at him. "Oh really. Well then, I guess I'll just have to torture that information out of you some night, slave!"

Wolf just chuckled; "Promises, promises!"

As we drove the rest of the way home, I planned out some of the activities that I would like to try out tonight with the two hot black musclemen. Both Wolf and I really enjoyed one on one sex with each other, but having the chance to play with other hot men sometimes was exciting as well.

When we arrived, Jamal and Ricardo followed my car around the circular drive to park in front of the house. When we went inside, I showed them around the house for a few minutes while Wolf was preparing the dungeon area for a session of use, turning on the sauna and hot tub, making sure there were water bottles in the fridge, and whatever else needed to be done. He knew the drill.

When Wolf came back upstairs and told me he was finished, I ordered him to serve our guests some drinks and snacks while I changed my clothes out of the uniform I wore to the party. I dressed in my usual dungeon attire, chaps, boots, jock pouch and vest.

When I led our guests down the stairs into the dungeon, they both whistled in appreciation. I had spent a lot of time and money upgrading the entire play space from the way Mike, my first master and lover had set it up. I had increased the size of the dungeon from one room to a full three rooms, plus the sauna area and had enlarged the cell under the stairs to the house.

Jamal leered at Ricardo, saying "I'm getting all hot and bothered just imagining what we can do to you and Wolf in here."

I grinned at his expression. "Whatever you can imagine, we've probably already tried it at least once! Maybe even twice, if it was really fun!" They both chuckled knowingly.

With that, I ordered Wolf to strip out of the loincloth and boots he wore to the party, leaving him naked except for the choker around his neck and the armband. His hair was still done up in the braids and feathers, which only added to his exotic look. Jamal told Ricardo to strip as well, then to put his boots back on.

When the two bottom boys were stripped down, I ordered them to stand together back to back with their hands down at their sides while Jamal and I circled them. They made an interesting pair, the deep ebony of Ricardo's skin contrasting with the golden bronze of Wolf's body. Ricardo's multiple braids hung down over his shoulders, as did Wolf's two long braids. As we scrutinized the boys, their cocks began to swell and enlarge, until both dicks were fully erect. Ricardo had a truly impressive erection, standing at least a full ten inches long, and as thick as my wrist.

I reached down to stroke his massive black cock while telling Jamal "I think I'd like to work on him for a while, if you want to work on Wolf. You can torture him any way you want, just as long as you don't cum inside him. I hope you understand."

Jamal smiled and said "Sure, no problem. We're both negative and healthy, but we play safe as well. We wouldn't have sucked you guys off at the gym today if you hadn't said that you both were safe."

With that, he ordered Wolf to kneel in front of him and clean his boots. I led Ricardo over to the cross and within two minutes had him tightly stretched, spread-eagled helplessly in front of me.

I looked over to where Jamal had Wolf down on his knees and said "I have an idea of how we can drive both of these boys crazy at the same time."

Jamal grinned, saying "That sounds like fun. What do you have in mind?"

"Bring Wolf over here, and I'll show you."

It only took me a few minutes to have Wolf spread out facing Ricardo, stretched in the chains hanging from the overhead beam. The two slaves could only stand looking at each other's body, about four feet away. Next I strapped gags around both their heads to keep both slaves quiet. Finally, to prepare both bound boys for the session they had to endure, I fastened nipple clamps on their chests. Wolf moaned into his gag as I applied the biting alligator clamps to his pumped, brown nipples. Ricardo watched with an expression of anxiety mixed with lust as Wolf writhed in pain as the clamps bit deeply into his tits.

Ricardo's breathing started to grow more rapid as I approached him holding another pair of nipple clamps. He closed his eyes and moaned with a mixture of pain and pleasure as I attached a pair of lighter, but still painful clamps to his thick chocolate brown nipples. The silver chain connecting the clamps contrasted with the glistening ebony of his skin, rippling muscles flexing as he adjusted to the unfamiliar pain of the nipple clamps.

Jamal breathed "Shee-it, that's hot. I like the look of that!"

Both slave's cocks were totally hard and throbbing from the combination of the bondage, the pain of the nipple clamps, and the sight of each others hard, muscular body helplessly spread eagled.

When the slaves were bound and gagged, I stepped between them and smiled at Jamal. "Come over here" I told him while I was stripping off my vest. He licked his lips hungrily and stepped up to me, wrapping his thickly muscled arms around me. The heat radiating from his sculpted, chiseled physique was really turning me on.

I thought I heard Wolf moan into his gag when Jamal kissed me deeply. I knew watching me make love to another hot muscleman would drive Wolf totally bonkers, especially when he was bound and couldn't do anything but watch.

Jamal stroked his strong hands up and down my back, murmuring in my ear "God, you have such a hot body. I want to make love to you right here!"

I kissed him deeply on the mouth and said; "So do you, stud. Go for it!"

He stepped back and leaned over to suck my right nipple into his mouth. I growled in my throat at the feel of his hot mouth on my tit. His teeth began to nip at the flesh of my tit, causing it to immediately harden. As I moaned louder, I stole a glance at Wolf. He was staring at the two of us with a look of total, uncontained lust in his eyes. His cock was absolutely rock hard as he whimpered softly into his gag. I knew he was suffering from not being able to do anything while I was being muscle worshiped by another man. This was always a great way to mentally torture Wolf. The frustration he felt was almost as bad as actual physical pain. The great part of doing this to Wolf was that there wasn't any jealousy involved. Both of us knew who we loved, and we both knew that playing with others was sometimes part of a scene. Besides, it was fun to watch Wolf suffer this way. Actually, it was fun to watch Wolf suffer any way, but mental torture was especially entertaining. As I had told him several times, mental torture was almost as much fun as physical torture. I loved to mess with his mind at times.

I closed my eyes, giving in to the feelings of pleasure from Jamal's hot mouth working back and forth across my chest from nipple to nipple, playing with my tit rings while his strong hands stroked and caressed every muscle on my torso.

I enjoyed the feel of Jamal's sculpted physique under my hands as I began to return the attention. His nipples were hard as I sucked them, licking the sweat from his pecs and abs before tonguing out his deep, shaven armpits. His sweat had a somewhat different taste than Wolf's. It seemed to be a bit muskier. Not unpleasant, but different.

I stroked my hands down Jamal's back, feeling every bulge of solid, sculpted muscle while I was kissing him deeply, his hard chest and abs pressed against my torso.

I unfastened Jamal's belt and undid his denims, allowing his massive cock to stand out from his opened fly. Within moments, he had slipped out of his pants, then put his boots back on.

Jamal and I made love to each others hard, sweat glazed bodies for a good ten or fifteen minutes in front of our bound and helpless slave boys. I could see from the expressions on both boys' faces that they were both totally aroused by the sight of our passion. The fact that both of their cocks were totally erect and throbbing was another clue as to how turned on they were.

Finally I stepped back from Jamal, while still gently stroking his huge erection with the tips of my fingers.

"I think it's time to go to work on these hot boys, don't you?" I leered at the helpless muscle slaves bound in the dungeon. Both of their stretched bodies were totally gleaming with sweat, their chests rising and falling with each breath.

I turned towards Ricardo while Jamal stepped in front of Wolf. Ricardo moaned softly into his gag when I stroked my fingers lightly down his chest and across his abs.

I trailed my hands down the glistening ebony body until I was holding one of the thickest and longest cocks I had ever seen. The bulbous head was a lighter shade of brown then the rest of the shaft, which was lined with veins. I gazed at the huge shaft for just a moment before I dropped to my knees and began licking the length of the giant cock. Ricardo moaned again into the gag when I stretched my mouth open as wide as I could and worked the huge head of the cock into my mouth.

I licked the swollen cockhead for just a few minutes before standing up and leaning against Ricardo's stretched, sweat glazed body while stroking my hands up and down his rippling ribcage.

"That's a nice cock, boy." I leered at him "How much torture do you think it can take, humm? Enough to make you scream, boy?"

Ricardo just nodded his head silently.

His eyes opened wider when I leaned closer to him and whispered into his ear "I guess we'll just have to find out tonight, boy. And yes, you will be screaming by the time I'm done with you! By the way, you are a 'boy' tonight. It doesn't matter to me if you're black, white or green! You haven't earned the right to be called 'slave' yet, boy."

Ricardo began to moan louder into the gag as I began to pull on the chain between his nipple clamps with one hand while I started to squeeze his cock with the other.

"I bet I can get at least two dozen clothespins on that dick, boy, and maybe another dozen on your balls. What do you think?" I growled to Ricardo while working his tits and cock. He just closed his eyes and nodded his head again.

"Yeah boy, we're gonna find out just how much pain you can take tonight. Is that what you want, boy?"

Ricardo nodded his head harder while moaning lustfully into the gag again.

At the same time, Jamal was starting to work on Wolf's hard body and swollen tits. He turned to me and said "I think I'm gonna take him into the other room for a while. Maybe I'll see what I can do to him on the rack."

Wolf moaned when I said "His record is six inches of stretch. That's twelve clicks on the winch. Have fun."

Jamal grinned at me before starting to unhook Wolf's restraints from the chains. When he had Wolf free, he told him to kneel. When Wolf was on his knees, Jamal unstrapped the gag from his head and told Wolf to open his mouth. When my slave's mouth was opened as wide as possible, Jamal slowly drove the swollen head of his dick into Wolf's hot mouth while holding both sides of his head. Wolf moaned around the thick shaft as his jaws were stretched wider than they had ever been.

Jamal gasped "Oh yeah, that's a good mouth. I'm going to stretch him out and see just how much of my cock he can swallow! I love fucking a hot slave mouth."

He pulled Wolf back from his cock and ordered him to his feet. Fastening Wolf's wrist restraints together behind his back, Jamal led my slave into the room of the dungeon containing the rack.

I turned back to Ricardo. His hard-muscled ebony physique was spread-eagled in front of me, awaiting whatever torture I decided to inflict on him.

I stepped close to Ricardo and reached out to the clamp on his right nipple. He watched my every move intently with a look of apprehension in his eyes. A jolt of pain shot through his body when I unclipped his tit, causing his muscles to flex and ripple as he strained against his restraints.

Ricardo began to whimper and cry into the gag when I leaned down and began to work his already sore tit with my teeth. I could feel his body writhing on the cross while I was torturing him.

I worked his nipple with my teeth, chewing and stretching the tit, while my hands explored his sweat-soaked torso, feeling every muscle as they strained and bulged as he futilely tried to escape his taut bondage.

Of course, my biggest joy came from torturing Wolf to the limits of his endurance and strength, but I also took great pleasure in working on other guys on occasion, such as now. Variety was the spice of life, and all that!

I chewed on the nipple for a few minutes before unclipping the other tit clamp and repeating the torture on Ricardo's left nipple. When I was done with his nipples, I ran my tongue through his open, spread armpits, enjoying the taste of his sweat. When I finally straightened up and stepped back from him, Ricardo was gasping for air and softly sobbing into the gag.

"What's the matter, boy?" I taunted him. "We're just getting started. You haven't even started to hurt yet, boy! You told me you wanted some torture tonight. Well, that's what you're going to get! I'm gonna love hearing you try to scream into that gag, boy!"

He just moaned softly and nodded his head again.

I walked over to the shelves holding my supplies and picked up a small canvas bag that held my supply of clothespins. Ricardo's eyes widened when I showed him the contents of the bag.

"They're all going on that cock and balls of yours, boy. Is that what you want?"

He closed his eyes and merely nodded his head one more time, with a resigned air.

Ricardo's head rolled back and a muffled groan came from him when I clamped the first of the clothespins on his low hanging balls. Each additional clothespin brought a similar reaction until I had at least fifteen clothespins on his ballsack.

In spite of the pain, or maybe because of it, his cock was totally hard. I was amazed when I hefted the thick, swollen shaft in my hand.

"God, that's a beautiful cock. I've got to torture that huge dick." I breathed, partly to myself.

Ricardo began to whimper louder and louder as I started clamping clothespins on the skin of his ebony shaft. I started on the bottom of his dick near the base and ran a line of clothespins all the way up to just under the thick head. Then I started to work my way around his throbbing cock, adding one clothespin after another. It took almost ten minutes to use all the clothespins in the bag.

By the time I was done, there were over thirty clothespins on his cock, including two on the very tip of his cock, pinching the piss hole closed.

Tears were running down Ricardo's face as he sobbed weakly into his gag. His chest rose and fell, glistening in the light of the dungeon as he gasped for air, his breath ragged with pain.

I stood back, admiring the sight of the sculpted, black bodybuilder helplessly bound in my dungeon, enduring extreme cock and ball torture. Every rib and muscle in his chest and abs was highlighted by the look of the streams of sweat trickling down his torso.

I just watched him enduring the burning pain in his cock and balls for a few minutes before I stepped closer to his helpless body again. I lightly stroked my hands over the straining, bound muscleman's body for a moment before I leaned close to his head and whispered "Is this what you had in mind when you said you wanted to be tortured tonight, boy?"

Ricardo nodded his head weakly and grunted a muffled "Uh-huh."

I asked him softly "Do you want more, boy? Do you want to take more pain, boy?"

He nodded and grunted in the affirmative again.

I grinned wickedly at him and strode over to the toy shelves again. Ricardo groaned when I picked up one of my favorite floggers. He seemed to be dreading what was coming next, while at the same time desiring his imminent torment.

"That's right, boy. It's time to see just how much you can take."

I draped the flogger across his chest, in the same way that Wolf loved me to do whenever I was getting ready to flog him. Ricardo moaned loudly into the gag and flexed every muscle in his rock hard body. His body was ripped and vascular in the way that only a few pro bodybuilders could achieve.

He gasped and writhed when I started to work the flogger across his chest and abs, slowly working the intensity up over the next few minutes. Every time I lashed the cat across Ricardo's solid physique, his muscles bulged and flexed, especially his thick, veined biceps as he strained against his restraints, and his washboard abs as he struggled to breathe.

I flogged his chest and abs until Ricardo gasped into the gag and made the stop signal with his hand that we had agreed on as a safe gesture. He sagged down as I set the flogger down and looked into his eyes, asking him "Are you all right, boy?"

He nodded his head, signaling that he was.

I smirked and told him "You just wait there, boy. I'm going to see how Jamal and Wolf are getting along. While you're waiting, just remember one thing. It hurts a lot more taking the clothespins off than it does putting them on! Especially if they've been on for a while. And I think I'm gonna leave em' on for quite a while!"

He just groaned and sagged down further against his restraints. I gave him an evil smile and went into the next room to check on my boy and his torturer.

When I went into the next room, there was Wolf stretched out tightly on the rack. Jamal was just getting ready to pull the chains on his restraints tighter with the winch. Wolf gave a short yelp of pain when the winch clicked for the next tighter setting. It looked like Wolf had already been stretched out to the fourth or fifth click of the winch.

Both of their naked bodies were drenched with sweat from the heat of the dungeon.

Wolf looked great, as usual, but Jamal's body was absolutely amazing looking. His rich chocolate brown body glistened in the light and his muscles flowed under his skin like the muscles of a sleek black panther stalking his prey in the jungle.

I stood and watched for a while as Jamal stroked and licked Wolf's stretched torso and pulled on the chain connecting his nipple clamps. Wolf howled as his thick nipples were savagely stretched by the biting clamps digging deeply into his flesh. The size of his throbbing erection, however, showed me that he was thoroughly enjoying his torture.

Jamal then climbed onto the rack and sat straddling Wolf's abs. He reached down and began to dig his thick fingers into the pressure points in Wolf's armpits.

Wolf writhed and struggled in vain as he was tortured by the ebony muscle god sitting on his helpless body. He was gasping for air and straining his muscles as each new wave of pain shot into his body from the expert ministrations of Jamal's hands.

Jamal worked his way down the sides of Wolf's torso, sliding down further and further onto Wolf's legs until he was digging his fingers into the joint and nerve insertion points on each side of Wolf's crotch, just next to his cock. By now Wolf was howling in pain. His struggles were verging on the frantic as he worked to escape the torture. He was gasping in total agony. Just when I thought that even he couldn't take any more, Jamal leaned back and ended his torture of Wolf's body.

As Wolf was sobbing in relief, Jamal leaned over Wolf's head and asked him softly "Do you want it, boy?"

Wolf softly moaned "Yes sir. Please."

At that, Jamal bent down, lowering his massive chest over Wolf's face until my slave lifted his head up and tried to suck on his left nipple. Jamal began to tease Wolf by keeping his chest just out of reach of Wolf's licking tongue. Wolf moaned and strained as far as he could against the pull of the rack, but Jamal stayed just out of reach.

Within moments, Wolf was desperate with frustration. I knew having a hot, muscular body just out of reach was driving Wolf absolutely nuts, having tortured him this way myself many times.

Jamal looked over to where I was standing in the doorway and gave me a grin just before he finally lowered himself down enough for Wolf to suck his left tit into his hot mouth. Jamal moaned with pleasure as Wolf began to work the tit with his teeth and tongue.

Satisfied that my boy was in good hands, I returned to the cross where Ricardo was writhing and twisting in pain as the feel of the clothespins on his cock and balls inexorably increased, causing him to suffer more and more.

He groaned loudly into his gag and strained his muscles as I unclipped the first clothespin from his cock.

"One down and only about forty five more to go, boy." I leered up at him. He just groaned again and closed his eyes, apparently steeling himself against the oncoming pain.

I stood up and in a quick movement clipped the metal nipple clamps back onto Ricardo's tits. He gave a muffled howl of pain, which increased when in quick succession I pulled four clothespins from his ballsack and three from his cock.

Every muscle in his amazing physique began to strain and writhe as I knelt in front of him and began randomly pulling the clothespins from his dick and balls.

Ricardo screamed into the gag for almost the entire two minutes it took me to remove all the clothespins. Just when he apparently thought his torture was finished, however, I brought over my small cock flogger and began to use it on his huge black cock and his low hanging ballsack.

Every muscle in his sculpted ebony torso was rippling and bulging under his glistening black skin. The veins popped out across his thick pecs, across his ripped washboard abs, and out the entire length of both of his widespread arms as he struggled to escape from his bondage. As he howled into his gag, he threw his head back and forth while I flogged his cock and balls, his long braids whipping back and forth across his chest and shoulders.

His massive thighs bulged and strained against the heavy leather restraints holding him helpless and exposed for my torture.

He screamed into the gag again and again as I worked over his cock and nuts, then screamed a final time when I unclamped his thick tits and twisted them as hard as I thought he could stand.

When I released his tits, Ricardo sagged down on the cross as his knees gave way, leaving him supported only by his wide spread arms. I unbuckled the gag from his head and gave him a deep, hard kiss.

"Oh my God." He moaned when I finally let him go. "Oh my God. That was incredible, Sir. Thank you."

I grinned into his face and said; "I told you that I was going to make you scream, boy."

I knelt down and released his feet from the restraints on the bottom of the cross. He slowly worked his feet together before I started to free his wrists.

When I had Ricardo totally released from the cross, he knelt down and began to kiss and lick my boots while murmuring "Thank you, Sir. I really loved that. Thank you." He slowly straightened up and began to lick and suck my cock. His mouth was hot and he had a great tongue. I groaned with pleasure as he worked my dick. Now I knew what Wolf had felt earlier in the steam room at the gym!

I held onto his head while I fucked his mouth, enjoying the different feel of the cornrows in his hair, and the tightly woven braids of hair, so different from Wolf's thick, flowing mane.

I let him suck me for a few minutes before I told him "That's enough, boy. We need to go into the other room and go to work on Wolf."

Ricardo smiled up at me and said "Yes Sir. It'll be a pleasure."

I asked Ricardo "Does your cock still hurt a bit from the clamps?"

He grinned and said "Yes Sir, but it's a good hurt!"

"Good. I know where we can find a hot mouth for you to fuck to make it feel a bit better, if you think that will help" I told him smiling.

Ricardo's smile widened. "Yeah, that'll help, Sir."

We headed into the room where Jamal was torturing Wolf on the rack to see how well my slave could endure three on one torture! I knew that Wolf loved to show off while being worked over in the bars, but now he had a chance to show off for just me and our guests as we took him right to the edge, and beyond!

Chapter 5

Threesome

Ricardo and I stepped into the next room of the dungeon in time to see Jamal sliding his chest back and fourth across Wolf's sucking, licking mouth. Wolf was licking the sweat from Jamal's rock hard, sculpted pecs as fast as he could. Jamal's entire naked physique was glistening with a coating of sweat, and drops were constantly falling down onto Wolf's body and into his face. Jamal's muscles rippled as he held himself above Wolf in a pushup position, lowering his torso down into reach of Wolf's tongue and then lifting himself back up out of reach, causing Wolf to whimper and moan in frustration as he strained to reach the hot body above him. I could see the cords and tendons in his neck strain and bulge as he stretched his head up in a futile effort to reach the gleaming, ebony body suspended over his face. I knew that this was driving him nuts with feelings of desire and lust.

Wolf's cock was totally hard as he endured the frustration of only being able to touch the amazing body above him with his tongue while enduring the stretching of the rack.

I knew that the one thing Wolf would really love to be able to do at this moment would be to wrap his arms around the hot black muscleman that was torturing him, and worship every muscle on his body. I loved to tease and torment him in this way whenever I was in the mood, so I had a pretty good idea of how he was feeling. The feelings of frustration and unfulfilled desire were almost as much of a torture to Wolf as actual physical pain.

Ricardo and I watched Jamal torture and torment Wolf for a few minutes before I gruffly said "I think it's time that we show this slave boy what it really means to suffer. Don't you two agree?"

Jamal lifted himself up from the rack, hopped down, grinned and said "Yeah.

I think he needs some real pain."

Ricardo added "Let's see you really torture him. I want to watch that!"

Jamal and Ricardo stood off to one side stroking and feeling each others bodies while I looked at the markings on the winch on the rack. I saw from the settings that Wolf was at the fifth notch of the rack. I grasped the handle of the winch and gave it a pull, stretching Wolf's body another two clicks of the winch. The sound of the chains tightening on the drum of the winch, combined with the subtle creaking of the leather restraints on my slave's wrists and ankles, was very erotic. He had endured being pulled out a full twelve clicks, which was six inches of stretch, so this was nowhere near his limit.

As he gasped in pain from the torture on the rack, I brought over one of my favorite floggers. I reached out and in a quick motion, removed both of the nipple clamps from Wolf's now tender nipples.

He shrieked at the sudden burst of agony in his nipples. When I began to squeeze and twist the tender knots of flesh on his tautly stretched pecs, Wolf screamed louder and strained his thick muscles in a futile effort to escape his torture. As he howled in pain, I swung the flogger and began to use it on Wolf's tightly stretched torso. He strained and writhed on the rack, every muscle and rib bulging as I laid the tails of the flogger across his chest and abs over and over, harder and harder.

As I flogged my slave, I started screaming at him "So, my cock isn't enough for you, boy? You need to have two cocks to satisfy you now? You ungrateful son of a bitch! I should throw you out of my home, you worthless pile of shit! You slut! How dare you! You thought you knew what pain was before, boy, but you have no idea!"

I was hollering louder and louder at Wolf with each stroke of the flogger. He looked at me with confusion in his eyes for just a moment before he suddenly caught on to what I was doing. I was putting on an act for our new friends by pretending to be insanely jealous.

Wolf winked at me, and started screaming "OH FUCK-OH FUCK, OH SHIT, SIR. HURT ME, MASTER! TORTURE ME, PLEASE SIR. OH GOD, SIR, I'LL DO WHATEVER YOU WANT, SIR! PLEASE, SIR, HURT ME, HURT ME, SIR!! I'M SORRY, SIR. I DIDN'T REALLY MEAN IT, MASTER!! YOU KNOW I'LL ALWAYS WANT YOUR COCK, MASTER!!"

Not surprisingly, his pleading and begging was really turning me on, as it always did. I began to flog Wolf harder and harder until I was swinging the cat with almost all my strength. My focus shifted from showing off for our guests, to concentrating on torturing my helpless slave for real. He strained and flexed his muscles while shrieking in pain with each stroke of the cat as I tortured his already tender chest and nipples and his washboard stomach and thick thighs, until his skin was red and striped with marks from the cat. In spite of his obvious agony, however, Wolf's cock was still rock hard, arcing up over his abs.

Finally I set the flogger down, my chest heaving, and my body dripping with sweat from the exertion of the flogging, turned to Ricardo and Jamal and asked them "You two studs want to help me torture this ungrateful slave? Get over here and start chewing on those tits. The harder you bite them, the better. I want to hear him screaming in agony."

The two ebony musclemen stepped up to the rack and bent down to each suck one of Wolf's swollen, brown nipples into their mouths. They began to suck and bite Wolf's tits, chewing on them while my helpless slave screamed in pain.

"Yeah, that's it. Work those nipples. He loves it. Bite 'em harder. Torture that pain pig. Make him hurt!" I was encouraging the guys while they worked Wolf's tits.

His chest was heaving, every rib rippling under his skin, while his washboard abs were flexing with every shuddering, gasping breath. The veins were actually standing out across Wolf's heaving stomach muscles, as well as across his solid, straining pecs.

His screams of pain grew louder and louder as the brutal torture of his nipples continued. I could see Wolf's tits being stretched as the two musclemen bit his nipples and pulled back from his chest, pulling the thick knobs of flesh away from his pecs with their teeth.

Jamal and Ricardo both were sucking and chewing on his nipples while they were feeling his straining muscles with their hands. The sight of four strong hands stroking and exploring my boy's body while he was tightly bound and stretched was extremely erotic. The fact that color of their hands was such a contrast to the golden brown of Wolf's body was somehow even more of a turn-on for me than usual. I had only ever seen a few African-Americans working on my boy, so the sight was extra hot.

After a few more minutes of teasing and torturing Wolf's nipples and body, I asked the guys if they were ready to make Wolf really suffer. They both lifted their heads from his heaving, straining chest and grinned. Jamal said "What do we need to do, Sir?"

"Release that slave and drag him over here to the corner" I ordered.

Within minutes, Wolf was helpless in the strong grip of the two musclemen, kneeling in front of me.

I could tell from both the expression on his face, and the fact that his cock was totally hard that Wolf was really enjoying submitting to three men at the same time. I had to admit that I was enjoying watching one of Wolf's favorite fantasies come true as well.

Jamal and Ricardo held him with his arms widely stretched as I coldly looked down at my suffering slave, and told him "Now you're gonna get what you told me you wanted, boy. Two hot black cocks in you at the same time!"

Wolf moaned as he looked at over twenty inches of hard, swollen ebony cock standing out in front of his face.

I stepped up to my kneeling slave and forced him to look up into my eyes.

"Be careful of what you wish for, boy. You might just get it!" I snarled.

I removed the choker that was tied around Wolf's neck, then ordered the guys to hold Wolf in position while I fastened his wrists and neck in between the hinged boards of the stocks. When he was tightly restrained, he was bent over at the waist with his hot ass totally exposed, and his mouth just at waist height. Next, I fastened a spreader bar between his ankles to keep his legs spread and his ass open.

I looked at Jamal and Ricardo and simply invited them to; "Fuck him. Both of you at the same time. I don't care if one of you does his ass and the other does his mouth, or if you can figure a way to put both cocks in his ass at the same time, but I want to see both of those huge dicks in him." As I told the guys that, Wolf just moaned loudly. I grinned and winked at the two muscle studs, knowing that Wolf couldn't see my face.

Jamal stepped behind Wolf and skinned back his throbbing cock. He slipped on an extra large condom before starting to lube up Wolf's hot hole with his thick fingers.

As Wolf moaned even louder at the probing of his ass, Ricardo walked in front of Wolf and said "I don't think we need to hear all that complaining, slave boy."

He pushed the thick head of his dick against Wolf's lips, until Wolf opened his mouth, allowing the head of the massive shaft to slip inside.

Jamal pushed the head of his cock against Wolf's ass at almost the same time, finally forcing his way past my slave's stretched sphincter.

The muscles in Wolf's back and shoulders began to ripple and bulge as he felt himself being fucked in both ends at the same time. He moaned as loudly as he could around the huge cockhead filling his mouth. It seemed to be a moan of both suffering, and of sheer sexual delight.

It was incredibly hot to watch the thick licorice black cocks driving into my boy's helpless body. Jamal's huge shaft gleamed with lube as it was driven in and out of Wolf's ass, and Ricardo's equally thick cock slid into Wolf's mouth. Wolf's lips seemed to be trying to mold themselves to every vein on the huge cock.

Both of the thick, veined ebony shafts slowly worked deeper and deeper into his body. Jamal's torso glistened in the light as he drove his cock in until it was totally buried inside Wolf's tight ass, his incredible washboard stomach muscles flexing and bulging, along with his pecs. He grasped Wolf's hips and began a slow, deliberate thrusting in and out, pulling his dick out until just the head remained trapped inside Wolf, then firmly drove the entire length of his massive cock into my boy's ass, causing Wolf to strain and struggle even harder, every muscle of his back and shoulders rippling with each thrust.

Meanwhile, Ricardo was slowly opening up Wolf's throat, forcing him to take the biggest cock in his mouth that he had ever sucked. Wolf finally began to choke and gag, gasping for air around the thick dick.

Wolf was easily able to take my entire nine inch cock into his throat without struggling, so this just brought home to me how much bigger Ricardo's cock was than mine.

I was totally enjoying watching Wolf take the two huge cocks at the same time. I decided it was time to add to his pleasure torture. I had already warmed his chest and abs, so I picked up my medium weight flogger and began to use it on Wolf's bent over back.

He strained and struggled as the cat began lashing the glistening skin. Every muscle in his torso began to bulge and writhe as I hollered to Jamal and Ricardo "Yeah, that's it. Fuck him! Torture him with those cocks! I want to see that slave suffer!"

As Jamal began pounding his dick into Wolf's ass harder and harder, Ricardo continued slowly forcing his cock deeper and deeper into Wolf's throat, finally cutting off his air altogether.

I told Ricardo "Pull out just enough for Wolf to take one long, deep breath, then shove that cock back into his throat. He's not going to be able to breathe until I say that he can!"

Wolf sucked in a huge lungful of air around Ricardo's cock when he could, then I told Ricardo to "Plug up that slave's throat. Now he's gonna suffer!"

I then turned to Jamal and said; "Fuck that ass. Hard. I want to see you pound that ass with that huge cock. Rape that slave while he can't breathe."

I knew Wolf loved hearing me order someone else to hurt him. It really turned him on, as another part of his being totally subservient to my will, to hear me order more pain for him, especially when I told someone else to rape him. Even though this was exactly what his cousin and his gang had done to Wolf several years ago, I think that he knew that I wouldn't let anything happen to him this time. It was another fantasy of his to be forced to relive his rape session, but without really being in any danger.

Wolf began to struggle in earnest against the unyielding wood of the stocks, trying to endure being fucked by a thick, long cock while not being able to breathe. I glanced at the clock to check the time. I wanted to be sure he didn't go too long without air. The muscles in Wolf's broad back, shoulders, and arms began to flex and bulge harder and harder as he began to suffer from the lack of air.

Both of the hot ebony musclemen were dripping with sweat as they double fucked my bound, helpless slave. Wolf's flexing, straining torso was drenched as well as he endured the feeling of the huge cock pounding in and out of his ass while his throat was totally plugged by the other massive shaft.

It was amazing to watch the muscles of the torsos of the two bodybuilders flex and ripple as they tortured Wolf with their cocks.

In just under two minutes, Jamal began to gasp "Oh shit, I'm gonna cum!"

I said "Pull out and shoot all over that slave's back. Cover him with your load!"

Jamal pulled his cock out of Wolf's stretched asshole and, stripping off the condom, began furiously pumping his cock with one hand while pulling and twisting his own nipples with the other.

At the same time, Ricardo backed up from Wolf's head, pulling his cock out of Wolf's mouth. As Wolf gasped and choked down frantic breaths of air, Ricardo started jacking his own cock as well.

Within seconds of each other, both of the ebony gods shot huge loads of hot, thick sperm all over Wolf's glistening, rippling back. Wolf gasped; "Oh yeah. Oh fuck yeah!" as he felt the jets of thick man seed spraying in thick streams across his flogged, sensitive skin.

When the guys had finished shooting, they bent over as one and began licking their mixed loads from my slave boy's muscled back. The sight was so hot that I had to step in front of Wolf and order him to open his mouth. As soon as he did, I drove my cock all the way into his throat and began fucking his mouth as fast as I could. Wolf moaned in his bondage as he felt the two hot tongues licking the mixed sperm and sweat from his body while my cock reamed his throat.

It only took about a minute before I groaned "Get ready, boy!" just before I filled his mouth with my load of cum.

Wolf coughed and sputtered around my cock as he swallowed my load. Finally, I pulled my spent cock out of his mouth. At just about the same time, Jamal and Ricardo apparently finished cleaning the cum from Wolf's back and stood up. They were both breathing heavily from the exertions of their huge orgasms.

Wolf sighed with pleasure when I released his head and hands from the stocks, allowing him to straighten up from his awkward, bent over position. He smiled at me even as he dropped to his knees and began licking my boots.

Jamal and Ricardo wrapped their arms around each other and kissed deeply, feeling each others hard bodies. As they broke the kiss, they then stepped over to me and both guys wrapped their arms around me, hugging tightly while Wolf continued licking my boots.

"Thanks for a really great time" Jamal said.

Ricardo added "Yeah, that was really hot. I haven't had anyone torture me like that in quite a while. It felt great!"

I hugged them back and said "I'm glad you had a good time. I love watching someone else work on Wolf for a change, and I enjoy a different hardbodied bottom boy as well."

I then removed the spreader bar from around Wolf's ankles and ordered him back up onto his feet. I said "I need to just relax for a while. Let's go sit in the sauna for a bit." I stripped off my chaps and boots, then headed for the sauna.

We all grabbed towels from the rack by the sauna door, then made ourselves comfortable. Within moments, all four of our bodies were running with streams of sweat in the heat of the sauna. Ricardo groaned softly as he stretched out on one of the benches.

"Oh God, this feels great." He said, taking a deep breath, which caused his muscular chest to expand dramatically. Jamal lowered himself down next to his lover and began to gently stroke the solid, gleaming black body, feeling every muscle, then began to lick the shiny ebony skin of his chest and abs.

I sat on one of the lower benches, then Wolf surprised me by sitting directly behind me and starting to massage my shoulders and neck. The feel of his strong hands working on my hard muscles was wonderful.

We sat in the sauna for a few minutes before I said "I think it's almost too hot. Let's go outside for a while."

We stepped over to the corner shower just by the outside door and took a quick rinse before stepping out onto the deck by the pool. The chill of the late October air was quite a shock after the heat of the sauna. Quickly all four of us got into the hot tub, which was bubbling quietly and steaming into the night air.

"Oh man" moaned Jamal. "Heaven!" He was right. The feel of the warm water circulating around my body and the feel of my hot slave boy's hard body wrapped in my arms was heaven, indeed.

Wolf and I sat in our usual position in the hot tub, with me in a corner alcove, and Wolf sitting between my spread legs, leaning his back against my chest. I had my arms wrapped around his chest, gently rubbing and feeling his hard nipples and sculpted pecs.

Wolf was sighing with pleasure at the feel of my hands. Sometimes we could sit like this for what seemed to be hours, just enjoying each other's company and companionship without saying a word.

Jamal finally broke the silence. "Man, I wish we had a setup like this back home. This is great. Unfortunately, we just don't have the room and the owner of the condo complex might not like it if we dug up his courtyard."

I grinned at him. "What, no sense of humor?"

Ricardo laughed. "Nope, not him."

"So, where exactly do you guys live, anyway? I know it's somewhere in the L.A. area but that's a really big place." I asked.

Jamal said "We actually live in West Hollywood, in a really gay neighborhood."

"Hollywood? So, I guess you're both in the movie business." I said with a grin. "After all, everyone in Hollywood is in the movies, right?"

Both guys laughed. "Oh yeah, that's what everyone thinks." chuckled Jamal. "All though, in our case, that's not too far from the truth. We don't actually work in the movie business, but we both have a lot of contact with show business people. I actually write for an advertising agency that does a lot of movie business."

I looked at Ricardo. "So, what do you do? Do you write as well?"

Ricardo laughed "Oh no, I don't have any talent for that. But, my job is just as much fun and I manage to get a lot of inside dirt on people. I'm a personal trainer for a lot of actors and actresses."

I looked down at Wolf. "Wow, no wonder he's in such great shape."

Wolf was grinning. "So, how many hot hunky actors have you had?"

Ricardo smiled. "You'd be surprised at how many supposedly straight guys that you always see in the tabloids with the starlet of the hour, or the trophy girlfriend, that I've had down on their knees in front of me with my cock in their mouths, or bent over in the gym taking me up the ass."

Wolf stared. "I was kidding!" he said.

Ricardo said "I'm not. There are a lot of really hot, young actors in the business today that play straight, but really enjoy men a lot more. When I do a session of personal training with an actress it's strictly business, but lots of guys ask for me because they like a good stiff dick!"

Ricardo told us of some of the guys in movies and television that he had had sex with as a part of working with them, including a couple of my favorite young stars. Also, he told us that he occasionally worked with some music groups, including some of the more popular boy bands.

He grinned; "You know how some people wonder about some of the guys in those groups? How many of them are gay, how many are straight, and so forth? I don't have to wonder because I know how many of them love a hard cock up their ass or deep in their throat!"

When we were done chatting, and it was time to head back inside, Ricardo said "I hope you will keep what I told you about these guys to yourselves. This could cause a lot of trouble if any of this ever got out. I hope you understand."

I told him, "Not a problem. We know what could happen. Your secret is safe with us. And, if word ever does leak out, you could always come back and torture Wolf until he confesses to being the one who told, because I sure won't tell anyone!"

Wolf turned to me with a totally shocked look on his face, which changed into a huge grin before he broke up laughing when I stuck out my tongue at him.

"Oh, you're gonna pay for that, smartass." He groused, but with a grin.

Ricardo and Jamal were laughing as well when Wolf reached out and smacked me in the shoulder with his fist, forgetting one of our house rules. When we are alone, we can have fun and mess around with each other like lovers do, but Wolf must always purport himself as a trained slave whenever we have company, or whenever we are out in public.

As his master, I have the right to needle and insult him, as part of the mind games of being a master, without his having the right to say anything back to me without permission as a slave. His 'smartass' comment was bad enough, but actually striking his master in front of company was over the limit. Way over the limit!

I looked at him with a shocked expression.

"You forget yourself, slave. That's gonna cost you several hours in the dungeon, enduring the most painful tortures I can think of! How dare you strike your master in front of company!"

Wolf's face actually fell when he realized what he had done. I guess the fun mood of the last hour or so in the hot tub and sauna had relaxed him a little too much.

He immediately dropped to his knees and bent down to kiss my feet.

I looked at Jamal and Ricardo, saying "I'm sorry you had to see that. I assure you, he will be punished."

I then looked down at the slave kissing my feet. "What do you have to say for yourself, boy?" I growled.

He rose to his knees, but kept his head down. "This slave is truly sorry, Sir. He just forgot his training for a second. He knows he deserves to be punished, but wishes to deeply apologize to our guests, and to his master. Please accept his humble apology."

Jamal said "We understand. It was just a slipup. Eric, you are the best topman, and you have the best slave that we've encountered in a long time. We know a lot of leathermen in L.A. who could really learn a lot from both of you. Consider it forgotten."

I looked at them and said "I appreciate that. I guess I could let it go, just this once."

I told Wolf "Stand up, boy." He immediately shot to his feet and stood in front of me, ramrod straight. I stepped up to him and glared into his eyes, steaming mad.

"If you ever do anything like that again in front of company, or in public, you will experience punishment unlike anything you have ever endured in your life! Our guests have been gracious enough to forgive your breach of training, and for their sake, I'll do the same thing. You only get one screwup, and that was it. If it ever happens again, you have no chance of being forgiven. You will be tortured beyond anything you have ever felt before! Do I make myself clear, slave?"

Wolf softly said "Yes, Sir. This slave understands. Thank you, Master."

He turned to our guests. "Thank you, Sirs, for forgiving my mistake. This boy assures you that it will never happen again." He looked back down towards the floor.

There was a brief, awkward silence before I said "It's getting really late. It's actually almost 4: 00 in the morning. Do you want to head back to the city, or would you rather stay here tonight? We have plenty of room."

Jamal said "I think we'll go back. We do have our friends that we were visiting. They were going out tonight as well, but we told them that we'd meet up with them later today."

I nodded, and said "Well, you do have the phone number here and my e-mail, so if you ever want to come back up and visit, please just let me know. You'll be welcome anytime. Isn't that right, boy?"

Wolf nodded his head, and softly said "Yes, Sir."

We all went back into the main room of the dungeon, where everyone's clothes were. Once Jamal and Ricardo were dressed, I told Wolf to wait for me in the dungeon while I walked our guests out to their car.

When they were gone, I strode back into the dungeon and told Wolf to stand. He stood in the center of the dungeon, his head bowed and his wrists crossed behind his back. I could tell that he was upset about his breach of discipline. He had made some mistakes before, but never in front of guests or while at a bar. His only previous breaches of discipline had occurred while at home, and then only while he was still being trained as a new slave. Wolf's lower lip quivered, and he seemed to be on the brink of tears.

"Well boy, what do you think I ought to do with you? Have you learned anything tonight, or do you need to be punished? I told our guests that I would let it go, but now you need to tell me if you can forget the incident as well, or if you think you need punishment. I'll let you decide, boy."

He softly said "Punish me Sir. I screwed up and I need to pay for my mistake. Whatever you want to do to me, Sir, I will accept."

"All right, then, boy. Over here."

He stepped over to one of the vertical beams supporting the floor above. I fastened the padded wrist and ankle restraints to his limbs. I told Wolf to stand with his back against the pillar. When he was positioned where I wanted him, I stretched his arms above his head and pulled them to the rear of the pillar, stretching his chest and shoulders. The restraints were fastened to eyebolts in the pillars.

Next, I fastened Wolf's ankles to the base of the pillar the same way, leaving him tightly stretched, his arms and legs pulled behind the pillar and his torso stretched taut.

I wrapped a rope several times around his flat, hard stomach, securing him fully to the pillar. Other ropes were then tied around his thighs, upper arms, and finally one was wrapped around his head, holding a leather plug gag in Wolf's mouth. The gag was in tightly enough that he couldn't force it out of his mouth, but not tightly enough to interfere with his breathing.

I stood in front of my totally immobilized slave, eyeing his hard, muscular body that was already beginning to streak with sweat. I would have loved to start to suck his nipples or his hard cock, but I had to remind myself that he was being punished. I realized that he hadn't cum during our session with Jamal and Ricardo, so I knew he would be horny as hell all night.

I leaned in and growled "I think staying like that the rest of the night will give you time to think about what you did. Now I'm going to bed. When I get up, I'll decide if you need any more punishment, or if I'll just have to refresh your training."

Wolf just whimpered and sobbed softly into his gag, as a single tear trickled down his cheek.

I climbed the stairs, flipping off the light as I left the dungeon, and went to bed, my heart heavy with regret. I hated to have to discipline my slave in this way.

I loved torturing him for our mutual pleasure, but I wasn't happy having to punish him for a breach of his training. I resolved that starting in the morning I would have to start being more firm with my boy. I loved him so much that I was sometimes guilty of letting his training and standing as my slave slip.

Well, not any more. Tomorrow, it would be back to basics for my slave.

Chapter 6

Discipline

After a restless night, I grabbed a pair of gym shorts and walked back downstairs to contemplate what were going to be the consequences of Wolf's breach of discipline. I realized that it was in all probability an innocent accident. We were both excited by having two hot black bodybuilders in the dungeon with us, but Wolf should have been able to control himself.

It was already after noon, so I prepared myself a light breakfast, then headed down the stairs into the torture chamber where my slave had spent the night in tight bondage.

He stood just as I had left him, with his arms stretched tightly around the pillar he was bound to. His head was bound tightly to the pillar as well, so even if he had managed to fall asleep, his head would remain upright. Wolf's body was streaked with sweat from the warmth of the dungeon, and his eyes were open, He watched me intently as I walked towards him.

I stopped about five feet from him and just stared into his brown eyes, with a stern expression on my face. His expression was unreadable, as he had a wide leather gag in his mouth, tied to the pillar. Secretly I was amused to observe that as I stood staring at my bound slave, his cock began to slowly swell and lift, until it was fully erect. I knew that Wolf was probably as horny as hell. He hadn't cum last night, even after being tortured on the rack by Ricardo, and then being fucked in his ass and mouth simultaneously by Jamal and Ricardo. I stepped close to Wolf and grasped his swollen cock.

"Did I say you could get hard, slave?" I snarled, even as I started to squeeze his dick tightly.

Wolf just moaned into his gag and closed his eyes in pain. I kept on tightening my grip until Wolf started to whimper.

Finally I released his cock and loosened the rope wrapped around his head. Once the rope was off, I pulled the gag out of his mouth.

Wolf worked his jaws to relax the muscles, but he didn't say anything to me. I was a bit surprised but also proud that he had remembered his discipline training. I stepped back from his bound body and just looked into his eyes again until he lowered his head in a gesture of submission.

"Well slave, do you have anything to say?" I asked him gruffly.

He spoke without lifting his head. "This slave is truly sorry about his mistake, Sir. He is ready to accept whatever punishment you feel he deserves."

I was glad to see that Wolf remembered that whenever a slave boy spoke about himself to his master he should refer to himself in the third person, to remind himself that he is less than a whole person in his master's eyes. It was just another form of mental discipline that was part of a good slave's training.

I lifted up Wolf's head so he was looking directly into my eyes.

"This will be your punishment, boy. You will undergo a week of remedial slave training. If you make it through the week without any slip-ups, you will have your full rights restored. Until then, consider yourself a new slave undergoing your first training."

Wolf nodded his head in agreement as he softly said; "Yes, Master."

I could see the look of shame and sadness in his eyes. I knew that he felt badly about his slip-up. He didn't make many mistakes, and he had never screwed up in front of others, but I knew that the few mistakes that he had made always bothered him greatly. It had always been a point of pride to Wolf to always try to avoid even the smallest error in his behavior as a properly trained leather slaveboy.

"All right then, boy. I'm going to untie you now. Your retraining starts as of this minute."

He silently nodded his head again as I began to loosen the ropes binding him to the pillar.

When he was completely untied, Wolf slowly lowered his arms down to his sides, then dropped to his knees in a posture of submission in front of me.

"The first thing you need to do, slave, is to go upstairs and clean yourself up. You stink. Take a shower and unbraid and wash your hair. When you've finished, report to me in your bedroom. Now go."

Wolf immediately rose to his feet and headed upstairs. I waited only long enough to pick out a few items from my toy box before I followed him.

When Wolf had finished in the bathroom, he walked into the bedroom that I had given him after he had moved into the house. Without saying a word, he knelt in front of me, awaiting whatever I was going to do.

I walked to the closet and, opening the door, reached in and took out Wolf's chaps and his combat boots.

"You will get these back when you've earned the right to wear them again, slave." I growled.

Wolf just watched me, a look of deep sadness in his eyes. I could remember how happy Wolf was when I presented him with his chaps just before I branded his nipples at the torture ranch we had visited earlier in the year. Now, he had lost the right to wear his leathers, and would have to earn that right all over again.

"O.K. boy, follow me." I ordered. I took the chaps and boots and put them in my closet, then led Wolf downstairs.

"Are you hungry, boy?" I suspected he was ravenous, not having eaten anything since yesterday afternoon.

Wolf nodded his head. "Yes, Sir."

"All right boy. Never let it be said that I starved my slaves." I told him while pouring out some cereal into a large stainless steel dog bowl. I added some milk and set the bowl on the floor. "Eat" I commanded.

Wolf dropped to his hands and knees and, lowering his face, began eating the cereal directly from the bowl. I watched him carefully trying to eat while making as little of a mess as possible. When he was done, he automatically washed out the bowl, dried it and replaced it in its proper place in the kitchen cupboard. Wolf then knelt in front of me again, awaiting his next orders.

"Since it's Sunday, boy, I'm going to want to relax a bit today. You will therefore only have to work a little bit in the house today. First things first, though."

Wolf was totally naked as he knelt at my feet. He wasn't wearing his regular collar since I had replaced it with the choker for the party. His expression clouded slightly when I held out the thick leather training and posture collar I had brought up from the dungeon. This collar was almost as thick as a surgical neck brace. It had a cutout in the front for the wearer's chin, but the rest of it was almost 6 inches high.

I buckled the collar tightly around Wolf's throat as he held his hair out of the way. When it was on, he couldn't move his head more than an inch or so in any direction. If he wanted to look at something, he had to turn his entire body. This collar was very, very uncomfortable to wear for more than a few hours or so. I knew, because Mike, my first master had made me wear it on many occasions!

When the collar was on, I ordered my slave to follow me. We went into the living room.

"Footstool, boy" was all I said. Wolf immediately dropped down onto his hands and knees in front of my favorite spot on the couch.

I sat down to read the paper, stretching out my legs and setting them on Wolf's broad back. He knelt there for the next hour or so, reduced to a piece of furniture for my comfort! This was a very effective way of letting my slave know exactly what his role now was in the household. He was there only to serve his master. His feelings, his thoughts, his needs and wants now meant nothing. The slave existed only as an object, not as a person.

The thick posture collar made it impossible for him to see anything other than the carpeting directly in front of his face since he could now only look straight down while he was on his hands and knees.

When I had finished with the paper, I slid my feet off of Wolf's back before standing up.

"Up, boy" I ordered.

Wolf shot to his feet and stood ramrod straight in front of me, awaiting my next order.

I held out the other item I had brought up from the dungeon. Wolf looked at it with an expression of resigned acceptance. I bent down and quickly slid his soft cock into the metal cage of the slave chastity device I was holding. I had waited to surprise him with the device because it was almost impossible to put it on when the slave's cock was hard.

The cock slipped into a metal frame surrounding it tightly without any room for the cock to expand, therefore making it very painful for whoever was wearing the chastity device to get an erection.

The frame was attached to a thicker metal ring that was hinged around Wolf's balls and then locked into place with a small padlock. The entire unit was then fastened to a leather belt strapped tightly around his waist.

"I'll take this off only when you've earned the right to have it removed. Understood, slave?" I told Wolf when I stood back up in front of him.

"Yes, Master." He softly said.

"Good. Now, for your first task. Clean the kitchen. I want it to be spotless when you're finished. Go to work, slave."

Wolf silently bowed slightly and turned to go to work. Part of his normal everyday duties at the house was to do all the cleaning, laundry, yard work, and so forth, so this wasn't that unusual of a job for him to do. Wolf always kept the house immaculate anyway, so I knew I would have to think of different tasks for him to do as punishment.

While Wolf was cleaning the kitchen, I went into my office to catch up on some e-mail that I needed to send. I worked for about an hour or so until Wolf silently padded into the office and knelt next to my chair.

I finished the message I was sending before turning to my waiting slave and asking "Are you finished, boy?"

Wolf softly replied "Yes, Master."

I logged out and turned off my computer and stood up.

"Let's go see what kind of a job you did, slave." I growled to him. "I hope for your sake you did good."

Wolf silently followed me into the kitchen. At first glance, everything looked to be in order. As I looked closer, I began to see that Wolf had outdone himself. The entire kitchen including all the cabinets, countertops and appliances were perfect. The brushed stainless steel range top and refrigerator doors gleamed, the polished black granite countertops looked like they had been buffed, and even the cherry wood cabinets shone. I was very impressed with the effort Wolf had put into his job, but I kept it to myself. I had to remind myself that he was being punished at his own request.

"I guess it will do, slave." I told him in a grudging tone of voice. "Follow me."

We walked down the stairs into the dungeon. I told Wolf to kneel in the middle of the floor in the main room. When he was kneeling in front of me, I unbuckled the posture collar from around his neck. He didn't say anything, but I knew that he was relieved to have it off.

"Open your mouth, boy."

As soon as Wolf did open his mouth, I dropped the gym shorts I was wearing and stuffed my thickening cock deeply into his throat. I moaned softly at the feel of his hot mouth surrounding my cock. No one that I had ever known could suck my cock as well as Wolf. He could swallow the entire shaft without choking or gagging, and he also could work his tongue and throat muscles unlike any other guy's mouth I had ever had my cock in.

I grasped his head as I began to fuck my slave's mouth harder and harder. I was glad to see that Wolf was remembering his discipline training, and keeping his hands crossed behind his back. I knew how much he loved to feel my muscles while I was fucking his mouth, but he didn't move his hands at all. I also suspected his cock was hurting, trapped as it was in the chastity cage. I had never seen Wolf suck cock without getting a raging hard on.

My face fucking of my slave continued for about five minutes or so until I couldn't hold out any longer, and with a gasping moan of pleasure, I filled his mouth with a hot load of cum.

Wolf moaned as well as he swallowed my load, his tongue working my entire cock, ensuring that he got every drop of my sperm.

I finally pulled my cock from his mouth, panting from the release of his always excellent blow job. "Stand up, slave." I ordered.

Wolf rose back to his feet and stood in his posture of supplication. Now that the collar was off, he could keep his head bowed, with his eyes downcast towards the floor. I saw that his dick was straining at the cage surrounding it, just as I suspected it would be.

"Did you enjoy that, slave?" I barked.

"Yes, Master." Wolf said softly.

"Well, I didn't hear a thank you, slave. That makes me think you didn't really want my load!" I growled, keeping up the act of being a hard ass. "I guess you need another lesson in proper behavior, slave!"

I enjoyed playing with Wolf's head this way. He actually was correct in not saying anything after taking my load until I told him to. For the week of his retraining, though, I was going to switch the rules around enough to keep him off-balance.

"Over here, slave." I snarled, heading towards the St. Andrews cross. Within minutes Wolf was bound to the cross, facing it with his arms and legs spread and his broad back spread in front of me for my pleasure.

I flipped his hair forward over his broad shoulders and stroked my hands down the broad v-shaped taper of his back. His skin, a flawless golden bronze except for the fading marks from his previous whipping, felt like warm silk covering his solidly developed muscles and rippling ribcage. I enjoyed feeling his helpless body spread out awaiting whatever I chose to do to him.

I slipped a gag around Wolf's head and ordered him to open his mouth. Pulling the straps tight, I buckled the gag in place.

I leaned against Wolf, enjoying the warmth of his back pressing against my chest. I reached around Wolf's torso and, sliding my hands along his body, I began to gently squeeze and twist his nipples. He moaned into his gag as I worked his tits.

"You know you've got a hot body, don't you slave?" I murmured into his ear as I continued to roll his nipples between my fingers.

He could only grunt a reply around the gag and nod his head.

"Well, I know a way to make it even hotter, slave." I said with a sadistic chuckle.

Wolf could only moan softly as I stepped back from his bound body and slowly rotated the cross forward until he was spread eagled face down.

I stepped to the shelves holding my supplies and picked up a box containing a dozen small votive candles. I also grabbed a longer candle and some matches.

Wolf didn't know what I was about to do to him until he heard the sound of the match striking, and smelled the faint smell of sulfur. Then he moaned into his gag, knowing what was about to happen.

I lit the longer candle then held it out over Wolf's bronze back. His muscles flexed and strained as the first drops of molten wax began to drip onto his skin. The wax was hot enough that it would really sting for a few seconds until it cooled, but not hot enough to burn his skin.

Wolf moaned louder and louder as I slowly continued to drip the wax onto his back. I loved watching the muscles writhe and ripple as I tortured the broad expanse of my helpless boy's shoulders and back.

I took some of the smaller candles from the box and began to attach them to his skin, using pools of wax to anchor them down. It took almost fifteen minutes to stick all twelve of the candles to his body, from his shoulders all the way down to the back of his thighs and calves. He was sweating so profusely by now that it took two and even three tries to get the candles to stick to his skin.

Wolf was gasping for air by the time I had finished.

"You like that, slave?" I taunted him, knowing that he couldn't answer. "You want more?"

Wolf could only nod his head to reply.

"Good, because you're gonna get more, slave!" I snarled in his ear.

Wolf began to moan in anticipation as I began to quickly light all the candles that were attached to his skin. I then sat back in the master's chair to watch what would happen next.

Wolf began to struggle harder against his bonds as the hot wax began to run down the candles and spread across his skin. Each movement of his body would cause some more wax to flow from the small pools just under the wick of each candle. This wax was even hotter than the wax I had dripped onto him. It was a vicious cycle. Every movement added to the torture by hot wax, and each new spread of wax caused him to flinch and flex his muscles, spilling more wax which caused him to struggle more, spilling more wax.

I was thoroughly enjoying watching my muscle slave enduring the torture. His ribs were rippling under his skin as he gasped for air every time more of the molten wax flowed into his body. Sweat shone on the skin that wasn't coated with a layer of wax.

Streams of wax began to flow down the sides of his torso and down from his thighs and calves as well. I also knew that as the candles burned down closer and closer to his skin, the wax was getting hotter and hotter.

I sat and watched my slave struggle and suffer until the last of the candles had burned down to the point where there wasn't enough of a wick to stay lit. Wolf had been moaning into his gag constantly for the last five minutes or so, as the wax was now so hot that it was on the point of burning his skin, without actually hurting him. I was always careful to use pure white candles with no scent added, as the addition of either dyes for color, or perfumes for scents, would raise the melting temperature of the wax hot enough to burn skin.

When the last of the candles had gone out, I let Wolf rest for just a few minutes. I knew that the sensation of having the solidified wax coating his skin was unusual, and rather erotic, having experienced it myself on several occasions.

Finally I rotated the cross back upright and gently ran my hands over Wolf's wax encrusted back.

"We need to get this stuff off, don't you think, slave?" I growled into his ear.

Wolf could only nod in agreement, knowing what was coming next.

I stepped to the shelves holding my toys and picked up a pair of thick rubber gloves that had been dipped in liquid rubber, then coated with crushed bits of stone and shell. Originally designed for fishermen to use to scale fish, they were also great for abrasion torture.

I rubbed one hand across the width of Wolf's shoulders. He howled into his gag at the feel of the rough surface scraping his sensitive skin. Grinning to myself, I started to grind the wax from Wolf's body with both hands.

Every muscle in his back and shoulders was flexing and bulging as I slowly and torturously worked my way down his torso. He was screaming continuously into the gag in his mouth. The skin of his back began to look like it had been sandpapered, with red stripes streaking the golden bronze surface.

It took almost ten minutes of constant rubbing to remove the majority of the wax from my slave's spread body. When I finally stepped back from him, Wolf was whining and sobbing into his gag. I knew he was in real pain from the gloves, and I also suspected his cock was probably hurting badly as well, being trapped in the chastity cage.

If I knew my slave as well as I hoped I did, I figured he was incredibly turned on by the painful torture he had endured. I decided to take him over the top, to the limit of his endurance.

"O.K. boy, it's time to get the rest of the wax off." I snarled in his ear.

Wolf only groaned as he felt the tails of the flogger stroke across his already tender skin. At the first slashing impact of the leather on his back, he grunted loudly into the gag as every muscle in his sculpted physique stood out in sharp relief.

Again and again I worked the flogger across Wolf's body until the last of the wax had been knocked off of his now reddened, striped skin. He was writhing and struggling on the cross as I continued to torture his helpless body.

Wolf began to scream into the gag again as I increased the intensity of the flogging until I was smashing the tails of the cat across his welted back as hard as I could. The sweat was flowing down my body as I tortured my slave to the limit of his strength. Again and again the leather impacted Wolf's skin with a vicious *SMACK!* sound, in concert with a muffled scream from Wolf. Every muscle of his back and shoulders was flexing and straining as Wolf desperately struggled to escape the burning, slashing pain of my flogging his tenderized skin.

He finally gave me the hand signal to stop that we used when he was gagged and couldn't speak. I immediately stopped flogging Wolf, knowing that he wouldn't have signaled unless he really needed me to stop.

Wolf went limp on the cross, supported only by his widespread arms, as his legs buckled.

I quickly rotated the cross horizontally again and carefully released Wolf from his bondage.

He was moaning constantly as I gently removed the gag from his mouth, then supported his head until he had recovered enough strength to slowly crawl down from the cross.

I lowered him down to the floor of the dungeon, then sat down next to him, holding my exhausted slave as he began to weep.

I knew that his crying after a heavy torture session was a way for him to release the emotional stress from being tortured, so I always let him cry himself out.

We sat on the floor for about ten minutes or so with Wolf wrapped in my arms and his head resting against my chest. Finally his breathing slowed to normal and he lifted his head. Looking into my eyes, he weakly smiled at me then kissed me.

"Thank you, Master. This boy knows he deserved to be punished for his mistake." He softly murmured. "This boy will accept whatever discipline Master decides."

I told him gently "Any other discipline can wait until you have recovered. It doesn't do any good to work over a slave so hard that he gets sick or is unable to function. Then he's useless to himself, and becomes a burden for his master. You will come upstairs with me, and I will allow you to clean yourself up and rest for a while. Don't think for a minute, however that this is the end of your punishment, boy. You still will have to come back down here and clean up all the wax that's all over the floor."

Wolf bowed his head in acknowledgement. Rising stiffly to his feet, he silently padded up the stairs into the house, following me.

That morning set the pattern for the rest of the week. Wolf would be used as a footstool while I caught up on my e-mail and read the paper, then he would be given a task to accomplish in the morning, such as scrubbing the bathrooms in the house with a brush attached to a gag strapped around his head. That even included using the gag brush to clean the toilets! When he was finished, we would head into the city to do our workout at the gym. Since we both were in serious training for the bodybuilding competition, I decided that our workouts were too important to miss. While we were at the gym, Wolf was allowed to speak without permission. As far as the other guys at the gym knew, there wasn't anything special happening between Wolf and myself. While at the gym, Wolf had to wear a tee-shirt to hide the whip marks on his chest and back from the twenty five lashes he would get on both his back and chest each night on top of whatever other torture he had to endure. As he endured the fifty strokes of the flogger, Wolf had to recite the list of house rules I had drilled into him when I had first trained him. I wanted to be sure he wouldn't forget any of the rules again!

Once we were back home, however, Wolf's retraining continued. All of his meals were eaten from the dog dish on the floor in a corner of the kitchen. Then we would go to the dungeon for his daily torture session, sometimes as early as seven in the evening, with the sessions lasting until nearly midnight. Then he would be chained up in the slave irons and left in the cell in the dungeon in total darkness to try to get some sleep.

The torture sessions included such punishments as Wolf being strapped to the bondage chair with the wires from my TENS unit attached to his nipples, and the connections from my modified relaxicisor on his balls. Wolf was forced to endure extreme electro torture until he was screaming into the hood, his entire body thrashing and writhing, every muscle bulging against the restraints, as the electricity slammed into his tits and nuts.

The other tortures Wolf endured over the week pushed him to his limit, such as being suspended from his wrists and hung from the overhead beam in the dungeon. I left him hanging for one entire night in total darkness, with his entire body weight stretching his torso. It made it very difficult for Wolf to breathe, especially since he also had the bit gag in his mouth. The gag caused him to drool saliva all over his chest as he fought to breathe.

Also, one evening he was bound standing up on the St. Andrew's cross with over forty pounds of weight suspended from his balls for an hour. Wolf gasped for the air the entire time. With that much weight pulling on his nuts, he was trying desperately to keep from throwing up from the sheer agony burning through his guts.

Another night he was stretched on the rack to the previous maximum that he had ever been pulled apart, twelve clicks of the winch, which was a total stretch of six inches. Then I forced the winch one more click, with Wolf screaming in absolute agony the entire time. To add to the torture, I left him pulled out that tightly for almost ten minutes before releasing him. At the end of each torture session, I would then force my exhausted slave to suck my cock until I pumped a load of my cum down his throat, but not let him cum himself. Then he would get his flogging while he recited the rules to me.

For the entire week, Wolf wore the cock cage which allowed him to be able to keep himself clean and piss whenever I gave him permission. But he couldn't get a hard on, or could he cum, or even play with himself. I knew his nuts would be swollen and incredibly sore by the end of the week from not cumming.

The hardest part for me was the fact that I forced him to sleep in the irons in the cell in the dungeon when he wasn't bound in some other form in the torture chamber. I truly missed having my lover in bed with me and feeling his hard body against me when I awoke in the morning.

I also missed the great spontaneous sex we would have first thing each day. But, I knew that Wolf was really upset about disappointing me with his breach of training and really wanted and needed this retraining, so I made the sacrifice.

By Saturday afternoon, Wolf was nearly exhausted from the constant demands I had made on him and the even harder than usual torture sessions in the dungeon. I hadn't worked him this hard even while I was training him after we had first met at the Eagle. In spite of his fatigue, however, he hadn't complained at all.

Also, except for the flogging following his waxing, Wolf had not called out one of our safe words, or signaled me to stop during his extreme torture sessions. He seemed to be trying to endure whatever I did to him, even if it pushed him past the previous limits of his endurance.

Wolf also had not slipped in his discipline once, and the house was even more immaculate than usual.

I decided that this evening, we would celebrate Wolf's successful refresher week of slave training. Of course, I didn't tell him that. He just knew that I had told him he had one week of retraining to endure.

I made a couple of quick telephone calls to Danny and some other friends in town while Wolf was giving the dungeon a final clean-up after he had endured an extended session of exquisitely painful inverted flogging. I had suspended him by his ankles and spread his arms widely out and down towards the floor before giving him a full one hundred lashes on his chest, and another hundred lashes across his back immediately upon our return home from the gym.

He had no idea of what I had planned for him! Tonight was going to signal Wolf's return as my public slave. I could only hope he would endure what I was planning for him. It wasn't particularly painful, but I knew Wolf would hate it even more than brutal torture. Of course, Wolf didn't hate to be tortured, at least not physically. Mental and emotional torture, well, that was something else!

Chapter 7

Redemption

The day was fading into a dreary, damp and misty night when I announced to Wolf that he had one last night of retraining to endure before he would have his previous status restored to him if he could endure the final punishment.

He looked at me from his kneeling position at the side of the chair I was sitting in, his expression of anticipation mixed with desire. However, he didn't say a word, not having been given permission to speak. He was looking really drawn and haggard, having been worked harder then usual for the last week and not having been able to sleep properly while wearing the shackles and being chained up in the cell most nights. He also hadn't shaved for a week which left his normal faint five o-clock shadow much more noticeable. Usually he only had to shave about every two or three days, since his beard grew so slowly. Secretly, I thought that the stubble shading his face made him look even hotter than usual, but I wasn't going to tell him that! At least, not until the appropriate time.

I knew he was anticipating whatever I had planned for him tonight. Usually, Wolf enjoyed the challenge of trying to endure my tortures. Tonight, however was going to be a bit different. I suspected that he would really end up hating what I was going to make him endure by the end of the night. Of course, that was all a part of being punished and tortured at his own request.

After we had eaten dinner and Wolf had cleaned up the kitchen, I just relaxed for a bit in the living room. I read and did a bit of work on-line, while Wolf silently knelt next to my chair, naked with his hands crossed behind his back, looking down at the floor. I knew just kneeling and not being allowed to speak was really tough mentally on a slave, having had to do it many a night myself while being trained by Mike. However, it was also a good way to practice mental discipline for a slave, plus it gave him time to think about his error in judgment.

At about ten o' clock, I closed the computer and stood.

I said "Slave, you will kneel here while I get dressed, understood?"

Wolf softly answered "Yes, Master."

I walked upstairs and put on my leather jeans, my vest and my engineer boots. I picked out what Wolf was to wear tonight as well. When I strode back downstairs, he was still kneeling in exactly the same spot.

I dropped his cutoff shorts in front of him and growled; "This is all you get to wear tonight, slave."

I then bent down and locked the posture collar around his throat. I knew that Wolf didn't like it very much, but he accepted it as part of his punishment.

I just sat down on the couch and waited for the evening's events to get started. Wolf continued to kneel on the floor with a questioning look on his face, but he didn't say anything. He knew better than to question what I was doing.

In about another five minutes I heard a car pull up in the driveway, followed almost immediately by another car. In a few seconds the doorbell rang.

"Answer it, slave." I growled to Wolf.

He rose to his feet, pulled on the cutoffs, and opened the door. In strode Danny my best friend, in full leathers, being followed by his slave, Eddie, and another couple, also in leather.

This was Joe Cook, another topman friend of mine and his slaveboy, H.J.. Joe was a recent arrival in the city, having moved here from South Carolina with his boy about a month earlier. He and his boy had purchased the piercing business from Frank, a friend of Mike, my late master. Frank was the man who had given me my nipple rings several years ago. He had since decided to retire and move out of the city.

Joe had a friendly face with an easy smile surrounded by a mop of shaggy brown hair that hung down to his shoulders, and a neatly trimmed goatee. He spoke with a pronounced slow southern drawl that belied his abilities as a hard core leatherman. Both Joe and his boy had applied to join the leather club that Danny and I, and our boys, were members of.

Danny and Joe both gave me a hug, their boys paid their respects to my boots, then we all turned to where Wolf had resumed his position on the floor next to my chair. I had explained the whole situation to Danny several days earlier, so he knew exactly what was happening between Wolf and myself.

"Master Eric, do you think this slave is ready to pass his final test?" Danny asked.

I looked down into Wolf's face and growled; "He better be. He's getting his due, whether he's ready or not!"

Wolf just moaned very softly. He had no idea that I had set this entire evening up to test him and to welcome him back as my partner if he endured tonight's tests.

I said to Wolf; "Over here, slave,"

He immediately rose to his feet and walked over in front of me. Wolf then knelt in the center of the room, head held up by the high collar, but with his hands crossed behind his back. Danny, Joe and I stood in front of him, while the two boys knelt off to one side.

"Slave, you committed a grave breach of your training. What do you have to say for yourself?" I snarled down into Wolf's face.

Softly, hesitantly, he said "Yes master, this boy made a mistake. He is very sorry and hopes he can be forgiven. He will do whatever it takes to earn your pardon, Sir."

I turned to the other guys. "I've been working him hard all week, and I think he's about ready to show us if he's serious." I snapped "Up, boy!" to Wolf.

He immediately shot back to his feet and stood at rigid attention. His back was ramrod straight, his head erect and his eyes were locked straight ahead. Danny and Joe ordered their boys up as well, and all six of us headed downstairs into the dungeon.

When we were downstairs I ordered Wolf to stand in the middle of the floor while I collected some items from my supplies. I buckled a pair of restraints with attached chains around his wrists, and another pair around his ankles. I led Wolf to the outside door. He followed, the chains dragging on the floor. We stepped outside into the chilly, drizzling night. Wolf immediately started to shiver since he really disliked the cold. I occasionally would use ice cubes or gel freezer packs to torture his nipples and his chest, or even his cock and balls while he was helplessly spread out on the cross. He really hated that, which was why I enjoyed subjecting him to that particular torture!

Whenever we would go skiing in the mountains of Colorado or Lake Tahoe, I would always needle him about looking like an overstuffed snowman, since he would be wearing so many layers of clothes. Wolf always half jokingly claimed he was so hot-blooded because of his ancestry, being half Apache Indian and half Mexican-American, so this made him extra sensitive to the cold.

I led my shivering slave over next to the pool area and told him to lay down on one of the lounge chairs. He gasped as his still welted back came in contact with the cold water on the slats of the lounge. As soon as he was stretched out, I attached the chains on his restraints to the lounge, leaving him stretched out full length totally exposed to the elements, except for his shorts. Within a minute or two he was soaked by the chill, misty air and light drizzle. Wolf began shivering harder and whimpering softly.

"Shut up, slave!" I snarled into his face. "The more noise you make, the longer you'll be out here alone in the cold!"

With that, I stood and turned to walk back inside, leaving Wolf bound, helpless and all alone in the cold, wet night.

When I walked back inside the dungeon, Danny asked me "Well, what do you want to do while the slave chills?"

I grinned at him and said "Well, let's see. We're in a well equipped torture chamber. There are two young, strong slave boys. We are three horny topmen. I think we might be able to think of something to do, don't you?" Danny and Joe both gave me wicked grins, turned and looked at their boys, kneeling along one wall, waiting.

Within a few minutes, both boys were naked and being bound by their masters.

Joe was spreading H.J. facing the St. Andrew's cross in preparation for a hard flogging of his back and shoulders. H.J. had a swimmer's build with a spray of dark hair across his pecs and down across his stomach, not much definition, but still solid muscle. H.J.'s head was covered with a short stubble of black hair. Joe had told me that he had shaved his boy's head when they got together, since H.J. had let his hair grow out into tangled masses of curls that were almost impossible to get a brush through. Once his head was shaved, Joe decided to keep it that way.

Danny took Eddie into the next room and was fastening restraints on his wrists before ordering Eddie onto the rack. Eddie had a lean, ripped physique that looked fantastic when he was pulled tight. Every muscle, tendon, and rib stood out on his torso when he was being tortured on the rack. I was a bit surprised to see that Eddie's hair was still cut into the Mohawk stripe that Danny had shaved during Eddie's torture session when he was being punished for his misbehavior at the Eagle. I had thought that Danny would let it grow back after the Halloween party we had attended earlier.

Sitting in my chair in the corner of the dungeon's main room, I kept an eye on the clock so as to not leave Wolf bound in the cold for too long. I wanted him to be miserable, but not get sick from exposure or hypothermia.

I sat and observed the two slave boys being tortured by their masters. Joe was working his boy's body with some of my cats, leaving angry looking welts across his writhing and twisting back muscles. I could tell by his flogging style that Joe was a really experienced topman, with a good grasp of how to torture a slave with a flogger.

Danny was slowly stretching Eddie on the rack, pulling him tighter and tighter, while Eddie shrieked in agony at each click of the winch. When Eddie was drawn out as taut as he had ever been pulled, Danny stood over him and started to work on Eddie's pecs and abs with a riding crop. Each stroke of the crop left a livid red welt across Eddie's bulging, rippling ribcage and incredible lean, hard abs.

I sat listening to their screams of pain and pleasure, for about half an hour or so before I went outside to get Wolf. The drizzle had intensified into a light but constant rain that was bone-chillingly cold. Wolf was shivering and writhing on the lounge. He was whimpering and crying softly, but he made an effort to quiet himself when he saw me approaching.

"Are you ready to go back inside, boy?" I asked.

"Y-Y-Yes, S-S-S-Sir. P-P-Pl-Please!" he stuttered between chattering teeth.

I bent down and released his restraints from the lounge chair. Wolf slowly rolled onto his side and worked his way up onto his feet. He stood in front of me, his head held up by the posture collar, but every other part of his body was the picture of misery and dejection. His hair was stringy and unkempt; glued to his body by the rainwater.

I led my thoroughly dispirited slave back into the warmth of the dungeon. When the heat enveloped his body, Wolf finally broke. He sank to his knees and began to sob.

"Oh God, Master, I'm so sorry. I'm sorry. I was disrespectful to you. I'm sorry!"

He was totally breaking down by now. I had never seen Wolf come this unglued, even during his initial training, over 16 months ago. I guess the full week of hard training and heavy tortures, combined with Wolf's own guilty feelings was finally too much for him to bear. The exposure to the cold was the final straw that broke through his dam of self-control, and now all of his buried feelings were coming to the surface.

Danny and Joe had released their boys from their bondage, and all four guys were standing to one side watching silently. I think that they all knew that this was a critical moment in Wolf's discipline and retraining.

I snarled down at my absolutely wretched looking slave; "Tell these other masters and boys what you did, slave, and how you feel now, boy!"

Wolf continued to sob, tears now running freely down his face. "I struck my Master in front of others. I didn't really mean to, but I did anyway. I love you, Sir. I would never want to do anything to hurt you. Please, Sir, please forgive me. It was an accident, Sir. Oh God, I'm so sorry! I'm sorry!"

By now, Wolf was bawling, his entire body shuddering; wracked by spasms. He had totally lost control of himself. I had completely broken him down over the last week.

I looked at the others standing watching Wolf cry. Tears were running down Eddie's cheeks at the sight of his friend breaking down. Eddie knew what Wolf was going through, having been recently subjected to severe discipline and retraining himself.

Finally the sight was too much for me to bear any longer. I thought; "Screw it!" as I dropped to my knees in front of my slave. I reached out to him and unbuckled the stiff collar from around his throat. As soon as the collar was removed from Wolf's throat, I wrapped my arms around him and pulled him to my chest.

The chill from his body struck me. I hadn't realized exactly how cold Wolf had gotten tied up in the rain.

"Shh, boy, it's all right. It's over." I comforted him as we embraced. "It's over. You're forgiven. You made it."

He snuffled and looked at me through red-rimmed eyes. "Really, Sir? You mean it, Sir?"

I smiled at him. "Yes, really. You've done everything I've asked of you and more. Now it's time to come home. I hereby declare in front of these witnesses that you are once again my slave in good standing. Welcome back, boy."

Wolf lowered his head onto my shoulder and began to cry again. This time, however, his tears seemed to be tears of relief. I held my boy until he cried himself out. It was an extremely emotional moment.

When I looked at the other guys, Eddie had his arms wrapped around Danny and was sucking one of his nipples, while H.J. and Joe were kissing deeply.

I held Wolf a few minutes more before I said; "Lets get those shorts off, boy. They're soaking wet."

Wolf stood in front of me while I unbuttoned his cutoffs and let them drop to the floor. I then used the key to unlock the cock cage from the ring trapping Wolf's nuts that he had worn almost constantly for the last week. Wolf moaned in pleasure and relief as he felt the chastity device being removed from his dick, which immediately began to swell in front of me. In less than a minute, Wolf had a raging hard-on.

I stood up facing my slave and in a mock gruff tone, growled "Did I say your cock could get hard, boy?"

Wolf smiled sheepishly, saying; "I'm sorry, Sir, but you know it's always had a mind of it's own."

I smiled back and asked him; "Well boy, do you know what you have to do to a disobedient cock?"

Wolf looked puzzled and merely shook his head.

I grinned. "What else? You beat it!"

Wolf looked at me for just a moment before bursting into delighted laughter. I couldn't help but to start laughing along with him. The joke wasn't really all that funny, but I think Wolf was just working the stress of the last week out of his system.

I hugged him to me and just held him tightly. I could feel that Wolf was still chilled from his exposure torture.

"Come on, boy, let's see if we can warm you up." I said as I started to slip out of my vest.

Wolf said; "May I, Sir?"

He helped me out of my vest, folding it neatly and laying it out on a chair. He then knelt in front of me to unlace my boots. He looked up and smiled at me before bending down and beginning to lick the last spots of rain water from my boots.

There was always something really sensual and sexy about having a hot man tongue clean my boots, and no one did it better than Wolf. I could swear that I could actually feel the warmth of his tongue even through the thick leather of my boots. I loved a good bootlicking almost as much as I enjoyed having a well trained bootblack shine my boots in a bar.

When my boots were clean, he helped me slip out of them, then reached out and unfastened my belt and unbuttoned my pants. Wolf stood and waited while I finished undressing, folding my leather pants with the same care and respect he always showed to my leather.

When I was stripped, I said, "Let's go, boy. You guys can come too, if you want."

Danny, Joe, and their boys stripped off their own clothes and followed us into the next room and into the sauna

Wolf moaned with pleasure as we entered the 195 degree heat. We all found places to sit on the benches. Within minutes, all of our bodies were dripping with sweat.

As I sat watching, Danny pulled Eddie to him and ordered his slave to start licking. Eddie loved to worship his master's hard, rippling physique. He leaned in and ran his tongue down the valley between Danny's solidly developed pectorals. Then he worked his way down to Danny's washboard abs.

I turned to Wolf and said "Looks like a good idea. Go to it, boy."

Wolf softly moaned "Oh God, thank you Sir" as he immediately began sucking on my left nipple.

Danny, Joe, and I sat in the sauna for about ten minutes or so, our three slave boys working to lick and suck up all the sweat they could from our bodies. The feel of Wolf's hot tongue sliding across my skin while his hands stroked and caressed my body was incredibly sexy. The look of the other two masters being worshiped by their boys was also totally hot, as everyone's body was dripping wet with sweat in the red light of the sauna.

It only took another couple of minutes before Joe started to mouth fuck his slave. Joe had a lean, sculpted physique and a thick, hard cock. H.J. was kneeling in front of Joe, his head being held still while Joe thrust the length of his cock in and out of his boy's mouth. Joe's hair was matted with sweat and stuck to his shoulders. It wasn't as long as Wolf's hair, but I still thought it was very sexy nonetheless. I had told him on our first meeting that I thought that he was hot, but I also respected his standing as a top. I also told him that if he ever wanted to get together with me as equals in bed for some hot man to man sex, all he had to do was ask! I had the feeling that sometime it was going to happen. Danny and I had had sex many times as equals, so it wasn't unusual for two topmen to enjoy each other's company at times.

Wolf sat between my legs as we watched the muscles on Joe's torso ripple under his gleaming skin until, with a groan of pleasure, he shot a thick stream of cum into his boy's sucking, eager mouth.

I nudged Wolf and said; "They have the right idea. Now it's your turn, boy."

My boy knelt between my legs and within seconds he had the entire length of my cock in his mouth. I groaned in sheer pleasure as I felt the muscles in my slave's throat begin to work on my shaft. I had really missed being able to have my cock sucked for the sheer pleasure of it, instead as part of a punishment or torture, as I had to do for the last week.

By now, Eddie was deep-throating Danny's cock as well. The two slave boys worked almost in unison, their heads bobbing up and down. Danny was sitting next to me on he lower bench of the sauna, and as we were getting the blow jobs from our boys, he leaned over and kissed me deeply. The feelings were almost too much to bear, the hot sucking mouth of Wolf on my cock, and Danny, tongue kissing me in the heat.

I heard Joe softly drawl; "Gawdamm, that looks great!" as the muscled backs of the two slaves glistened in the red light of the sauna, with streams of sweat pouring down their torsos. Within another minute, Danny pulled back from me and groaned; "Aw shit, I'm gonna cum!" just before grabbing Eddie's head and holding it still while pumping a load of his hot sperm down his boy's throat. That triggered my own orgasm and I growled "Oh yeah, take it, slave" as Wolf's mouth was filled by my load of cum.

Wolf moaned in sheer pleasure as he swallowed my seed, licking my cockhead to be sure he got every last drop of my load. Finally he leaned back and smiled up at me, his face glowing with happiness. His hair was a mess and he needed a shave, but in my eyes he was beautiful. Wolf had endured the week of hard retraining and strict discipline that he himself had requested after his slip-up, and I felt that we both were stronger for it.

I ordered Wolf to stand up. He rose up and stood at attention, his rock hard cock standing straight out in front of him. Next to him, Eddie stood as well, his own dick throbbing.

Joe said; "Eric, I want to thank you for inviting us over here tonight. This is an incredible dungeon you have here. I know I've never seen such a great set up, and I don't think H.J. has either." His slave didn't say anything, but merely nodded his head.

Joe continued; "To show you guys how much we appreciate the welcome you gave us to the leather community here, I want my boy to take care of those hard cocks if that's all right with you. We're the new guys in town, and I'd like my boy to learn just where he stands in the order of the slaves around here. I figure there's no better way for him to learn that then to suck a couple of senior slave cocks and swallow some slave cum."

I looked at Danny who smiled and said; "Sure. Tell him to go for it."

Joe merely looked down at his boy and nodded. H.J. knelt in front of Wolf and Eddie. Opening his mouth, he sucked the head of Eddie's dick into his mouth. Then he reached up and grasped Wolf's thick shaft and gently pulled it towards his mouth as well.

Wolf and Eddie started to stroke and caress each others bodies as they stood together in front of the kneeling slave. Finally they wrapped their arms around each other and began to kiss deeply as H.J. succeeded in getting the heads of both of their cocks into his stretched mouth at the same time. Hs arms were wrapped around the legs of the muscle slaves standing in front of him. Wolf and Eddie both were moaning as their tongues explored each others mouths and their hands felt each others hard, gleaming muscled bodies. It only took another minute or two before Eddie began to moan louder as the muscles in his incredibly ripped abs began to flex and ripple as he approached his orgasm. H.J. sucked both cockheads into his mouth as far as he could just before Eddie's load shot into his mouth. Apparently Eddie's cumming triggered Wolf's load. H.J. choked and gagged on the two loads of slave sperm filling his mouth at the same time. I had to guess that Wolf's load was huge, since he hadn't cum in over a week. The two slaveboys hugged and kissed deeply until both orgasms were spent.

Joe's boy finally pulled back from the two cocks stretching his mouth. He licked his lips, trapping a small dribble of cum that was running down towards his chin. H.J. smiled and turned towards where Danny and I sat.

"Thank you, Sirs" he said, bowing his head at the same time. "That was wonderful. Both of you have exceptional boys. It would be an honor to serve either one of them, or either of you, Sirs, anytime my master would allow me to, Sirs."

I nodded my thanks at his compliment. "You would have to have your master's permission, obviously, but you are welcome, boy."

Joe grinned as he sat down next to Danny and myself.

"I hope sometime we can all get together again to have some fun. Unfortunately, we have to leave soon, since we have to get up kinda early in the mornin'. I really do want to thank you for inviting us over here tonight. Sometime we'll have to come back so we can give these boys a good workin' over. H.J. can take some pain, but I've never found out exactly how much. I bet we could find out here, though."

I grinned back and told him; "You're always welcome to visit. Maybe we can have a torture contest between these slaves some day and find out exactly how much each one can take. There's a shower in the bathroom just outside to the right. Speaking of the bathroom, I really gotta take a leak!"

Joe looked at me and said; "How about you let H.J. take care of that for you, so you don't have to go out."

I grinned and said; "Sure, if that's what he wants to do."

Joe answered; "He loves it. Almost nothing he loves more than a bellyful of hot piss!"

H.J. knelt in front of me and took my cock into his mouth. Within seconds I felt the stream of piss begin to flow into his mouth. H.J. moaned in pleasure even as he was swallowing my entire load of piss.

When I was done, H.J. pulled back and softly said; "Thank you Master Eric. That was great. It tasted so good, Sir."

I told him "Glad you enjoyed it, boy."

Joe grinned at his boy, then turned to me and said; "Now, what was that about a shower?"

Danny turned to me and said "I'll show him. We really have to get going, too. I hope you don't mind if we run."

"Hey, not at all. We enjoyed having you guys over tonight. But before you leave, I think Wolf has something to say." I looked expectantly at Wolf.

He cleared his throat and softly said; "Sirs, and fellow boys. This slave made a mistake and embarrassed his master in front of company. His master was gracious enough to offer to forget it, but this slave felt that he needed to be disciplined. He knows that he's learned his lesson, and this slave wants to apologize once again to his master."

With that, Wolf knelt down in front of me again and kissed my bare feet.

I waited until he straightened back up in front of me, then I cupped his chin in my hand forcing him to look directly into my eyes.

"Your apology is accepted, boy. Now, let's get out of here before we cook."

The six of us exited the sauna. Danny, Joe and their boys took turns in the shower, cleaning up before getting dressed. Wolf and I stayed naked. I ordered Wolf to straighten up the dungeon while our guests were dressing. When they were ready to leave, I called Wolf back into the main room of the dungeon to bid our company a proper farewell. He kissed the boots of the two visiting masters, and thanked the two boys.

I told Danny I would call him in a few days to discuss some business I had with him, and told Joe he was welcome to call and arrange a visit anytime.

After our company had been shown to the door by Wolf, I called him to me.

"Boy, its now just after midnight. That means that it's now Sunday, the first day of a new week. It's also the start of your new freedom. I just hope we don't ever have to do this again!"

Wolf smiled a bit sadly.

"Believe me, Sir, I don't ever want to have to do it again either. It wasn't the pain that I minded as much as the fact that I disappointed you, Sir. I also missed being able to sleep with you. I love you, Sir." Impulsively, he wrapped his strong arms around me and hugged. I hugged him back just as hard.

"Let's go get a shower, boy, and then I want you to clean yourself out with the shower shot. I think you need a good fucking, and first thing in the morning, that's what you're gonna get!"

Wolf looked into my eyes and smiled.

"Yes, Sir." was all he said.

It was all he needed to say. My slave lover was back.

Chapter 8

Renewal

I awoke later that morning to the soft susurration of Wolf's breathing as he slept. It was unusual for me to wake up before he did, but I suspect he was exhausted from the week of retraining. I lay next to him for a while as he lay on his back. I enjoyed watching the gentle rise and fall of his chest as he breathed. Finally, I gently laid my head on his chest, trying not to awaken him. I heard him murmur softly in his sleep.

I lay like this for a while before being lulled back to sleep by the rhythmic beating of Wolf's heart. When I awoke again, the first sensation I felt was Wolf's hand gently stroking my hair. I turned my head slightly and gently began to suck on his right nipple. The pressure on the back of my head increased gently as I heard Wolf softly moan; "Oh yeah. Oh yeah. Mmm, that's nice."

I had missed being able to make love to my slave / lover for the sheer pleasure of it for the last week. Some old school leather top men said that falling in love with a slaveboy was wrong. They claimed that a topman was supposed to keep an emotional distance from his slave. I had to totally disagree. I felt that to be able to control whatever a topman did to his bottom boy, the top had to have a deep emotional attachment. Without that emotion, there would be nothing to stop a top from torturing his bottom to the point of physical injury, or even worse!

I also thought that a deep emotional attachment was necessary from a slave to his master. His sense of duty, of loyalty and even love was necessary for a truly deep relationship.

Wolf was without a doubt the best thing to happen to my life since Mike had saved me from my bout of self-destruction after the loss of both of my parents in the plane crash. I truly loved him deeply. That was why having to torture and discipline him for his error was so difficult.

I slowly increased the level of the sucking of Wolf's right nipple, while at the same time I started to gently play with his left nipple with my free hand. I was rewarded with a moan of pure pleasure from him.

After a few more minutes, I raised my head from Wolf's chest and slowly slid up until I was face to face with my lover.

"Hi" he grinned to me.

"Hi yourself" I smiled back before kissing him.

"God, I missed this." Wolf softly said. "I'm so sorry about what happened, and I promise that it'll never happen again."

"That's all right, boy. It's over now. You've been forgiven. I think you learned your lesson." I told him, while hugging him to me.

"Thank you, Sir. I hope that I did. If not, I guess you'll just have to beat it into me again." Wolf said, but with a merry grin. I knew things were back to normal and that Wolf's sense of humor was starting to reassert itself.

I gave him a mock glower and slid my hand down his hard body to grasp his swollen cock. Wolf moaned with pleasure as I started to squeeze his thick shaft.

"It looks like parts of you still haven't learned their lesson. I guess that I'll just have to keep on reminding it who's in charge around here! Like I said last night, if you have a disobedient cock, the only thing to do is beat it." I said gruffly while starting to slowly jack Wolf's dick. He moaned in pure pleasure and lay back, his hands under his head while I continued to stroke the fat eight inches. I loved working my lover's cock in my hand. The entire dark brown shaft was silken smooth, with thick veins running the entire length. Wolf moaned again in pure delight as I finally bent down and slipped the plum shaped head of his cock into my mouth.

I sucked Wolf's cock for a few minutes before I pulled back and slid up until I was laying on top of him. I gazed down into his brown eyes and softly said; "Do you remember what I said I was going to do to you this morning, boy?"

Wolf smiled up at me and said; "Yes Sir. You said that I needed a good fucking and that you were going to give it to me." He lifted his head up and kissed me before continuing; "I'm ready for you, Sir. Please fuck me, Master. Fuck me hard and long. I've really missed being fucked by the hottest, sexiest bodybuilder leatherman in the city, Sir!"

I lifted myself off of his body so Wolf could roll over. He lay across a pillow that he pulled under his hips, so his butt was sticking up. He spread his legs as I lubed my cock up and worked a finger deeply into his hot hole. Wolf moaned in sheer pleasure as my cock slipped inside his ass, stretching his sphincter. I worked the entire nine inches of my shaft into his ass, then just lay down on top of my slave, remaining still for a few moments. I loved the feel of his warm, muscular back against my chest, and the clean, fresh smell of his hair. I wrapped my arms around his torso, my fingers playing with his nipples as I slowly started to rock my hips up and down. Wolf growled in sheer ecstasy as I slowly continued to fuck him for almost fifteen minutes in just this one position before I told him it was time to try another.

Wolf rolled over onto his back again and lifted his legs. I grasped his ankles and held then wide spread while he guided my dick to his willing asshole. Wolf gave another moan of pleasure when I slowly, teasingly reentered him. The sight of my muscle slave's body writhing and flexing in ecstasy as I began to thrust into him was unbelievably erotic. Wolf's entire torso was rippling with muscle as I began to drive faster and faster.

I groaned in pleasure when Wolf reached out and began to stroke my chest and run his hands over every part of my body he could reach.

"God, I love your muscles. Fuck me, please, musclemaster. Fuck this slave as hard as you can, Sir. Please!" Wolf gasped as I started to pound into him.

I wanted to prolong our sex session and try some new positions for fucking, but the sight and feel of Wolf's body was just too much for me to control myself. I started to slam my cock into his hot, willing ass harder and harder as I growled and grunted with the effort of ravaging his ass.

Wolf began to squeeze and pull on my nipples and run his hands up and down my abs as I pounded his ass harder and harder with my cock. He cried out a wordless howl of pleasure on each thrust of my dick.

I continued my relentless driving into his hot hole, until with a cry of "Oh fuck, boy, I'm cumming. Take it!" I pulled out of his ass.

Wolf immediately slid down under me, while at the same time opening his mouth. His hot mouth covered the head of my cock just as a huge load of sperm jetted out. I threw back my head and bellowed "Oh yeah, Oh yeah. Aww, fuck, boy! Take it, slave!"

Wolf loved swallowing my loads of sperm. He had often said that he thought it was a bit of a waste to shoot a load of cum into someone's ass, since they couldn't taste it that way. And he loved the taste of a good, hot load of cum!

Wolf pulled on my nipples as I filled his mouth with my cum, only letting go when my explosive orgasm was spent. Finally, I had to pull out of his mouth, as the feel of Wolf's tongue working over the now exquisitely sensitive head of my dick was too much for me to take any more. I lowered myself back down on top of my slave boy's hot, sweaty body. I could feel the pounding of both of our hearts as Wolf wrapped his arms around my back and kissed me deeply. He held the kiss for what seemed to me to be minutes before finally pulling back.

"Oh God, I missed that" he moaned softly.

"You and me both, boy." I gasped as I lay my head back down on Wolf's rock hard pecs until my breathing slowed to normal.

I lifted my head up and looked deeply into his eyes. "See what happens when you fuck up, boy? You don't get to enjoy my cock inside you. Now, are you going to behave?"

A mischievous gleam came to his eyes as he grinned; "Yes, Mother. Whatever you say, Mother. Nag, nag, nag."

I stared down at him with a mock stern expression. "Now you listen to me, young man. You're not too big for me to put across my lap for a good spanking!"

Wolf giggled; "Whenever you're ready, Mom."

I rolled off of his body and grabbed one of his shoulders, flipping him over onto his belly. I stroked my hand down his sweaty back until I came to his firm bubble butt. I ran my hand over the golden brown globes of Wolf's beautiful, solid ass, then without warning, I slapped my hand down hard on his right ass cheek with a loud SMACK! It left a perfect hand print that looked like it had been painted on. I quickly slapped his other ass cheek with another SMACK! Wolf gasped in pleasure as I began to give him a good old fashioned ass warming. Within seconds, we had changed positions so that he was laying across my lap as I sat on the side of the bed, slapping his quickly reddening ass with my hand. He moaned and growled with pleasure each time my hand smacked against his ass. I felt Wolf's dick getting harder and harder against my leg as I continued to spank him. It took about five minutes of continuous spanking before Wolf gasped "Please Sir, Yellow." That meant that he couldn't take any more of whatever I was doing to him, but that he wanted to continue our scene.

His ass was bright red when I let him up off my lap. When he stood up, his dick was rock hard and throbbing.

"Awright, boy;" I growled. "On your back."

Wolf lay down on the bed. I next ordered him to flip his legs up and over his head. Wolf was very flexible for a bodybuilder because of all the stretching exercises we did whenever we worked out. He could flip his legs up until they went over his head and back down onto the bed. In this position, he could lift his head up and suck the swollen head of his cock into his own mouth. I absolutely loved watching Wolf give himself a blowjob. He moaned softly as he licked and sucked his own cock. Slowly he stretched his head up and slowly bent his body down until he managed to slide most of the length of his cock into his mouth. His head began to pump up and down on his shaft.

His selfsucking continued for a good five minutes, during which his entire torso began to glisten with sweat. Finally, he started to moan with pure pleasure.

"Jack that cock off into your mouth, boy." I ordered. Wolf immediately began to pump his dick with his right hand while twisting his own nipples with the left. Within a minute Wolf was gasping and moaning in ecstasy as thick streams of cum began shooting into his mouth from the head of his own dick! He managed to get every drop of his load into his mouth. The sight of my slave boy selfsucking himself and swallowing his own sperm was incredibly erotic to me. I had been forced to do it myself by Mike, my first and only master on several occasions. Actually, he only had to force me to do it the first time!

When his orgasm was spent, Wolf let himself down onto the bed with a groan.

I grinned at him. "See what happens when you sass me, boy? I'll teach you to keep a civil tongue in your mouth!" I said in a fake, whiney old lady voice.

Wolf started to giggle again, then said; "I'd rather keep my uncivil tongue in YOUR mouth, Sir!". Within moments, we were both howling with laughter. It was a sort of a feedback loop. I would look at Wolf and he would laugh harder, which caused me to laugh harder myself, which would send Wolf into even harder laughing.

It took a few minutes before either of us was able to stop laughing. Finally, we managed to calm down enough so that we could lay together, our arms wrapped around each other, just enjoying each others company.

"I'm glad you learned your lesson, boy." I smiled into Wolf's eyes. "And, since you've been so good and so diligent about accepting your retraining, I have something for you."

I reached into the drawer of the nightstand next to the bed and pulled out a long envelope, handing it to Wolf.

"Happy birthday, boy. This is for you."

Wolf looked surprised for a minute before he said; "I'll be damned. This is my birthday. I had completely forgotten what the date was. Thank you, Sir."

He opened the envelope and read the card that was inside. I knew his sense of humor, so I figured the sillier the card, the better. I also knew a sappy, sentimental card wouldn't have worked as well as a goofy one, so I went for goofy. Wolf laughed at the card, but then a huge smile split his face when he saw what else was in the envelope.

I had included a gift certificate for $500 from Shackles, the biggest leather shop in the city.

Wolf turned to me with a smile on his face. "Oh God, thank you. Thank you so much, Sir. This is wonderful."

I smiled back and told him; "Well boy, you've earned it over the last year and a half. Now, go fix us some breakfast. Tomorrow if you want, we can go into town and see what you want to get at the leather shop."

Wolf kissed me again before he hopped out of bed and headed downstairs. I lay back in my bed and just thought about how my life was different since Wolf had joined me as my lover and my willing slave. We had been together since that day in early June almost a year and a half ago, when he first walked into the Eagle and professed his desire to be my slave. Now, I couldn't imagine my life without him in it.

My musings were interrupted by Wolf's announcement that breakfast was ready. I got up out of bed, slipped into my gym shorts and headed downstairs. I was surprised to see Wolf kneeling next to my chair at the dining room table, a delicious looking breakfast waiting. As I walked into the dining room, Wolf rose smoothly to his feet and pulled out my chair. I sat down and he slid my chair in and then dropped back to his knees and assumed the posture of a subservient slave boy waiting for any orders from his master. He used to do this regularly when we had first gotten together, but as we progressed from master and slave to lovers, our behavior with each other had become much more casual, at least in private.

I reached out and ruffled my slave's thick, luxuriant mane of raven black hair.

"Thank you, boy." I told him.

He bowed his head and softly said; "You are welcome, master. This boy hopes you enjoy your meal."

I ate, then when I was finished, I ordered Wolf to have his own meal. I gave him permission to use a regular plate, and not use the dog bowl he had been eating from over the week of his retraining.

When he had finished, and had cleaned up the kitchen and done the dishes, we went into the living room so I could read the paper. I usually only glanced through the paper during the week, but I read the Sunday edition through, concentrating on the business section. Wolf surprised me again when I sat on the couch to read. He handed me my paper, then knelt in front of me and simply said; "Sir?"

I looked at him as he dropped to his hands and knees in front of me, voluntarily offering himself as a footstool. I lifted my feet up and set them across Wolf's solidly muscled back. He gave a soft, almost silent moan of pleasure as he felt the weight of my feet on his body, as he served as furniture for his master's use.

I had forced him to do this while being retrained, but this was the first time Wolf had offered himself as furniture voluntarily since I had first trained him up as my slave over a year and a half ago. Then, it was a regular part of his discipline training as a new, first time slave. I guess his period of retraining had brought back memories of how a slave was supposed to behave around his master.

It wasn't just Wolf's fault that our relationship had grown more casual. I had fallen so deeply in love with this wonderful man that I had allowed him to behave much more informally around me than a slave normally would. Maybe Wolf's retraining would be a point of renewal for the both of us. I would have to try to act more like Wolf's master, as well as his lover, since Wolf seemed to be trying to fall back into his role as my slaveboy.

I continued my musings while I read through the paper. It took over an hour, during which Wolf patiently served as my footstool for the entire time, not saying a word. I could feel the gentle rise and fall of his back under my feet as he breathed.

Finally, I set my feet on the floor and stood up. Wolf immediately rose to his knees and awaited whatever I was going to order him to do.

"Follow me, boy" I told him as I headed upstairs. I led him into my bedroom and told him to kneel. Wolf immediately did as instructed and watched intently as I slid open the drawer of one of the nightstands by the bed. He smiled when I pulled out his studded slave collar. He hadn't been allowed to wear it since his screwup.

I turned to him, saying "You know what to do, boy."

He immediately gathered up his hair from behind his head and held it up out of the way. I held out the collar at the height of his throat and Wolf leaned into it. I buckled the collar firmly around his throat, hearing a small sigh of pleasure from my slave as the small padlock on the front of the collar clicked shut.

Wolf smiled as he let his hair drop, covering his shoulders. Without saying a word, he bent down and kissed my feet. When he straightened back up, he softly said; "Thank you, Sir. I will do my best to honor what this collar means."

Since it was a cold, dreary day with intermittent rain showers, I decided that we would just stay at home. I asked Wolf; "Well, what do you want to do, boy? I'll let you decide."

Wolf said; "I'd love to just spend some quiet time with you, Sir. I know we're going to be busy for the next few weeks, what with the holidays and everything coming up, not to mention the gym workouts. I really want to just be with you, Sir."

I smiled at him. "Well, normally I would order you to clean the house since you're going to be inside all day, but over the last week, this house has been cleaned within an inch of it's life! So, I guess some quiet time isn't a bad idea, boy."

Wolf grinned at me as he led me over to my bed. "I'd like to show you just how much you mean to me, Sir, if I may."

I lay down on the bed face down, as Wolf asked me to do. As I lay there, I felt him climb up and sit straddling my lower back. I groaned softly in total delight as Wolf's strong hands began to massage my shoulders. He worked on the muscles of my shoulders for just a few minutes before saying; "I think I need something to make this a bit easier."

I could hear him rustling around on the shelves of the headboard before I heard the distinctive sound of the pump bottle of massage lotion I liked to use.

I moaned again even louder as Wolf started to massage me again, only this time with the lotion on his hands. The feel of this fingers digging into my shoulders and back was pure ecstasy. I let go of any of my cares and worries, and just lost myself in the sensual delight of my slave's hands.

I had learned how to give a therapeutic massage from a friend of mine who was a professional massage therapist, and over the last year or so, I had taught Wolf how to give a great deep massage as well.

His totally glorious massage of my back lasted for the better part of an hour. Wolf worked his way from the top of my neck all the way down to the soles of my feet. When he was done, there wasn't a square inch of the backside of my body that he hadn't worked his magic on. At least, that's the way it felt to me. I was amused to feel that Wolf's cock had gotten hard during my massage. I could feel it laying on my back and sliding along my skin when he moved.

Finally, Wolf slid off of my back and said; "Whenever you can, you can turn over, Sir."

I groaned a bit as I slowly rolled over, not really wanting to move a muscle, I was so relaxed. When I was settled on my back, Wolf moved in to straddle my abs. He looked totally hot, with his hair down and flowing around his pecs and his shoulders. The exertions of the massage had caused a sheen of sweat to glow on his torso, highlighting his muscles.

Wolf repeated the entire sensual massage on the front of my body, working every muscle in my arms from my shoulders to the tips of my fingers and then working all the way down to the soles of my feet. When he was done, he knelt between my legs and bent over to take my cock into his mouth. I groaned from pure pleasure at the feel of his lips surrounding my hard, throbbing cock. He sucked my dick for a few minutes before sitting up and sliding up to straddle my legs once again.

Holding himself over my cock, Wolf reached down to guide my cock as he slowly let himself down, slowly impaling himself with the entire nine inches. He moaned as the shaft slid slowly into his ass.

Finally he sat on my hips with his ass stuffed with my hard cock. Wolf's entire body was now streaked with sweat as he began to slowly ride my cock. Every muscle in his hot, incredible torso rippled with his every movement.

I just lay back for a few minutes and let Wolf ride my dick before I reached out and began to work his nipples. He groaned with pleasure as my strong fingers began to twist and squeeze the thick brown nubs. Wolf's cock stood out rock hard over my abs as I slowly began to rock my hips up and down, fucking his ass for the second time that day.

Wolf gasped; "Oh God, harder, Sir. Fuck me, please."

He started to moan louder and louder as I increased the speed of my fucking while at the same time I was working his nipples harder and harder. Wolf reached out and began to feel my muscles as I fucked him, finally reaching my nipples. He started to work on my tits even as I was torturing his tits with my hands.

Finally I reached out and held his hips as I pumped a load of cum into my slave's willing ass. When I came, Wolf threw his head back and moaned loudly as, without touching his cock, he jetted a thick load of his sperm onto my chest and abs. His body writhed and flexed as the cum kept shooting from his dick onto my body.

Finally, with his orgasm spent, Wolf rose off my cock and let himself down. He slowly began licking his load of cum off of my body, along with the sweat coating my muscles.

I closed my eyes and reveled in the sensual delights of having my body worshipped by my hot, horny muscle slave. I could feel Wolf's tongue working to lap up every drop of his sperm from my skin as he worked across my torso with his hot mouth. After a bit, I knew he had all the cum from my body, and now he was just making love to my muscles. I allowed him his indulgence, if for no other reason then that it just felt so damned good!

Wolf finally lay down on top of me and kissed me deeply. I worked my hands up and down the broad planes of his solid back muscles as Wolf's tongue explored the inside of my mouth. We held the kiss for what seemed like an eternity. I was so passionately in love with this man that I felt that we could stay like this forever!

Wolf pulled back from the kiss and softly said; "I love you, Sir, and thank you for being here for me. Believe me, Sir, I'm so sorry about what happened last week and I'll never let anything like that happen again."

I smiled up into his face as I told him; "I know you won't boy. It was just a mistake. Everyone makes mistakes. Just in your case, a mistake could result in days and days of painful torture and punishment!"

I could actually see the mischievous gleam come into Wolf's eyes as he grinned down at me and said; "Promises, promises, master!"

I laughed and growled; "Come here, slave" as I pulled him back down on top of my body.

"Are you gonna start being a smart ass all over again, boy? Do I need to tie you up and torture you for a while again, boy? You know I can do it, slave."

Wolf giggled and said; "Prove it!"

Within two minutes Wolf was stretched tightly spread-eagle on my bed, bound hand and foot to the posts of my bed frame. I looked down at my helpless slave, his chest rising and falling.

"So you want me to prove what I can do to you, slave?" I snarled in a mock threatening tone. We both knew that we were having fun this afternoon, and neither one of us were taking any of this foolishness seriously. Wolf and I enjoyed playing when the mood was right, and it was certainly right today! After the last week of Wolf's retraining, we both needed a session of pure silliness and fun.

I reached out and began to gently stroke my fingers into Wolf's exposed armpits. He moaned a bit when he figured out what I was going to do. His moans turned into giggles as I began to tickle his ribs, my fingers beginning to dig into his sides. Wolf started to struggle and strain his muscles as my tickle torture began to become more intense.

Within minutes Wolf was howling helplessly as I worked his body from his armpits to the soles of his feet. Gales of laughter were being torn from my bound slave, as every muscle in his sculpted, gleaming torso strained and flexed to its limit. Tears were running down his face as he struggled to breathe between bouts of laughing. Watching him laugh was making me laugh as well. The entire scene escalated as Wolf laughed each time I dug my fingers into his armpits, or tickled his ribs, or even worked the insides of his knees. As he laughed and squirmed under me, I would laugh harder as well.

This scene lasted a good ten minutes before Wolf gasped; "Yellow, Sir. Please."

I stopped tickling my slave and waited as he struggled to catch his breath, before he weakly moaned; "You win, Sir."

I flopped down on top of my still bound slave and snarled: "Damn right, boy. I always win. And don't you forget it, slave."

He looked up into my eyes with a wicked grin and said; "At least until the bodybuilding contest. Then, you're gonna lose!"

My eyes flew open wide and without another word, I sat back upright and started Wolf's tickle torture all over again, which I'm sure was his intention.

This time I added some new means of tickling my helpless slave, such as running a feather down his sides and across the soles of his feet. When I used the sharpened end of the feather shaft on his feet, Wolf literally screamed with laughter, even as he squirmed and twisted desperately. I grinned as I watched him struggle frantically, even as he laughed so hard that he was having a hard time catching his breath.

I also used my Wartenburg pinwheels on his stretched body. These were small metal wheels that looked kind of like the rowels of a spur on a short handle, except that the points sticking out from the wheels were sharp pins. They had been created for dermatologists to use to test skin sensitivity, but they made great torture toys, as well. I loved using them in Wolf's spread, exposed armpits and across his thick pecs.

He shrieked with laughter and writhed in his bondage when I started to roll the wheels across his swollen, brown nipples and up and down the length of his fat cock.

Finally, when Wolf was almost in hysterics from laughing so hard and for so long, I decided to show him a little mercy. I lay back down on top of his sweat coated torso, feeling his heart pound in his chest. Without a word I started to lick the sweat from his solid pecs. Wolf gasped and moaned when I started to lightly lick his left nipple, before I sucked it into my mouth. I worked the tit for just a few moments, just enough to have Wolf moaning and writhing in ecstasy before I switched and started to repeat the teasing on his right tit.

I shifted my position slightly and started to run my tongue lightly down the side of his sculpted torso, feeling every rippling muscle and rib on Wolf's right side. I loved the feel of his muscles under my tongue, as Wolf began to squirm and strain again, even as he started to laugh again. I was actually tickling my helpless slave with my tongue. I tormented him this way for a few minutes until I decided to shift to his left side. I was totally enjoying the taste of Wolf's hot, salty sweat, and the feel of his muscles quivering under the glistening bronze skin of his fabulously ripped and muscular torso.

When he was moaning constantly in sheer pleasure. I pulled back from his chest and looked down into his deep brown eyes. He smiled up into my face before I kissed him deeply on his full, sensual lips.

"Any more smart-assed comments, slave?" I growled into his ear.

He weakly shook his head. "No Sir."

I untied my bound boy, then we spent the rest of a long, rainy afternoon gently making love to each other, as only two men who truly were in love could do.

Chapter 9

Seduction

The next morning, after Wolf and I had made love again, we both had breakfast and showered together. We headed into San Francisco for some shopping and our Monday workout at the gym. Since we were going into the city for our shopping, we were going to the gym off of Folsom street. Normally, we used the smaller, but still well equipped health club nearer home.

Our first stop was at Shackles, the leather shop so Wolf could use his gift certificate. He was like a kid in a candy shop as he bounced from one department of the shop to another, trying out different items like new types of restraints, various styles of leather gear, and even some rubber wear. I wasn't really a big fan of rubber clothes, but I had to admit that Wolf looked really hot in a scoop cut red rubber tank top. The thin latex shirt really emphasized the spread and width of his lats and the amazing shape of his pecs, while showing off his washboard ab muscles like a second skin.

It took him a while to decide, but he finally selected a classic cut leather biker jacket and a bar style leather vest that was cut so that it hung down on his chest with the edges just showing his nipples and framing his washboard abs and the deep valley between his thick, sculpted pecs. We both thought that the vest and coat would look really great along with Wolf's chaps and boots. The store clerk that was helping us even complimented Wolf on how hot he looked in the vest with no shirt under it, and his hair hanging down over his shoulders. I certainly had to agree with him there!

I took the opportunity as well to pick up some equipment for the dungeon while we were in the shop. I bought a pair of grip style wrist restraints, which were a pair of heavy leather restraints equipped with a separate padded hand grip fastened to the wrist straps with short lengths of chain on either side. From the ends of the grips, longer chains led up to a connecting ring in the middle. When attached to a slave's arms, they allowed him to have a place to grab onto and help support his weight, without causing his hands to become numb. Wearing the restraints, a slave could hang by his arms for hours. I planned to see how well they worked at our first opportunity!

I picked out some other toys as well, and suggested to Wolf that he should get the rubber tank top, since he looked so good in it. He told me that he wanted to, but that it would take the total of his purchases over the amount of the gift certificate.

"Oh please, do you really think that I'm worried about a few extra dollars?" I told him with a grin. "I can always take the difference out of your hide back in the dungeon!"

Wolf laughed, and the clerk said; "Wow, I'd sure love to see that!"

I gave him a smile and handed him one of my business cards.

"Just give us a call, and we'll see what we can arrange sometime."

He looked at my card and said; "You're Eric Kurtz? Roger, my boss talks about you all the time. I'm so pleased to finally meet you. My name is Bill. I'm kinda new here."

He turned to Wolf and practically gushed.; "And you must be Wolf. I've heard stories about you. I just want to say that you have to be the luckiest boy in all of San Francisco to have the master that you do!"

We shook hands, then I asked Bill; "Where the hell is Roger, anyway? I figured he'd be here cracking the whip, so to speak, on the help."

"He's on a buying trip somewhere trying to get a deal on a load of new leather hides. I guess the shop needs them for new goodies." Bill shrugged.

"Well, you tell him we were here. We'll see you around sometime. Just remember that you have our number, and you're always welcome to call." I grinned. " We have to head for the gym so I can see how far I can push Wolf. He's such a wimp that I have to watch him all the time to make sure that he's not goofing off !"

Wolf raised an eyebrow and gave me a shocked look, then began to laugh when I stuck out my tongue at him. However, after what he had endured the previous week, he knew not to say anything.

After we left the leather shop, we went to the gym for our chest workout, which was my favorite. I loved watching Wolf's pecs flex and bulge as he strained at the weights. I also loved the feel of my own chest working at our various exercises, from several versions of bench presses, flat, inclined, and declined, to dumbbell flys and cable flys, just to name a few. Working with the amount of weight that both Wolf and I could use while working our chests was emotionally satisfying. I was also proud of how much more weight we both could throw around after only a short time of serious training as well. It helped that Wolf was almost as strong as I was, since it really helped the intensity of our workouts to have a partner who could spot each other with the weight that we both could lift.

Since one of my greatest fetishes was working on a guy's nipples, I loved seeing a man with a really well developed set of pecs. My chest had always seemed to be really well developed, ever since I had played football in high school. I really enjoyed the way that the veins would pop out across my pecs, and the striations in the muscles would ripple whenever I would do a pose that really showed my chest off. When I would flex my pecs, my nipples were almost on the underside of the curve of the muscle, so my nipple rings would hang down from my tits.

Also, I was really impressed with the way Wolf's chest had grown and developed in a relatively short time. His pectorals were thick and defined, with sharp vasculinity and well defined striations in the muscles. They looked like they had been carved from a block of dark walnut wood, with his high riding, pumped and enlarged nipples surrounded by the markings of his brandings. I figured it wasn't going to be much longer before I gave Wolf his own set of nipple rings. I was looking forward to the scene where I would torture his tits as hard as they had ever been worked, only to finish off by having his nipples pierced, much as mine had been done several years ago.

After a hard three hour workout, Wolf and I practiced our posing at the gym, then showered off and headed out to complete our various errands around the city.

That sort of became our routine for the next few weeks. Unfortunately, we were so occupied with our training and all the other distractions around the holidays, we didn't have too much time to spend in the dungeon. Wolf told me that he understood that we were going to be really busy over the next couple of weeks, and that he could do without our sessions in the torture chamber for a while.

"The anticipation of what you will do to me when we get back to a regular schedule is good enough for me for a while, Sir. I don't mind waiting." He told me that one evening when I had fallen into bed dog tired. I told him how much I loved him, and that I would make it up to him as soon as I could.

I would do my computer work in the morning while Wolf took care of whatever chores needed to be done around the house. Then we would usually go to the local gym for our workout, except on our off days. Then, we would have other activities to occupy ourselves, such as finishing up the last details on my newest car in the collection at the restoration shop over in Oakland that was attached to the warehouse where my cars were being stored until I could get a garage for them built on my property behind the house.

My 1931 Cadillac roadster was just finishing up a total restoration from the frame up.

As we worked our way towards the holidays and all the activities surrounding them, I thought that it might be a perfect time to show off the Caddy. There were going to be parties thrown by some of our friends, as well as larger gatherings.

One supposed highlight of the holiday season was attending a formal Christmas party and fund raiser given by several of the larger gay charities and civic groups in the city on the 23rd of December. I usually thought that this affair was a bore, having had to attend it for several years, just stuffy people standing around congratulating themselves on being so high class!

However, it was my first opportunity to get to see Wolf dressed to the nines in a fitted and tailored tuxedo. When I first saw him walking down the stairs in the house in his tux, I could only hold my breath. He looked magnificent! His tux jacket emphasized the spread of his shoulders and the taper to his waist, and his hair looked gorgeous, drawn tightly back like a black skullcap and pulled into a high ponytail that flowed down his back. The golden bronze color of his skin contrasted with the crisp white, pleated shirt he wore and his gleaming white teeth when he grinned at me. His shirt had turquoise studs, which were echoed by the color of a sterling silver and turquoise clip holding his hair back, and a bow tie and cummerbund in a rich deep turquoise color as well.

My tux matched Wolf's with the exceptions that my shirt studs and my tie were a deep ruby red, and I wore a vest instead of the cummerbund.

"God, you look great!" I told him.

Wolf smiled and said; "I was just about to say the same thing about you, Sir. That outfit is so sexy. I don't know exactly why, but you look so hot! I love you in leather, but that tux is almost as much of a turn on. I just want to make love to you right here and now!"

I smiled back and told him; "First things first, boy. We do have to put in an appearance at this high class wing ding. Then, I guess we'll see what happens later."

We put on a pair of matching cashmere topcoats to keep out the chill of the December night, and drove into the city in the Caddy, attracting a lot of attention on the way.

However, just as I was afraid of, the party was for the most part just groups of people standing around chatting. I felt it was a waste of a perfectly good Saturday night, when we could have been at the bar with people we really liked. The few highlights of the party were seeing the looks of awe from other partygoers and the valet parkers when we pulled into the drive in a gleaming two-tone green 1931 V-16 Cadillac roadster, and the admiring looks that we gathered as we strode arm in arm into the auditorium where the party was held. There were a lot of gay and lesbian couples at the party, so two men walking in arm in arm wasn't all that unusual. However, I enjoyed watching the heads turn in the crowd as people would watch Wolf as he would go to the bar to get us some drinks or to the buffet tables for snacks.

Several people at the party did ask me about "That gorgeous, handsome young man who is with you". I secretly relished to looks of envy on their faces when I would introduce Wolf to them and explained exactly who he was, then told them that; "Yes, he really is as hot and sexy as you think, but unfortunately, I don't share. He's mine, and mine alone."

Wolf would blush slightly, but he seemed to take it all with good humor. I was pleasantly surprised to see that Wolf seemed to be able to hold his own at a formal affair, and seemed to be good at the requisite small talk, even though I had never allowed him to accompany me to any of the previous parties I had attended.

For the most part, however, the affair was just as dull as I was afraid that it would be. After what seemed to be an eternity of dull small talk with various stuffy people, I couldn't wait to get out of there. I didn't mind supporting the charities, but I just wish I didn't have to put up with so many boring people to do it. At least before we left, several of the older gentlemen involved with the various groups that were throwing the party told me how envious they were that I was sleeping with "Such a good looking and personable young man." Wolf got a huge laugh when I told him that after we left the party.

We were both laughing when Wolf confessed to me that at least five times during the party he was openly propositioned by several of the older men at the party, including one who told him that he "Could make it worth your while to move in with me."

I looked at him with a gleam in my eye and said; "Did you consider his offer, boy?"

Wolf grinned and said; "Well, actually I did."

I glared at him for a moment before he chortled; "Yeah, for about a half a second or so."

"Gee, that long, huh? I'd have thought that you wouldn't have had to think about it!" I said with a huge grin on my face.

Wolf and I just roared with laughter.

For a change of pace, Wolf and I went into the Eagle before heading home. It was a real hoot going into a leather bar dressed in a full tux. I knew that both of us would have to put up with a whole shitload of good-natured razzing from our friends at the bar. Two men in tuxedos in a leather bar stood out like two penguins in a herd of cows. The chorus of wolf whistles and comments were deafening when Wolf pushed open the door and the two of us walked into the front room of the Eagle.

"Well la-de-fucking-da! Look at the fancy pants boys!" crowed Danny when he saw us walk into the bar. "Aren't you both just too fucking pretty. Good God, you both look like refugees from the Acme butler school! You can dress up all you want, but you'll still be just as homely as ever, Eric. But, I gotta admit that Wolf cleans up nice. And what the hell is with that antiquated land yacht you're driving? Where in the world did you dig up that relic?"

I knew Danny just couldn't pass up the opportunity to harass us. We were best friends and had occasionally had really great sex together, but we loved to needle each other occasionally. He would tease me about my 'collection of rusty old used cars', and I would sometimes razz Danny about 'that pile of moth-eaten old second hand clothes', referring to the uniforms he liked to wear, especially when he showed up at the bar wearing a kilt, which I always called a dress!

I knew he was joking with us and accepted his harassment with good humor, knowing that sometime soon I would get him back. I had told him on many an occasion that; " Just remember, I don't get mad, I get even!"

We hung around the bar for an hour or so, socializing with our friends, and enduring a lot of razzing about our tuxedos before I decided that it was time to head home. I just couldn't resist the opportunity to get in one final parting shot however.

"Attention, yon varlets. I believe that we shall be taking our leave of you now." I announced with an absolutely over the top upper crust British accent. "But when we get back to the manor, I'm probably going to spend the next few hours doing something you will never get the chance to do, namely fucking the hell out of my hot, handsome muscleboy here. What do you say, Wolf, should we leave the peasants here to their cheap and tawdry thrills while you and I go home and fuck like bunny rabbits?"

Wolf grinned at me, made a deep bow, and said; "Forsooth, my liege. I like the sound of that."

Most of our friends hooted and called out things like; *"Knock the bottom out of that boy!"* and *"Fuck him till he can't walk straight!"* as we left.

When we arrived home, Wolf surprised me by saying; "Please, Sir. May I have the honor of undressing you, Sir?"

"Go ahead, boy." I told him, wondering what he had in mind.

Wolf asked me to wait in the living room while he got ready. I sat on the couch for a few minutes before Wolf came back downstairs from his bedroom. He was still in his tux, but was carrying an armload of bedcovers and pillows. I watched as he went over to the fireplace and lit the gas fire and spread out a comforter and some pillows in front of the fireplace. Next he turned down the room lights until the only illumination in the room came from the fire and the twinkling lights on the Christmas tree in the corner. Finally, he put on some softly playing jazz on the stereo.

Wolf asked me to stand in the middle of the room, in front of the fireplace. He stepped in front of me and kissed me.

"I love you, Sir." he murmured as he started to slip my jacket from my shoulders. He laid the jacket smoothly across a chair and then untied my tie. After taking off my vest and laying it on top of my jacket, he stood close to me. Removing the top stud from my shirt, he leaned in and gently kissed my neck. I got an almost electric thrill from the feel of his soft, warm lips on my skin.

Wolf slowly removed the studs from my shirt, slowly spreading it open and gently kissing and licking the skin of my chest as it was slowly exposed. I was incredibly turned on by his slow, erotic seduction of my pecs.

It took Wolf a good ten minutes to just open my shirt. When he undid the last stud and pulled my shirt back over my shoulders, he bent down and began to gently, erotically make love to my nipples with his mouth. I moaned in sheer pleasure at the feel of his tongue stroking the sensitive tips of my nipples and gently playing with my nipple rings. Gently and ever so slowly Wolf worked his way down to my abs, kissing and nuzzling every muscle and rib on the way.

When he had worked his way down to my belt, I thought that he would undo it, but Wolf had a different idea. He stood up and walked behind me, to slip my shirt completely off. When it was off, he started to make love to every muscle on my back and shoulders. I groaned softly in total pleasure as Wolf spent almost fifteen minutes gently kissing and licking every square inch of my back. I flexed my muscles for him, causing the sweat to begin to shine on my body.

He then slowly worked out the entire length of my right arm. Wolf gently worshipped my thick tricep muscle before working his way to my peaked bicep.

When he had slowly and lovingly worked his mouth all the way out to the end of my arm, finishing up by sucking each of my fingers into his mouth one at a time, Wolf repeated the entire worship of my muscled left arm. I was panting with sheer lust when he finally finished with my back and arms, then knelt in front of me to remove my shoes and socks. When they were off, he bent down and began to orally worship my size twelve feet. God, that was so hot!

Wolf asked me to sit on the couch while he gently kissed and sucked on each of my toes. He hadn't done too much foot worship in the time we had been together, so this was a pleasant surprise.

I sat back on the couch, losing myself in the sheer pleasure of Wolf's foot worship. I totally lost track of the time, until Wolf gently asked me to stand up in front of him again. When I did, he reached out from his kneeling position and unfastened my trousers. He slipped them down and allowed me to brace myself on his shoulder while I stepped out of my pants, leaving me just wearing my jockstrap.

Wolf's incredibly erotic seduction continued as he slowly and gently made love to every muscle in my thick thighs and rock hard, sculpted calves. I had been working my legs hard in our workouts, and it really showed.

Wolf traced every vein and bulge of muscle with his tongue on both legs, until my legs were literally quivering from sheer pleasure. My cock felt like it was going to tear through the fabric of the jockstrap I wore, it was so hard.

I thought that I was going to explode in a helpless, spontaneous orgasm when Wolf slowly worked his way behind me and began to literally kiss my ass. He moaned softly as he ran his hot mouth over my butt. I cried out in pure sensual ecstasy when he spread my ass cheeks and buried his face between them, licking my asshole.

Finally, after what felt like an eternity of pleasure, Wolf took my hand and led me over to the comforter laying in front of the fireplace. He knelt back down in front of me and gently worked my jockstrap off, my fully hard cock springing upright against my hard abs. Wolf leaned in and lightly ran his tongue up the length of my shaft just once before standing back up.

"I love you more than you could ever know, Sir. I want to thank you for everything you've ever done for me, Sir." Wolf whispered in my ear, just before kissing me as deeply and as passionately as he had ever done. I held my lover's body tightly as we kissed for what seemed to be hours.

Wolf finally released me and gently asked me to lay down on the comforter. When I had made myself comfortable, he smiled a bit wickedly as he changed the music to a faster dance song with a disco beat.

Wolf grinned widely as started to undress himself while swaying to the beat of the music. I laughed when I realized that Wolf was going to treat me to a one man strip show.

I lay back on the comforter, propped on the pillows, while I watched my muscleboy lover slowly, sexily undressing himself for my enjoyment. Wolf teasingly removed his jacket and the cummerbund. Next he slowly began to unfasten the studs of his shirt. He stroked the skin of his chest as it was exposed before finally peeling the shirt off his broad shoulders leaving his body stripped just to the waist. He smiled at me as he caressed his own solid pecs and began to pinch and twist his nipples while sinuously dancing to the music.

I moaned lustfully when Wolf began to gently stroke and then slap his own abs while flexing and relaxing the washboard muscles, causing them to ripple under his skin.

He slowly began to flex his thick arms, pumping up the huge biceps by flexing and then relaxing the massive muscles. The veins popped out on the surface of his arms from his wrists all the way to his shoulders. His forearms looked almost like a road map with the rippling muscles covered with the veins and cords. Finally, Wolf did a full double bicep pose that he had learned for our contest. God, he looked spectacular! His torso tapered down from his huge shoulders and wide lats down to a flat, hard washboard stomach. Every muscle in his amazing body stood out in the flickering light of the fire. Somehow, the look of his body stripped to the waist in the tux pants was even more erotic than usual.

Wolf then started to show off his muscled physique to me using some of the posing routine I was teaching him for the contest, with some really sexy dancing mixed in. When we would go to a bar where there was a dance floor, Wolf's dancing made me feel like I was about as agile as a pig on stilts. Wolf said it was probably because he had been in some native dance groups on the Indian reservation he had been born on. I was okay on a dance floor, but Wolf was incredibly sexy to watch!

As he posed and worked his muscles, Wolf's body began to glow with a light sheen of sweat from his exertions. It was all I could do to keep from jacking myself off while I was watching his incredibly erotic display of his magnificent physique.

I growled; "Oh yeah, boy. Show it to me!" as he began to ever so slowly open up his trousers and tease me by showing a glimpse of his tanned, firm ass. He bent over and unfastened his shoes before kicking them off one at a time. As he bent down, his ponytail hung free, then lay across one shoulder when he straightened up. I moaned again when Wolf began to play with his thick black hair, rubbing the end of his ponytail across the broad plains of his pecs, and sucking the hair into his mouth.

Wolf finally stepped out of his trousers, leaving him wearing only a pair of tight spandex briefs. The black fabric shone in the light of the fire, and the shape of Wolf's totally erect cock was visible, trapped by the skin tight fabric.

He began to gently stroke his thick dick under the spandex, softly moaning; "Yeah, oh yeah!" as he worked his sensitive cock. I could see the thick head of his dick, and even the veins running the length of his shaft under the shiny fabric.

He was now so turned on that it was just a matter of minutes before Wolf finally peeled off the spandex underwear and stood totally naked over me, his throbbing cock standing straight out in front of his body.

The look of his physique in the flickering firelight was absolute perfection to my eyes. Every muscle in his torso rippled and flexed as he ran his hands over his dark bronze skin. I lay back with my hands under my head, just looking up at the almost unbelievably godlike figure standing over me. Wolf loved to show off his muscles for me, especially now that we were so heavily into the training for the bodybuilding contest, now less than three months away. His physique was responding to the weight training faster than most other guys I had ever trained with.

Wolf began to pose and show off his muscles even harder as his lust seemed to be growing. I could tell that he was really turned on by showing off for me, and I was just as turned on looking at his sculpted body. I knew that Wolf was an exhibitionist and loved to have guys watch him while he was being tortured in the bars, and I knew that he would probably love being on stage for the bodybuilding contest as well. Unfortunately for the fans coming to the contest, they wouldn't be able to watch either Wolf or myself pose totally nude. That was a pleasure we reserved for each other. Wolf loved to worship my muscled physique just as much, if not more, than I loved to worship his muscles.

Wolf sank to his knees, straddling my abs. I reached up and ran my fingers over his sculpted pecs just as gently and as sensually as he had done to me. Wolf growled in his throat when I licked my fingers and teased his thick nipples with my wet fingertips.

I then traced every ripple of his washboard six pack abs with a fingertip while Wolf groaned softly. He gasped and moaned when I used my little finger and stroked it across his navel. I had recently started to experiment with forms of navel torture, and had discovered that Wolf had a very sensitive navel. I had some plans of different navel tortures that I was going to use on my unsuspecting slave boy.

As I gently ran my fingers over Wolf's hard cock, nestled as it was between my pecs, Wolf moaned with delight. As I teased him, he reached up behind his head and unfastened the clip holding his hair in the ponytail. I moaned with lust and delight at the sight of his hair flowing down over his shoulders as he shook it down in a sexy cascade of flowing jet black hair.

Within a few minutes, Wolf slowly lay down on top of me. He just silently looked deeply into my eyes for a moment before he pressed his mouth against mine in a deeply passionate kiss. I sighed with pleasure as I began to gently stroke my fingertips up and down his hot, shiny hard muscled back. We didn't say very much for a while, as we just lost ourselves in the pleasure of exploring every square inch of each others body.

Wolf and I spent several hours in front of the fireplace making sometimes gentle, sometimes passionate love to each other. It was the most totally romantic night I could recall in some time. It wasn't just the incredible sex that we had. Wolf and I would spend long stretches of time between making love to just talk. We talked about everything from our pasts, revealing things that we still didn't know about each other, to our possible plans for our future together. I told Wolf that next summer I wanted to take him on a road trip back east, as I needed to go back to Indy to deal with some business in person. I thought that we could work in some bicycling trips along the way, as we were both avid cyclists. He thought that would be really fun.

Sometimes our conversations that night were deeply spiritual, and sometimes we were giggling like kids, as we talked about the silliest things.

Finally after making love for what seemed to be the fifth or sixth time that night, both Wolf and I fell asleep on the comforter in front of the fireplace, our arms wrapped around each other. We never did make it into bed that night, but neither one of us cared.

Chapter 10

Torment

I awoke early in the afternoon still wrapped in Wolf's arms. The fire was still crackling softly in the fireplace, as it was a gas fire and didn't need wood. Wolf was still sleeping soundly, so I was able to gently extricate myself from his arms without waking him.

I just sat for a while on the couch looking down at the sleeping form of the man who meant more to me than any other person in my life with the exception of my parents. I still loved my memories of Mike, my first and only master, but we had never been quite as close as Wolf and I were. Mike had always kept a subtle distance from me emotionally, as he thought there should be a distance from a master to his slave.

I padded upstairs and put on my robe before walking back downstairs. Wolf was just beginning to wake up. I sat back down and watched as he stretched lazily like a cat, every muscle rippling under his bronze skin.

"Good morning sleepyhead." I grinned down at him. "It's about time you decided to haul your butt up. Just look at the time."

Wolf smiled back up at me. "Well, if I didn't have to stay up so late trying to take care of a certain overly horny man, I could have gotten to sleep at a decent hour."

I laughed. "Get up, boy. I need some breakfast, and I suppose that you do too. Although, I guess we could just call it lunch by now. And if you're going to be a smart ass, I might just have to take you downstairs and beat some respect back into you."

Wolf's grin widened. "Promises, promises. You say that now, but what about later?"

I knew what he was doing. Sometimes after we made love just one on one without any S+M, Wolf was in the mood for a long session in the dungeon, just as I was. He enjoyed being forced to endure extreme pain, and he would try to goad me into torturing him. I was on to his little game, but since I was still in such a good mood after our night of romance the night before, I decided to indulge him and play along.. Besides, since I had let Wolf have his fun with his seduction and stripping, I thought that it was my turn to enjoy myself by indulging in my favorite activity, a session of extreme torture for my muscle slave. We hadn't had too much dungeon time for a while, what with working out and all the other activities surrounding the holidays.

"All right, wise guy, that's it. On your feet. NOW!!" I bellowed at him. Wolf shot to his feet and stood at attention. I stepped up to him and grabbed his right wrist and bent it behind his back. He gasped in pain as I twisted his arm up.

"You want to be a smart ass? Let's just see how much of a smart ass you will be in a couple of hours, slave." I snarled into his ear. "No breakfast for you, boy. All you get to do for the next few hours is suffer."

I marched Wolf down the stairs into the dungeon. When we got into the middle of the main room, I told him to kneel and keep his head down. Wolf instantly complied with my order, but I could see that he was already beginning to get a hard on in anticipation of an extended torture session.

I took off my robe leaving me stripped naked. I would go back upstairs and dress for our session after I had Wolf bound for his torture.

I took out the new grip restraints I had just purchased, and fastened them to the ends of one of my long spreader bars. I ordered Wolf to stand and grasp the handles of the restraints. I fastened the restraints around his wrists, leaving him with his arms spread in front of him as he stood. I pulled down a chain from the hoist on the ceiling and told Wolf to stand under it. I lifted the bar up and fastened the chain to the center eye on the bar. Using the hoist, I stretched Wolf's arms up until he was standing on his toes, his body stretched tightly in front of me, suspended from his widely spread arms.

I fastened ankle restraints on his legs before spreading his legs and fastening the restraints to eyebolts on the floor. When I was done, Wolf was spread out in front of me, his chest rising and falling erratically as he gasped for air. His entire body weight was suspended from his arms, as his toes now were a couple of inches off of the floor.

I stepped in front of my helpless slave. "Not so mouthy now, are you boy?" I growled. "I hope you're ready to suffer."

Wolf just murmured; "Yes, Sir. Whatever you want to do to me, Sir."

"Damn right I'll do whatever I want, boy." I snarled in his face. "And all you can do is endure it, slave!"

With that, I turned on my heel and stalked out of the dungeon and up the stairs, leaving Wolf to hang helplessly. I took my time eating a light snack before going upstairs and putting on my boots and chaps. I thought about taking Wolf's collar, but decided against it. It was a pain to put on when he was hanging by his arms, since his shoulder muscles were so thick.

By the time I went back down into the dungeon, Wolf had been hanging for the better part of an hour. His body was streaked with rivulets of sweat, and the muscles in his shoulders and back were quivering with the strain of supporting his weight. Unsurprisingly, however, his cock was totally erect, standing out straight in front of him.

I strode over to my suspended torture slave and stood in front of him. He looked at me expectantly.

"I guess you think that you're really hot, boy. Showing off for all those other men at the party. Flexing your muscles and everything. Well, now you're going to see just exactly what those muscles are for. They're there for my pleasure, and my pleasure alone! Don't you ever forget that, boy." I snapped at Wolf.

I stepped behind his stretched body and wrapped my arms around his torso. I breathed deeply with my face buried in his thick black hair, loving the clean, fresh scent.

Wolf moaned softly when I began to gently squeeze and twist his nipples with my fingers. I could feel the muscles in his back begin to flex against my chest as I played with his tits.

"Do you know what I gonna do to you now, boy?" I murmured into Wolf's ear.

He just shook his head.

"You remember I said I was gonna make it up to you that I haven't had time to work you over for a while, right, boy?"

Wolf softly said; "Yes Sir. I remember, Sir."

"I think I'm gonna spend the next couple of hours making you endure some good old fashioned torture, boy. We're gonna see just how much pain you can take!"

Wolf moaned; "Yes, Sir. Please torture me, Sir. I was showing off last night, Sir. I need to be punished for my arrogant behavior, Master. Please hurt me, Sir!"

Wolf knew that his pleading for torture would turn me on. I loved it when he would beg me to hurt his body. I also knew that this would probably be our last really heavy scene before our bodybuilding contest. I didn't want to mark up Wolf's skin with my floggers and whips and damage his chance in the contest, so I would have to get creative for this particular session.

I stepped back from his suspended body and went to my toy shelves. Wolf moaned when I picked up the alligator nipple clamps. He moaned again when I also found the light chain I used to connect the clamps. Wolf strained his muscles and gasped in pain when I

opened one of the clamps and clipped it on his left nipple. He gasped and moaned again when the other clamp was set on his right tit. Then, I attached the chain to the rings on the ends of the clamps.

I stepped back and admired the sight of Wolf's bronze chest rising and falling erratically as he adjusted to the pain of the torture clamps biting into his nipples. The silver of the chain between his pecs contrasted with the color of his skin. He looked incredibly sexy hanging in his bondage, his muscled physique spread for my pleasure.

I stepped back to the shelves and picked up a handful of my small lead weights. Wolf began to moan in pain as I began to hang the weights from the chain between his tits, stretching his nipples and causing the teeth of the clamps to bite deeply into his sensitive flesh. When I had about a pound of weight on the chain, Wolf finally began to howl as each additional weigh was added. I kept adding weights as Wolf screamed louder and louder as each one was added.

Finally, there were about six pounds suspended from my boy's stretched tits. The teeth of the clamps were digging deeply into the swollen nipples, biting them while stretching them cruelly. Wolf's head was thrown back, his eyes squeezed shut and his teeth clenched in agony. His chest rose and fell in short jerks as he fought to breathe with the intense pain ripping throughout his torso from his nipples.

I stepped back so I could admire the view of my slave. His entire body was streaked with sweat. His torso was shaped in a V-taper from his wide lats down to his hard, rippling abs. Wolf's shoulders had gotten thicker and wider as we had been working out so intensely for the last several months. His armpits were deeper and wider than I had ever seen them before. I just couldn't resist the temptation. I buried my face in Wolf's right armpit and began to eat out his pit. Wolf moaned loudly as I started to lick the sweat from his skin. I knew that he really enjoyed having his pits licked, probably as much as I did. While I was tonguing his armpits, I thought of another new way to torture my slave that I had never done before.

"Damn boy, those pits are hairy. No competition bodybuilder has hairy pits, slave. We're gonna have to do something about that." I growled in Wolf's ear. I was exaggerating, of course. Wolf actually had very small tufts of hair in his pits.

I walked to my toy rack and searched for a few minutes until I found what I was looking for. I turned back to Wolf holding a pair of tweezers. Wolf watched me with a mix of lust and anticipation in his eyes as I reached into his left pit with the tweezers and began to pluck out the hair in his pit! He threw back his head and screamed as each hair was ripped out. Sometimes I would grab two or three at a time. I would alternate between a quick yank of the hairs and a deliberate, slow agonizing pulling of the hairs until they tore loose from his sweat glazed skin. His muscles would flex and strain from the agony he was being forced to endure, which would cause his armpits to deepen and his huge biceps to bulge, while his chest heaved and his abs flexed and rippled.

Wolf's entire body would twist and strain as the hairs were ripped out of his pits, which caused the weights hanging from his nipples to swing and add to the pain in his tits. I was enjoying watching Wolf struggle to endure this totally new form of torture being inflicted on his body. He would gasp and groan as I began to slowly stretch each hair from his skin, before he would finally shriek in pain as the hair was torn from it's root. I knew that his lats were already sore from the strain of supporting his entire body weight for so long, so the pain of having his hair pulled out would just add to his agony.

It took almost fifteen minutes of slow, deliberate torture before all the hairs had been pulled from Wolf's deep armpits. He was gasping for air when I finally set the tweezers back on the shelf. When I turned back towards him, Wolf gasped out; "Oh shit, no!"

I was holding my small spray bottle of alcohol that I used to sterilize the sounds before inserting them into his cock. Wolf shrieked in agony when I sprayed a fine mist of alcohol into each armpit. The mist cooled his skin for just a moment before the coolness turned into a feeling of fiery pain.

I just stood back and watched the beautiful sight of Wolf hanging by his wide spread arms, his entire body writhing and twisting in agony, as the alcohol burned into the raw, red skin of his armpits. His chest was rising and falling as he gasped for air, the weights hanging from his swollen nipples swinging and banging against his ribs. His head was thrown back and his eyes were closed as Wolf struggled to endure the torture. However, to my total lack of surprise, his cock was totally erect and throbbing in time with the rapid beating of his heart. When his struggles against his restraints seemed to be slowly abating, as the burning sensations in his armpits eased, I would shoot another mist of alcohol into both pits, starting a new round of screams and struggles.

I tortured Wolf's armpits for about five minutes with the alcohol before I finally put the mister away. By now, Wolf was sobbing in agony, the tears streaming down his cheeks.

"Are you ready for something else, slave?" I snarled into his ear.

"Yes, Sir. Whatever else you want to do to me, Sir, I'll try to endure it, Sir." Wolf gasped softly.

"As I said before, I'll do whatever I want to you, boy. And you won't just try to endure it, slave, you will. Because you have no choice, boy!" I snapped at Wolf while I was slowly lowering him down to the floor from his hanging position.

Within five minutes I had Wolf tightly stretched out on the bondage table with his arms and legs spread wide. I had removed the weights from his nipples, but the clamps were still biting deeply into his tits. He moaned with unbridled lust when I gently stroked my fingers down his washboard abs and began to play with his navel. As Wolf's stomach muscles had developed and hardened, his navel had first flattened out and then had actually begun to protrude slightly.

Wolf moaned again when I took one of the Lucite tubes of his nipple suckers and attached it to the vacuum pump, then put the tube over his navel and turned the pump on. His navel began to be stretched up into the tube. He gasped in pain and pleasure as I began to gently tug on the chain between his nipple clamps while his navel was slowly being distended by the vacuum.

Wolf gasped; "Oh fuck, yes, Sir. Thank you Sir!" when I unclipped both of his tits at the same time and began to torture his nipples with my fingers. As I tormented my slave's tits, his cock was streaming with pre-cum. I could tell how turned on Wolf was by watching his body language, and the way he was responding to my ministrations.

After about ten minutes of working on his tits while the pump was sucking on his navel, Wolf was writhing in total ecstasy on the table. I finally released his nipples and started to concentrate on his navel. I removed the tube that was sucking on his navel and stroked the hard knot of flesh for a moment with my fingertips.

Wolf watched me with anticipation and lust in his eyes as I pulled on a pair of surgical gloves and picked up a small jar that had alcohol in it. Also in the jar was a moderately long needle with an enlarged plastic head. I pulled the needle from the jar with a small pair of pliers that had been sterilized as well.

Wolf groaned as I held the needle with the point facing into his navel, and slowly began to push the needle in. His abs immediately flexed rock hard as the needle began to pierce deeper and deeper into the puckered flesh of Wolf's bellybutton. He gasped and strained his muscles as I worked the needle in its entire length, until all that was visible was the plastic head. I stepped back and watched for a few minutes while Wolf gasped for air as his stomach muscles flexed under his shining bronze skin. He looked incredible as he struggled to endure this new form of torture. I had actually seen this being done to someone on the Internet, and had researched a few sites to see if it was actually safe to do to my slave, and wouldn't cause any permanent harm.

I decided to add to his torture and stepped back close to my groaning, gasping slave. He moaned louder as I gently began to wiggle the head of the needle with one finger. He moaned each time I would even touch the needle, but actually moving it from side to side would cause Wolf to scream in his combination of pure pain, and almost overwhelming delight.

"Do you like that, boy?" I growled into his ear.

"Oh fuck yes, Sir!" He groaned. "This feels so fucking good, Master! I love it, Sir!"

"Wait until you feel the needles piercing your nipples, boy, when I have your rings put in. Those needles are lots bigger, and they actually cut out a core to let the rings go in."

"God, I can hardly wait, Sir." Wolf moaned lustfully.

I immediately made a decision about Wolf's next torture.

"Well then, boy, maybe you won't have to wait." I stepped back to my shelves and picked up a small box. The box contained a collection of needles left over from Mike's having to take shots for his meds. Each of the hypodermic needles was still packaged in sterile wrappings, so I knew they were safe for what I was about to do.

I picked up the spray bottle and shot a fine mist of alcohol on each of Wolf's thick brown nipples. He writhed as the sharp pain shot through his tits for a few moments before slowly fading out.

I unwrapped one of the needles and held the point against Wolf's left nipple Wolf's eyes widened as he gasped out a soft "Do it, Sir. Please!"

I began to slowly and torturously push the needle into Wolf's tit. Every muscle in his torso flexed as he felt the sharp point pierce his flesh and begin to slide into his nipple.

"OH FUCK, SIR. OH FUCK. DO IT, MASTER! TORTURE MY NIPPLES, SIR! OH FUCK YES!! TORTURE ME, SIR" Wolf screamed! He continued to scream and shriek, every muscle in his body straining and flexing against the heavy restraints holding him spread helplessly on the table, as I pushed needle after needle into both of his nipples.

When I finally stepped back from the table to watch my muscle slave suffering extreme nipple torture, Wolf had to endure having four needles pierced through each nipple! The thin steel shafts stuck into the nipples at various angles, with the other end of each needle sticking out of the tit on the other side, kind of like the spokes on a bicycle wheel. Wolf lay on the table moaning and whimpering softly with pure agonized delight.

I watched him for a few minutes, just enjoying the sight of my slave boy suffering. I loved to watch whenever I could devise a new form of torture for Wolf to endure. Sometimes he would be very still as he struggled to mentally endure his pain, and sometimes he would strain and thrash against his restraints as the agony tearing through whatever part of his body I was working on would overcome his control, and all he could do was struggle to break free.

I searched for just a moment before I found the other needles I would need to finish Wolf's extreme nipple torture. He watched me, a look of both fear and almost overwhelming desire in his eyes, as I took the new needles, actually pins, and sterilized them in the alcohol. They were slightly thicker pins with a "t" shaped head, originally used as wig pins. I took one of the now sterile pins and held the point directly against the tip of Wolf's right nipple, facing directly towards his chest. Wolf's eyes widened as I started to push the thicker pin into his tit! Every muscle in his torso bulged and flexed, straining against the restraints even harder than before as the pin slowly slid deeper and deeper into his already tortured nipple.

Wolf gritted his teeth and tried not to cry out at the excruciating pain he was enduring. I knew that he really enjoyed being forced to endure extreme pain, especially in his nipples, and trying to endure the agony stoically and silently, added to his pleasure.

It took about ten seconds to push the pin deeply enough into his nipple so it would stay standing straight out from the flesh. Wolf gasped for air for just a few seconds before I repeated the final piercing on his left tit.

When I was done, I released the catch on the mount of the table and rotated it so Wolf was now standing almost upright. He looked incredibly hot and sexy. His body was shiny with sweat, every muscle totally defined under his skin. His chest rose and fell, and his washboard abs flexed with each breath as he gasped for air, trying to breathe against the excruciating pain that must have been ripping through his torso from his tortured nipples and navel. The needles piercing his nipples looked like a pair of exotic jewelry pieces attached to his thick, sculpted pecs. Of course, his cock was still totally erect, as it always was whenever he was forced to endure severe pain at my hands.

I let him process the pain for just a few seconds before I growled; "Ready for your real torture to begin, boy?" into his left ear.

Wolf just gasped out a soft; " Please, Sir, hurt me. Torture me. Make me scream and beg for mercy, Master!"

Damn, he knew how to turn me on!

"All right. You asked for it, boy." I snarled.

Wolf's eyes flew open wide when he heard me strike a match to light a small candle. I grinned sadistically at him as I brought the candle over to the bondage table and, without another word, held the flame under the end of the pin sticking out of Wolf's left nipple!

He threw his head back against the table and began to scream uncontrollably as the metal impaling his nipple began to get hotter and hotter!

"OH FUCK, SIR! OH YES! DO IT SIR! OH MY GOD! HURT ME SIR. HURT ME, HURT ME, AND HURT ME MORE, MASTER!! AW SHIT! OH FUCK, YES. TORTURE ME! OHGODOHGODOHGOD!" He was shrieking almost hysterically!

His screaming and struggling increased as I would alternate holding the flame of the candle under both of the pins in the tips of Wolf's thick brown nipples. Every muscle in his body was flexing and straining, from his thick, veined biceps all the way down to his sculpted calves. His chest would heave and flex each time a fresh wave of heat would flow down one of the pins in his nipples.

Finally I held the flame under the pin in Wolf's right tit and left it there! He shrieked at the top of his lungs as the metal got hotter then it had before. His struggles against the leather restraints increased until every muscle was straining at the limit of its strength. He looked magnificent being forced to endure the agony of the pins in his tits slowly cooking the flesh from the inside out!

I held the candle under the pin until Wolf shrieked out; "YELLOW, SIR!" I then immediately removed the flame from under his left tit, but before Wolf could relax, I moved it to the right one!

Wolf's flexing and struggling immediately renewed as the torture shifted to his other nipple. I knew he didn't want me to stop completely, because he didn't call out "red-light", our signal to stop completely. Amazingly throughout this entire session of torture, Wolf's cock hadn't softened a bit. It was still throbbing and pulsing, the plum colored head swollen and glistening with pre-cum.

Finally the agony in Wolf's nipple was too much for him and he screamed out; "RED-LIGHT!" Instantly I removed the candle and, using a small pair of pliers, gently removed the thick pins from each of his nipples. Wolf shrieked in pain as the pins were pulled out.

His head slumped forward onto his heaving chest when the pins slid out of his tortured nipples. I lifted his head up so I could look into his eyes and make sure that he was all right. Wolf moaned a little before he finally opened his eyes.

I asked him; "Are you O.K. boy?"

He smiled weakly and said; "Yes, Sir. That was incredible, Sir. Thank you, Sir."

I grinned sadistically at him and said; "Don't forget, boy. You still have a bunch more needles I have to get out. Your suffering isn't done, boy. Not by a long shot!"

I let him endure the needles for about ten more minutes before I gently and ever so slowly began to pull them out of his nipples, one at a time. Wolf gasped and moaned; "Oh fuck!" as each needle was withdrawn, leaving a single small drop of red at each of the piercings.

It took a couple of minutes before all eight of the needles were out. Wolf gasped for air when the last needle was pulled out of his right tit, but then he moaned loudly when I picked up the alcohol spray. I shot a fine mist of alcohol onto each nipple, causing Wolf to arch his back and shriek at the top of his lungs, straining and flexing his gleaming muscles. I thoroughly enjoyed his agonized struggles, knowing that the alcohol was hurting his nipples almost as badly as if I were branding them again, but it would help lessen the chance of his getting any infections from the multiple piercings.

To add to his agony, I shot another fine mist of the alcohol into each of Wolf's deep, sweaty armpits. He screamed again and again as the burning sensations ripped through his spread-eagled body once more.

It took a good ten minutes before Wolf's breathing slowed to near normal, and he was able to open his eyes and look at me standing next to the bondage table, slowly stroking my cock as I enjoyed the truly erotic sight of my muscleman slave enduring exquisitely agonizing torture at my hands.

"Did you enjoy that, boy?" I leered down at him. "Is that what you wanted, humm?"

Wolf gasped; "Oh God, yes, Sir. I love it when you torture me, master."

"O.K. then boy, let's see what you think of this."

He moaned loudly as I knelt down and began to deep throat his thick shaft. As I sucked his thick cock, I reached up and used one finger to gently wiggle the needle that was still impaling his hard navel. As the needle moved inside his abs, Wolf whimpered and growled deeply in his throat, sucking in air between tightly clenched teeth.

It only took a few minutes before Wolf gasped out; "Oh fuck, I'm cumming, Sir."

As the hot sperm began to shoot into my mouth, I slowly pulled the needle out of Wolf's navel.

He shrieked at the sensation of the length of sharp metal being removed from his body. Wolf arced his back and flexed his abs when the needle finally slid out of his navel.

"OH MY GOD, SIR!" he shrieked. It seemed that the feeling of the navel piercing caused his orgasm to be even bigger and stronger than it usually was. I kept his cock in my mouth until his cum finally finished shooting out of the swollen head of his dick. He gasped and moaned with pure pleasure as I gently worked the sensitive head of his dick with my tongue, adding to the intensity of his torture.

Just when he thought that his pain would end with his orgasm, I straightened up and used my right hand to slap his sensitive navel and rock-like, washboard ab muscles. Wolf shrieked once again at the sharp pain shooting through his torso. I kept slapping his abs until they were bright red, Wolf hollering and screaming each time my hand smacked down onto his tortured stomach.

Finally, I ended my torture of my helpless, spread-eagled slave boy. His entire body was soaked with sweat, streaming down his heaving, flexing muscles. My entire body was dripping with sweat as well, since torturing my willing slave always turned me on so much!

I decided to end the scene, since Wolf was quivering and shaking slightly, which he did whenever he was near the limit of his endurance. The shaking was from an overload of endorphins flooding his system. As a fitting finale to the scene, I released the catch on the bondage table and rotated it so Wolf was now upside down. Before he could say anything, I stuffed my hard cock deeply into his mouth and began fucking it.

Wolf moaned with pleasure as my dick slid in and out of his hot, sucking mouth. As I felt my cock building to an explosive orgasm, I drove my solid, nine inch shaft deeply down Wolf's throat, cutting off his air. It only took a few more seconds before my cock erupted with a huge load of sperm, shooting into Wolf's throat. He choked and struggled as my load flooded into him.

Finally I pulled back from my torture slave. Wolf gasped for air when my cock slid out of his mouth. I rotated the bondage table back into its upright position and began to unfasten my slave. I undid his ankle restraints first, as I always did. This allowed him to get his feet under him before I released his wrists.

Finally, Wolf was released from his bondage. He immediately knelt in front of me and began to lick my boots as he loved to do after a hard session of torture. The muscles under the glistening skin of his back and shoulders started to shake and shudder as he began to cry out his emotions as he usually did after being tortured. I let him lick my boots until his crying stopped. I knew he needed to do this to allow himself time to process his emotions. It was just one of the many things about my slave that I loved, the fact that he would let his feelings out, instead of keeping them bottled up inside.

I told Wolf to stand up, and when he had done so, I wrapped my arms around his hot, sweaty physique, loving the feel of his body in my arms.

"Was that what you wanted, boy?" I smiled down into his face.

"Oh God, yes." He moaned. "That was incredible, Sir. Thank you so much. I was actually seeing stars for a couple of minutes there! Unbelievable. I can hardly wait to get my nipples pierced and ringed now, Sir."

"So, you were seeing stars, humm boy? I always said that I would give you whatever I could, boy. Even the stars and the moon. Well, now you've seen the stars. I guess that leaves the moon." I grinned

Wolf grinned back. "Oh no, Sir. I've already gotten the moon from you many times, Sir. Just turn around in your chaps and I'll see it again, Sir."

I cuffed him along side his head as I broke up laughing and he started giggling.

"Smart ass!" I growled at him.

He giggled again as he said; "Hey, my ass is smart, and yours is sexy. It all works out, Sir."

"All right, so you've gotten the stars and the moon. I guess that just leaves the sky. You'll just have to wait for that, boy. Now, lets go get something to eat."

Wolf looked slightly puzzled for just a second before he smiled and said; "Yes, Sir"

What he didn't know was that I had just given him a huge hint as to what his big Christmas present was going to be. But he would find out tomorrow morning. It was going to be the biggest surprise I had ever given my lover.

Chapter 11

Christmas

We went upstairs after I released Wolf from his bondage, and had a late lunch. We spent the rest of the afternoon and the evening just relaxing around the house. Wolf wasn't able to do too much, since he was pretty exhausted, and still hurting from the intense torture I had forced him to endure. We both knew that this was probably going to be the last really hard torture session until our contest, so I had made sure that it was one Wolf would remember for quite a while!

The next morning, which was Christmas, I rose early and started my day by making a quick phone call to Danny, who was the sales manager of the dealership where I had purchased Wolf's big gift. He was expecting my call, as we had arranged for Wolf's present to be stored near Danny's home for a few days. He told me that he would be ready to have the gift delivered whenever I asked him to. I told him that any time would be fine, and he told me that he would be on the way within a few minutes. Wolf was still sleeping, since he was totally exhausted by the extreme nipple torture I had subjected him to.

After a short while, I heard the sound of a car turning into our driveway, immediately followed by another. I stepped outside to greet our visitors, since I didn't want them to ring the bell and wake Wolf up. I wanted to totally surprise him. I took delivery of Wolf's gift and wished Danny and his boy Eddie, who was driving Danny's car, a "Merry Christmas". I knew it would be one at our house, as soon as Wolf found out what I had gotten him!

Before they left, Danny invited us to come over to his house a bit later, as he was having a dinner and get together for some friends. He told me that he'd call me when everything was ready.

After about another hour or so, I finally heard Wolf stirring around upstairs. I went up to his room and stuck my head in the door.

"Merry Christmas, boy. I figured it was about time you were getting up." I grinned at him.

Wolf just groaned. "God, my tits and armpits hurt, Sir. And a merry Christmas to you too, Sir."

I just chuckled as I slipped into his bed with him. Wolf's groans turned into a soft moan of pleasure as my arms wrapped around him. I kissed my hard bodied lover deeply. He returned the kiss with enthusiasm.

"Come on, boy. Let's go get some breakfast, and then we can see what Santa left under the tree." I had to admit it, but I had always been a sucker for Christmas. I might try to be a hard-assed leather topman most of the time, but around the holidays, I was as excited as any ten year old.

Before we left Wolf's room, I told him to roll over and let me look at his nipples. I wanted to make sure that they weren't damaged too badly by the torture with the needles and the heat. His tits were a bit swollen, but there seemed to be no other problems. They both had slightly dark spots at the tips of the mounds of brown, swollen flesh, but it seemed that Wolf's nipples hadn't been too badly burned by the heated needles.

I gently kissed each of his tits and said; "Well boy, I guess you'll live. Haul your ass out of bed, and let's get downstairs so we can check out our loot. Come on, boy. Chop-chop. Hop to it!"

He gave me a totally exaggerated look of suffering and whined; "You torture and torment me as hard as you can, and then you just bitch when I try to rest up. What a cruel master! Oh why do I put up with you? You're so mean to me!"

I sneered; "Oh boo-hoo-hoo. Whine and snivel. Moan and complain. That's all you ever do. Bitch, bitch, bitch. Maybe I should just boot you out the front door with just the clothes on your back! That way I won't have to listen to you pissing and moaning all the time."

We just looked at each other for a moment before both breaking into laughter. I knew we were both being totally silly, and I loved it. I hugged him again as we were both almost helpless from laughing so hard.

When I could finally catch my breath, I kissed Wolf again and said; "Last one downstairs has to wait to open his presents!"

Wolf immediately leapt out of bed, grabbed his robe, and headed for the door, with me hot on his heels. We reached the foot of the stairs at the same time, so I laughed and said; "O.K. it's a tie."

We finally calmed down and had breakfast, before going into the living room and starting to look through the presents under the tree. There were a few from me to Wolf, and a couple from Wolf to me, of course, but there were also a few marked to the both of us from Santa. Obviously all of the Santa gifts to Wolf had been put under the tree during the night by me, but there were a few from Santa to me that I didn't recognize. I guess that Wolf had managed to get up during the night and put his own hidden gifts out. Wolf had the money to buy whatever he wanted, of course, since I paid him a weekly stipend equal to what I had been paying a lawn service, housekeeping service and the pool maintenance service before he moved in with me. I told him that I never wanted him to think of himself as a kept boy, but that if he continued to do a good job doing all the cleaning and yard and pool work, I would pay him a salary. What he didn't know was that I also put an equal amount into a trust fund each month for him. The money was invested by my stockbroker in the markets, so Wolf was becoming quite well off, even if he didn't know it at the time.

We started in on the presents under the tree. Most of the gifts were just small personal gifts to each other, such as a new money clip and wallet for me, and some new bicycling jerseys and shorts for Wolf. Surprisingly enough there were a matching set of jerseys and shorts from "Santa" to me.

I looked at them and said; "Gee, what are the odds that Santa knew exactly which jerseys to get me so we would match?" Wolf just gave me that "Yeah, Right!" look before we both broke up laughing delightedly.

We both loved to ride both road and mountain bikes, so this was something that both Wolf and I really needed. Besides, I thought that we both looked pretty good in skin tight spandex that showed off our muscular physiques!

Of course there were some leather gifts, as well. I gave Wolf a new, longer leash for his collar, and he surprised me with a new set of a different style of urethral sounds then I already owned. I grinned when I opened them up, and said; "Well, I guess I know who's going to be the first to see how they feel, right boy?" Wolf just smiled knowingly at me.

I also surprised Wolf with a custom made pair of leather pants, matching the ones that I already owned. He just grinned from ear to ear and thanked me effusively when he opened up the box they were in.

I told him; "Well now boy, we can match when we go out. These should almost finish up your collection of leathers. They should look great with your coat, vest and your boots, when you're not wearing your chaps. I have to insist that whenever I take my slave out in public, he has to look at least passably presentable!"

Wolf laughed and said; "Thank you, Sir. I love them!"

Finally, when we had opened up all the boxes under the tree, I made a bit of a show of feeling around in the pockets of my robe, while muttering; "Now where did I put that?" Wolf just furrowed his brow and said; "Where did you put what, Sir?"

Eventually I pulled a small box out of my pocket and, handing it to Wolf, said; "Here it is, boy. I almost forgot. This is yours as well."

Wolf looked puzzled but opened up the box. Lying inside on a bed of tissue paper was a single key. He looked up at me and said; "What is this for, Sir?"

I grinned and said; "Go look out the front door, boy."

Wolf's eyes widened as he stammered; "Oh-oh no. You didn't. Oh my God! Sir! You didn't!"

He walked to the front door and hesitated for a second before he opened it up. When he did, he just shouted; "OH-MY-GOD!"

Sitting in the drive outside the front door was a bright red Saturn Sky red line roadster! Wolf turned to me, totally speechless. His mouth moved but no sounds came out.

I smiled at him and said "Merry Christmas, boy. Now I don't have to haul your ass around or loan you the Magnum whenever you want to go anywhere. Now you can drive yourself in your own car."

Wolf just wrapped his arms around me as the tears started to run down his face. Finally he managed to find his voice.

"Oh God, Sir. That's just too much. I never expected anything like this, Sir. I don't know what to say. I could never give you anything to match this gift, Sir"

I just smiled down into his face, flushed with excitement and streaked with tears.

"You already gave me something worth much more than any car, boy. You gave me your love and loyalty. You allowed me to mark you as my slave. You are the best thing that has ever happened to me, boy. I just hope that this can help to repay some of the pleasure that you have given me ever since the first day that we ever met, boy. I love you, Carlos Greywolf, and I never want you to forget that!" The tears started to run down my face as well as I softly told my lover just what he meant to me. I meant every word of what I said to him. Wolf really was the center of my life now.

Finally I told Wolf; "Well boy, lets get dressed and we can go out and check out your new toy."

Wolf grinned up into my eyes and said; "You bet, Sir."

Before we could get dressed however, the phone rang. It was Danny, telling me that his dinner was going to be ready soon, if we wanted to start heading that way. I told him that we'd try to bring along something for dinner.

I said to Wolf; "Well boy, it looks like you will get a chance to show off your new wheels. I assume you'll want to drive to Danny's, right, boy?"

He just smiled; "Yes, Sir."

"Well, Danny says that dress is just casual, so I guess jeans and tee shirts will be all right with our leather jackets. Lets get going, boy!"

Once we were dressed, Wolf proudly opened the passenger door of his new car and held it for me while I shoehorned my 6' frame into the two-seater convertible. Since it was, after all, December in the bay area, we wouldn't be able to put the top down. Therefore it was a bit of a tight fit for me, but Wolf settled in behind the wheel like the car was built for him. Which, in a manner of speaking, it was. I had ordered it optioned up the way I thought that Wolf would like it.

I enjoyed watching Wolf work his way through the light traffic on our way down to the city and to Danny's house. Wolf was an excellent driver, having driven most of the cars in my collection at one time or another. We stopped off to pick up a couple of bottles of wine and some snacks at a grocery store that was open on Christmas before pulling up in front of Danny's house. There were a couple of other cars there, some of which I recognized as belonging to friends of ours.

I smiled at Wolf as I told him; "It'll be interesting to see what everyone thinks of your present. Eddie's probably totally green with envy!"

Wolf chuckled; "Yeah, but do you think he'll ever let Danny know that?"

We looked at each other for just a beat before we both shook our heads and said; "Naah!" at exactly the same time. Then we both just broke up laughing. It was almost like an old vaudeville routine.

When we got to the front door, we were both still chuckling. The door opened and there stood Eddie, Danny's slave boy and lover.

He saw us and smiled before he said; Well, if it isn't the luckiest boy in town, and his sugar daddy!"

Wolf's mouth dropped open, and he looked like he was just about to explode before Eddie grinned from ear to ear and said; "Gotcha!"

From inside the house we heard "EDDIE!" His face fell as he recognized the voice of his master. Danny stepped to the door and was just about to berate his boy when he saw that it was Wolf and I standing there. He then looked out into the street and saw Wolf's new car. He turned to us and grinned.

"I should have known it was you two. Couldn't wait to show off your new wheels, could you? Always causing trouble."

We laughed as Danny hugged us both, then turned to his boy.

"Don't worry, boy. There's no problem. It's these two troublemakers. It's all their fault. Wherever they go they leave chaos in their wake."

I glowered at Danny and growled; "Well, if that's how you feel, then I guess we'll just take our booze and leave. Come on boy, we know when we're not wanted."

Danny grinned at my act and said; "Whoa, whoa, you have booze? Well, that changes everything. Come on in."

We all laughed as we went inside. There were about six or seven other guys there already. Most of them were mutual friends of ours, including Joe and his boy H.J., so we just greeted everyone and wished each other a merry Christmas all around.

Over the next few hours we just enjoyed the company of some good friends, had a really great meal, and just generally enjoyed ourselves. We were able to let go the roles of master and slave, and just be friends for a while. Eddie and Wolf and a couple of the other guys went out and ogled Wolf's car while Danny and I and the rest of our friends just hung out and relaxed.

I felt that it was important to me, as well as to Wolf to just be able to be ourselves once in a while. As Wolf and I had joked, Eddie was really impressed with the Saturn, and we could tell he was just a bit jealous, but, as I pointed out to him, in his job as a driver for a limo service in town, he got to drive everything from stretched Hummers to a Rolls-Royce limousine worth several hundred thousand dollars. He grinned and said; "Gee, Sir, I never thought of it that way. I guess you're right. Still, that's a cool car."

Several of the other guys at the party told us things like; "Damn, you two are really getting built. We've never seen you looking that hot. Your muscles look like they have muscles!"

Wolf and I both thanked them and told them about the contest we had entered. I noticed that Danny and Eddie just looked at each other and smiled. Then I told everyone about the bet I had made with Wolf.

Danny grinned and said; "You know, I'm almost hoping Wolf wins. I'd love to see you getting your ass worked over for a change, instead of always being the one torturing this poor slaveboy!"

I gave him a mock glare, which he just responded to with a huge grin, and then he stuck out his tongue. I couldn't help it then and just started laughing.

The rest of the afternoon and the evening passed with everyone just enjoying a day of good friendship without any underlying sexual tensions or expectations. At one point a couple of the guys asked if we would mind showing off the results of our training, so Wolf and I both peeled off out shirts and gave them a short example of our posing routines. It was just a really fun and relaxing day. I figured if anyone wanted to have sex, they would, but no one pushed anyone else. Occasionally, though, a couple of guys or more would disappear into one of the bedrooms for a while, only to come back out a bit later somewhat flushed and breathing hard.

Wolf and I ended up sitting on the couch in our favorite position, with me leaning back against the cushions, and Wolf sitting between my legs with my arms wrapped around his body. Even Danny was much more casual and relaxed in his treatment of Eddie, who was still sort of on thin ice after his major screw-up in the bar several weeks earlier. I realize that it might sound corny, but there was a real holiday feel to the day. It was nice to have a day of good friendship and just plain old fashioned fun.

Finally, after everyone else had left, I told Danny and Wolf that I thought that it was time that we were heading back home over the bridge. Eddie looked at his master and Danny just nodded his head slightly.

Eddie walked over to where Wolf and were on the couch and dropped to his knees in front of us.

"Sir, before you leave, may I have permission to give you my gift?" he said softly.

I looked quizzically at Danny, who just smiled and winked at me. That let me know that he knew exactly what was going on.

I looked down at his boy and told him; "Sure, boy."

He smiled and said; "I would like to have the honor of getting both of you off, if that's all right with you, Sir. It's just my way of thanking you for helping me realize the mistake that I made, Sir."

I grinned and told him; "That's fine with me. What do you think, boy?" I nudged Wolf. He grinned at me then looked down at Eddie as well. "That sounds like fun."

Eddie's face split in a huge smile. Danny and I both knew that Eddie was totally hot for Wolf, and had been ever since the first time he had seen him. We knew it wasn't any way disrespectful to his master, but was just one man being really attracted to another.

I looked at Wolf and Eddie and said; "Why don't the two of you go into the bedroom and have some fun. Danny and I need to talk for a bit, then we'll come in and join you."

Both of them grinned, and headed for the rear of the house. Danny and I knew that they would really enjoy some time together before we headed in, so we just let our two boys spend a good half hour having sex before we undressed and walked into the bedroom.

Eddie was laying on top of Wolf, diligently running his tongue over every part of Wolf's hard, sculpted torso. Wolf was just lying back with his hands under his head and his eyes closed, apparently really enjoying Eddie's gentle ministrations, if the size of his hard-on was any indication! Wolf was softly moaning as Eddie gently ran his hands over the thick, bulging muscles of Wolf's arms while licking the bronze skin of his chest and abs at the same time. Apparently Wolf had told Eddie what I had done to torture his nipples the night before, as Eddie seemed to be avoiding playing with the still tender mounds of dark brown flesh.

Danny and I just stood and watched as our two boys just enjoyed the rare pleasure of being able to make love to each other. Finally, Eddie raised his head from Wolf's body and smiled up at us. Wolf opened his eyes and grinned as well.

I looked down at the two hunky muscular boys making love and said; "You two look like you're enjoying yourselves."

Eddie said; "Yes Sir. Thank you, Sir. We really are."

Danny said; "I have an idea how we can make this even more fun. Eric, do you mind if I take Eddie for a couple of minutes? I think you and Wolf can keep yourselves entertained for a bit." Then to his boy he said; "Come with me. We need to get you nice and cleaned out."

Eddie grinned at his lover/master and said; "Yes, Sir. Whatever you want, Sir."

As they headed off to the bathroom, I lay down on the bed next to Wolf.

"Having a good time, boy?" I smiled at him.

He wrapped his strong arms around my body and said; "Oh yes, Sir. This is the best Christmas I've ever had. I mean, wow, a new car, great friends, and the greatest master and lover in the world. What more could any man ever wish for, Sir. I'm the luckiest boy in the world to have you, Sir."

I hugged him to my chest as my eyes started to fill with tears of happiness. We just lay on the bed holding each other until Danny and Eddie walked back in.

"Whoa, whoa there. None of that, now." Danny chided us. "At least until we can join in! Eddie, on your knees between Wolf's legs. I want to watch you take that whole cock down your throat. Eric, I've got something special I'd like you to do. Do you see that hot ass in front of you? I want you to fuck it. Fuck that boy until he can't take any more, and then keep going."

Eddie moaned in a combination of delight and anticipation as he got on his knees between Wolf's spread legs. He bent down and slowly sucked Wolf's thick, streaming eight inches into his mouth. When Eddie was totally bent over, I positioned myself kneeling behind him. I lubed my cock and slowly started to press it against Eddie's tight ass. He moaned and then gasped in pain briefly when my thick dick finally slid into his hot hole. He groaned with pleasure around Wolf's cock as I slowly worked the entire nine inches of my shaft into him. He gasped at the sensation of having seventeen inches of dick impaling him from both ends. Eddie had a tight ass since very few people other than Danny ever got to fuck him. I had done it on several occasions, and I knew that Wolf had fucked Eddie as well, but very few others.

I grasped Eddie's hips and began to slowly thrust my cock in and out of his ass. He moaned around the thick cock filling his mouth, as I watched the muscles on his hard back flex and ripple under his skin. Wolf was softly panting with pleasure as his cock was worked by Eddie's hot, sucking mouth. He reached down and ran his hand down the strip of hair on Eddie's head before stretching his arms out to the side and surrendering to the pleasure of a hot cocksucking.

We both fucked Eddie for about ten minutes before Wolf started to gasp "Oh yeah, oh yeah. I'm gonna cum. I'm gonna shoot!"

Danny, who had been standing next to the bed, stroking his cock and watching his boy get double fucked, said; "Give it to him. Fill his mouth, boy."

Wolf grasped Eddie's head and began to fuck his mouth harder and harder, his hard abs flexing, until he hollered; "Oh fuck!" and pumped a thick load of his jizz into Eddie's waiting mouth. Eddie worked to swallow the hot sperm filling his mouth, even as I started to drive my cock into his ass faster and harder.

Danny knelt on the bed behind me, wrapped his arms around my torso and began to twist and pull on my nipples. I groaned at the feel of his hard chest against my back, and at the feel of his hands working on my tits.

"Fuck him, Eric. Fuck that boy's ass." He growled in my ear.

I started pounding my hard dick in and out of Eddie's hole faster and faster until I couldn't hold out any longer. With a loud, deep-throated cry, I shot my load deeply into the hot channel surrounding my dick. As I filled Eddie's ass with my sperm, Danny worked my nipples almost savagely. He knew what hard tit work would do to me.

Eddie howled as my load hosed into his ass. This was a rare treat for him, having two cocks at the same time.

After recently having had the pleasure of helping Danny torture Eddie in my dungeon, and watching Eddie's hot, ripped physique struggling to endure the savage electrical torture, it was a real treat to be able to watch his body in pure ecstasy.

I continued to pound Eddie's ass until my explosive orgasm was spent. Danny finally released my nipples and I slowly pulled my cock out of Eddie's ravaged asshole. He just gasped out a soft; "Thank you, Sir" as he flopped down on top of Wolf's hard body.

After a few minutes Eddie rolled off of Wolf and smiled up at Danny and me.

"Oh God, that felt great. Thank you again, Sir." He said.

Danny looked down and growled; "You're not done yet, boy. Open your mouth."

Eddie did so and Danny immediately grabbed both sides of Eddie's head and began to fuck his mouth. It only took a few more minutes before Danny gasped and shot his load of sperm into Eddie's mouth. Danny stood there, his chest heaving, as Eddie swallowed his master's load. Finally, Danny pulled out of his slave's mouth. Eddie softly said; "Thank you, Sir. Again. And thank you for allowing me to get our guests off, Sir. I hope they enjoyed it as much as I did, Sir."

Danny grinned down at his kneeling slave. "I think they liked it, boy. At least, I haven't heard anyone complaining." He looked to where I was now lying on the bed next to Wolf, watching two men who loved each other enjoy some hot sex.

I looked up at him and chuckled; "Nope. No complaints here. You know I always love a good tight ass, and I know Wolf loves a hot mouth as well. Eddie has both, so no complaints."

Danny laughed, even as Eddie grinned sheepishly while standing up. We all knew that Eddie really enjoyed sucking cock and getting a stiff cock up his ass, even if Danny was protective of who he would let fuck his slave boy.

Wolf surprised us by asking; "Danny, may I get Eddie off? It seems only fair that he gets to cum, as well. After all, he did a great job on everyone else."

Danny smiled and said; "Sure, why not."

Eddie grinned, and then moaned with pleasure as Wolf knelt in front of him and slowly sucked his long, but thin cock deeply down his throat. Eddie's cock wasn't very thick, but it was beautifully shaped and formed, a golden brown color, with veins tracing the entire length of the shaft, and a thicker head.

Eddie threw his head back and groaned in ecstasy as Wolf began to run his hands up and down his lean, ripped torso. Wolf's fingers rippled over the cuts in Eddie's incredible washboard ab muscles, then slipped up to his rippling ribcage, and finally began to stroke Eddie's taut, chiseled pecs and erect nipples.

Eddie moaned louder as Wolf began to twist and pull the hard knots of reddish brown flesh as his head began to pump faster and faster on the long cock sliding in and out of his hot mouth.

It only took another two or three minutes before Eddie grabbed Wolf's head and began furiously fucking his face, gasping and growling as he pounded his cock into the sucking mouth of my lover. Beads of sweat were running down Eddie's hard chest and abs, and streaming down his back as he threw his head back again and howled as he pumped a load of his hot, steamy cum deeply into Wolf's mouth. Every muscle in his ripped, wiry torso was flexing under his golden skin as he shot again and again into Wolf's waiting mouth.

When Eddie finally gasped and released Wolf's head, and pulled his cock out of his mouth, Wolf immediately stood up and clamped his mouth over Eddie's. I realized then that he hadn't swallowed the load of cum, but was transferring it back to Eddie, so he could swallow his own sperm! Eddie moaned again as the load of cum dripped from Wolf's mouth into his own mouth. I could see Eddie's throat muscles working as he gulped down his own seed.

The two boys stood, their bodies pressed together, their arms wrapped around each other's torso for a full minute, kissing deeply. Neither Danny nor I wanted to disturb them, since we both knew how much the boys loved each other. Finally, they broke the kiss. Eddie just gasped for air before saying; "Oh wow. That was great. Thanks, Wolf. And thank you, Sirs, for letting Wolf suck me off. That was just incredible!"

I told him; "You're quite welcome. We really enjoyed watching you. That was one of the hottest blowjobs I've seen in quite a while. What do you think?" I added, turning to Danny.

He smiled; "You're right. That was hot."

I said; "I hate to end the party, but we really do need to head home. Tomorrow, it's back to the gym as usual, since the contest is less than two months from now."

For the second time that day, I saw Eddie and Danny just exchange a quick glance and a brief smile. I began to suspect something was up, but I also figured it wasn't any of my business.

Wolf and I got dressed and after saying our final good-bys to Danny and Eddie, we headed home across the bridge. We were now into the home stretch of training for the contest, and we both knew that after new years, it would almost totally consume our lives until the day of the contest, in mid February. After that, either Wolf would endure his most intense tortures ever, or I would be his slave for a month! I could hardly wait to see how it would turn out! Either way, it was going to be fun.

Chapter 12

The Contest

The rest of the holiday season passed quickly, capped by a New Year's Eve party at our house. I invited all the guys from the various leather organizations we belonged to, and Danny asked some of his friends from the uniform club along, as well. There must have been nearly fifty guys at the house that night, some in leather, some in uniforms, and some just in street clothes. Wolf was kept pretty busy keeping the ice buckets filled, and the snacks supplied, as part of his duties as the host's slave. He was dressed in his new leather pants and his red rubber tank top, with his nicest studded collar locked around his throat. He looked amazingly hot, with his broad, flaring lats emphasized by the cut of the tank top, and his muscles rippling under his skin with his slightest movement. He had braided his hair for the evening, the tail hanging down to the middle of his back.

I was wearing what I liked to call my formal leathers. I had on my leather pants, my high biker boots, polished to a gleaming shine by Wolf, a pleated tuxedo shirt, my vest and a custom made leather bow tie.

Some of our guests used our dungeon facilities for play during the evening, but Wolf and I stayed upstairs. I was enjoying the company of our friends, and Wolf was doing his duties, taking care of our guests needs.

At midnight, all of us were gathered in the living room celebrating the New Year with a toast and lots of hugging and kissing. I stood in the center of the crowd with Wolf in my arms, holding him tightly as we rang in the start of another year together. Our actual anniversary was in June, but this was a time for celebration as well.

Someone called out; "Hey Eric, what's your New Year's resolution this year?"

I laughed and gave my standard answer. "My resolution this year is the same as it's been for about ten years. 'I resolve to not make any New Year's resolutions!', and it's been real easy to keep that resolution!"

Everyone laughed at my answer, since most of my friends knew it was a running joke with me. Then I held up my glass of champagne and told my friends; "Besides, what do I need to change? I've got my health, I've got my friends, and I've got the greatest lover anyone could want!"

Wolf actually blushed a bright red before I kissed him again while our friends applauded. Then Danny held up his glass and called out; "A toast to our host, Eric. The hottest and horniest topman in town. Not to mention the owner of one of the greatest pairs of pecs and nipples in the city."

I modestly said; "Aw, come on, my chest isn't all that great."

Danny chuckled; "Not yours, you idiot! Wolf's!"

This time it was my turn to feel the heat rising in my face as everyone laughed, raised their glasses and called out; "To Eric!" before drinking. Then one of our guests started singing "Auld Lang Syne" and slowly the rest of the guys joined in. It was actually a very moving moment, and I saw Wolf quickly wiping tears from his face.

I leaned in and whispered; "You mushball. I saw that" as I gave him a quick smile before I kissed him again. He just giggled softly and hugged me.

Finally after another half hour or so our guests slowly began to depart, until finally Wolf and I were alone at last.

"Come on, boy, let's go to bed. This mess can wait until the morning to get cleaned up." I told Wolf before leading him upstairs. When we were in my bedroom, he gently undressed me and hung up my leathers before undressing himself and sliding into bed with me.

"Well, boy, it's a new year. Time for new beginnings. Is there anything you want to change, boy?" I asked Wolf as he lay nestled in my arms.

He just smiled and said; "No Sir. I can't think of a thing I'd ever want to change. I've got the master I've wanted all my life, a great home and great friends. What more could I ask for?"

We made love gently for a while, both of us sucking a hot load from each others cocks before we both drifted off to sleep, still wrapped in each others arms.

When we woke up later in the day, Wolf and I had a late breakfast before he went to work cleaning up the debris from the party. I knew that the gym was closed on New Year's Day, so we couldn't go work out. I had some weights in an unused store room off of the dungeon, but it wasn't worth the trouble to dig them out. We both could use a day off, so we just hung out and watched some of the annual football games on television.

Starting the next day, however, it was back to our usual schedule of workouts. We were into the home stretch of our training, and I was trying to arrange our training and diets so that we would both peak at the time of the contest. We both were working on honing our bodies to the peak of our personal perfection, and we also were practicing our posing routines. We had chosen the music to accompany our three minute posing sessions in the evening part of the contest, and we had both purchased the posing briefs we were going to wear in the contest. Mine were red, and Wolf's were his favorite turquoise blue.

As I explained to Wolf, the contest was in two parts. The afternoon session was just for the contestants and the judges. Each contestant in all five of the categories came on stage one at a time and performed the compulsory poses for the judges. The top five contestants, if there were five competitors in a category, were asked back for the evening session, which was the part open to the public. Each contestant could do a three minute routine using their own music and choreography, as long as the routine contained all the compulsory poses. Then the top contestant in each category came back on stage for a final free-for-all pose down, to select the overall winner. The five categories in this particular contest were; Lightweight, Middleweight, which included Wolf, Heavyweight, my category, Masters, which were contestants over 40 years old, and Teenagers.

It was a slightly different format from a nationally sponsored event, since this was just a strictly amateur local contest. There were no national bodybuilding points at stake or anything like that. This show was strictly for fun and local bragging rights.

Our workouts continued right up to the last day before the show. We both had practiced our posing and our free form routines until we could do them flawlessly. I loved watching Wolf show off his tanned, sculpted physique, and I knew that he was just as excited watching me pose for him. The last night before the show, we did our final workouts and ate a light dinner before I led Wolf upstairs to my bedroom. We undressed each other and slipped into bed together.

"No matter what happens tomorrow, I want you to know that I am as proud of you as I have ever been" I told Wolf. "Win, lose or draw, you are and always will be a champion in my eyes, boy."

Tears of happiness were running down my face as I held his body closely to me. Wolf leaned in to me and kissed the tears away. Then I saw that he was crying as well.

"Thank you, Sir, for allowing me to be a part of your life." He softly said. "I can't imagine living without you."

We just held each other for a while, talking, before Wolf started to gently run his tongue over the planes of my pecs. I moaned with pleasure at the feel of his hot mouth gently surrounding my right nipple. He started to suck on my tit, while his teeth gently nibbled on the sensitive flesh.

He moaned with lust when I pressed my hand to the back of his head, forcing his face tighter against my chest while I flexed my pecs. His tongue work on my nipple got hotter and his teeth began to bite harder and harder on my tit. I groaned as he slowly reached up and stretched my arms over my head and held them there, leaving my chest spread out for his pleasure, and my armpits wide open and exposed for his eventual licking.

I lay back, Wolf holding me stretched out in mock bondage while he worshiped my sculpted torso from my biceps, down through my armpits, across my pecs and my thick ribcage, finally working his way down to my washboard abs.

He moaned; "Oh yeah" softly as I flexed my stomach muscles while he licked and tongued each thick, hard ridge of solid muscle. I had actually gotten my body fat down to an amazing four percent for the contest! Of course, Wolf's was almost never above seven percent most of the time, and by now, his body fat was down to an almost unbelievable three percent! We were both as ripped as we had ever been.

Wolf continued his worshiping of my physique, finally sliding down and gently running his tongue down my streaming cock. I groaned with pure lust when he finally slipped the swollen head of my cock in between his lips.

"Yeah. Suck it, boy. Suck that cock, boy!" I moaned as his head started to pump up and down on my throbbing shaft faster and faster.

I reached down, grasped his head and began to fuck his mouth. Wolf's hands slid up and down my torso, feeling my muscles flexing and rippling as I worked my dick in and out of his incredible mouth. He was moaning with pleasure and pure lust as I pushed his head down further and further on my thrusting cock, until I was driving my dick in it's full nine inches!

Wolf moaned again with lust when I threw my head back and howled; "Take it, boy!" as I filled his mouth with my cum. As I was shooting, Wolf reached up and squeezed and twisted my nipples almost savagely. His fingers rolled my tits and pulled the rings as I shot in his mouth.

Finally my orgasm was spent, and my head fell back on the pillows. Wolf finally let my cock out of his sucking mouth. He slid up next to me and kissed me passionately.

"Thank you, Sir." He whispered in my ear.

We were both breathing hard from my orgasm. I could only lay there for a minute before I could finally kiss him and ask him; "Well, do you want to get off too, boy?"

Wolf grinned and said; "Always, Sir."

I told him to sit on my chest. When he did, I slid him up until I could take his throbbing, thick eight inch cock into my mouth. Wolf groaned as I started to stroke his hot, sweaty torso while I was sucking on his cock.

He moaned again, even louder when I started to pull on his thick, pumped nipples. Wolf always loved it when I would work his tits while getting him off. I loved watching the muscles of Wolf's tight washboard abs flexing in front of my face, and listening to him moan with pleasure whenever I would suck him off like this.

It only took another couple of minutes until wolf started to gasp and groan in the way that meant that he was about to cum.

When he started to pump his sperm into my mouth, I rolled his nipples between my fingers as hard as I could. Wolf shrieked at the sudden burst of pain in his chest, but it was a cry of pleasure.

"OH FUCK, OH FUCK!" he howled, even while he was filling my mouth with his huge load of cum!

Finally I pulled my head back, releasing his cock. Wolf immediately lay down on top of me, his heart pounding in his chest from his orgasm.

"Was that what you wanted, boy?" I asked him, looking up into his soft brown eyes.

"Damn right, Sir!" He grinned down at me before kissing me deeply.

"I hope you enjoyed it, Sir, since that's the last time you will get to top me for a month. I'm gonna beat the pants off of you tomorrow, Sir, and then your ass is mine for a month!" Wolf gave me a wicked grin, before I rolled him over, winding up on top of him.

"Don't be so sure, boy. I might have a few surprises up my sleeve. And then you'll be in deep trouble, slave!" I growled at him.

Wolf giggled; "Promises, promised!"

We both broke up laughing, before we finally calmed down and dropped off to try to get a good night's sleep before our big day tomorrow.

In the morning we ate a light breakfast, then collected our gym bags and headed off to the auditorium where the contest was being held. Most of the other contestants were there already. As we registered, both of us got a major surprise.

"Well, well. Look who finally made it" came a familiar voice from behind us. I turned around to see Danny walking towards us, his face split with a huge grin. I was surprised to see him, but even more shocked to see Eddie, his boy walking alongside him. Eddie was just wearing a golden yellow posing thong, but what was even more surprising was the fact that the strip of hair running front to rear on his otherwise shaved head had been dyed a bright blonde that was almost the same color as his thong. Combined with his classically Asian features, the blonde Mohawk made him amazingly sexy looking in my eyes.

"What the fuck are you guys doing here?" I gaped.

Danny chuckled. "You two aren't the only hot bodybuilders around, you know. Eddie is going for the lightweight class."

I suddenly realized why they had exchanged those sly smiles with each other at the Christmas dinner at Danny's house.

I grinned at them. "You sneaky bastard. Why didn't you tell us what was going on?"

Wolf and Eddie both laughed when Danny said; "What? And miss the chance to see that look on your face? Not on your life!"

I turned to Wolf. "This doesn't change a thing, boy. I don't care who we're competing against, I'm still gonna clean your clock in the posedown!"

He chuckled; "In your dreams, musclehead!"

We both broke up laughing at the shocked expression on Eddie's face. If he ever talked to Danny like that in public, well, who knows what would happen? But Wolf had my permission to speak freely until we saw who won the contest.

Finally both our friends started laughing as well when I explained exactly what was going on.

"I guess we need to get in and get changed." I told Danny. "We'll see you later."

He smiled. "Seriously, good luck, both of you."

We walked into the area that had been set aside for the contestants and changed into our posing gear. There were about thirty other bodybuilders in the room. As I looked around, I thought that Wolf had a really good chance of winning his weight category, but that I was going to have a harder time. There were about eight or nine other heavyweights, and most of them looked amazingly good.

We hung out in the dressing room, some of the guys getting a final pump on their muscles and getting oiled up until each of the weight classes was called out to the stage for the prejudging.

As I expected, Wolf was among the finalists in the middleweight category, and Eddie was selected for the lightweights. I hoped I would do as well since there were more heavyweights than any other class.

I did my poses for the judges, and answered their questions, then nervously awaited their final votes. I was really surprised when they called my name out as the first of the heavyweights to make it into the finals.

Wolf and Eddie both wrapped their arms around me and gave me a big hug when I walked back into the dressing room. We dressed in our sweat suits and sat around chatting, waiting for the evening session of the contest.

We stood at the rear of the auditorium when the evening show started. The first competitors were the teenagers. There were only three guys in this class, but picking a winner was going to be hard. All three of the guys were amazing looking, considering that one was only fifteen, and the others were seventeen and eighteen!

I leaned over and whispered; "Boy, I can't wait until these guys hit twenty one and they're legal. Talk about new slaveboy potential!" into Wolf's ear. He just turned and gave me a shocked look until I grinned at him. Then he broke up as he realized that I was needling him.

Eddie had to leave to get ready to go on stage with the lightweights. We both wished him good luck as he left.

"Nervous, boy?" I asked Wolf.

"Just a little, Sir." He admitted.

The house lights dimmed again as the lightweight competition started. Eddie had drawn the first spot in the lineup. He strode out on stage and into the spotlight. My breath caught in my throat. He looked spectacular! Every muscle in his eight-pack abs and defined chest rippled and flexed under his glistening golden skin with every breath. Being a lightweight, Eddie didn't have much bulk, but I had never seen a human being so amazingly ripped and shredded.

I loved Wolf, and always would, but for just a few minutes, I was jealous of Danny, knowing that he got to sleep with this hot, wiry muscleboy.

Eddie went into his posing routine, and the crowd went nuts. His skin seemed to be paper thin over his flexing muscles. When he flexed his back, the Phoenix tattooed across his back and shoulders seemed to come alive, the wings seeming to flutter and move as Eddie's muscles rippled and flowed. He was even more ripped than the last time I had seen him being tortured in my dungeon. His physique was amazing! Apparently the crowd agreed, because when he finished his routine, they stood up and cheered loud and long!

We watched the next couple of contestants in the lightweights before Wolf had to go backstage to get ready to go on stage himself. We walked backstage where Wolf stripped off the sweat suit, and I helped oil him up. Before he finished, however he coiled his hair up into a tight bun at the nape of his neck, securing it with his sterling silver and turquoise hair clip. He told me that it was a good-luck piece given to him by his grandfather, the shaman.

Finally it was time for Wolf to go out. In front of everyone in the locker room, I gave him a quick kiss and whispered; "Break a leg" into his ear.

I watched from the side of the stage as he went into his posing routine. He looked like some sort of mythical American Indian God! His bronze body glistened in the lights, every sculpted muscle of his amazing physique bulging and flexing, the veins popping out across his ripped body, from his slab-like pecs, capped with his thick nipples, out the length of his massive arms all the way from his biceps to his almost frighteningly ripped forearms, and down to his sculpted, chiseled thighs and calves.

His routine was a wonder to watch, as he had incorporated some Native American music and dance steps in the mix we had recorded. The crowd cheered as he struck each new pose, almost raising the roof when he did a full rear lat spread, flaring his huge shoulders and upper back out to their full width, showing the amazing V-taper to his narrow waist. When Wolf turned around and finished his posing with a most muscular crab pose, highlighting his amazing pecs and abs, and the rest of his upper body, the applause and wolf whistles were deafening.

I could tell from the huge grin on his face that his previous nervousness had disappeared the second he hit the stage, and heard the first cheers of the crowd.

When he finally was done, the crowd stood up and cheered even longer than they had done for Eddie. At that moment, I knew that I had no reason to be jealous of Danny. We were lucky to have the two hottest, sexiest and most amazing slaveboys in the city, if not the entire state!

When he walked back into the locker room, most of the other guys applauded and congratulated him, as they did all the competitors. We all knew we were here to have a good time, so there wasn't much tension backstage.

I broke up laughing when Wolf wrapped his arms around me and gasped; "Damn, that's almost better than sex! What a rush!"

When I could finally answer, I said; "It's not over yet, boy. I'll bet that you and Eddie will be in the posedown for the championship!"

"What about you, Sir?" he said.

"We'll just have to see, boy." I told him.

All I could do now was wait for my turn to go on stage. I wasn't really interested in watching the rest of the middleweights, not that I didn't care, but I was actually getting nervous myself. I hadn't been on stage posing in several years, and I was really getting the jitters!

I peeled off my sweat suit and stood while Wolf almost lovingly spread the oil on my tanned skin. I actually had to concentrate on not getting a hard on from the feel of his hands caressing my body! I had seen bodybuilders pop an erection on stage while posing, and in a skimpy posing thong, it could be embarrassing, to say the least.

When the announcer finally called my name, for about a half second or so, I was afraid I was going to throw up! Then I walked out on stage, into the spotlight and started my posing. As soon as the music started and the crowd started to whistle and applaud at each pose, my nervousness suddenly fell away, and I felt a rush of excitement.

I started to feel stronger and stronger as the reaction from the audience built as I hit each pose. I could actually feel the rush of adrenaline pumping into each muscle! My routine flowed flawlessly from one pose to another. Each muscle had been pumped and sculpted, until I was in the best shape of my life.

The crowd cheered when I did my double bicep shot, showing off my 23" upper arms, the silver of my nipple rings shining against my chest.

My legs looked flawless in the spotlight, every muscle standing out in sharp relief when I hit the thigh and calf poses, while the veins almost seemed ready to pop right through the skin of my legs.

When I finished my posing with the traditional most muscular pose, the audience stood and cheered loud and long. I was gratified to see Danny in the second row standing and applauding wildly.

I was really pumped with emotion when I finally made it backstage. Wolf walked over to me and wrapped his arms around my gleaming body and kissed me right in front of everyone else in the locker room. There was a faint murmur of comments from some of the other competitors.

He looked up and announced to everyone there; "Hey, he's my lover, and I'm so proud of him. If you have a problem with that, well tough! Besides, I highly doubt that we're the only gay guys here!" He said with a huge grin on his face.

At that, Eddie piped up; "You know it, Carlos!", using Wolf's real name, then kissed him deeply on the mouth!

Now there wasn't anything else to do but await the judges scoring when the other heavyweights were finished posing. I still didn't think I was going to win the weight class, as some of the other guys seemed to be bigger than I was.

Finally, came the time when all the contestants were called back on stage to hear the judge's decisions. The first winner was Josh Perez, the seventeen year old teenage class competitor. Next, to our delight, Eddie won his weight class! I really felt that he should have because he was just so much more ripped and muscular than any of his competition.

I held my breath as the competitors in the middleweights were called out. I cheered when the announcer called out; "The winner in middleweight, Carlos Greywolf of Sausalito!"

He had done it! Wolf was going to be in the final posedown with Josh, Eddie and whoever won the heavyweight and the masters classes!

Next came the heavyweights. I nervously held my breath as the announcer called out the fifth place, fourth place and the third place finishers. I actually felt more and more of a rush of excitement as each name was called, and it wasn't me! Finally, the only two heavyweights left were me, and a huge black man named Lawrence, who reminded me of our friend Jamal, from Los Angeles. We stood side by side as the announcer stepped to the mike and said; "In second place in the heavyweight class... Lawrence Washington!

The winner of the heavyweight class is Eric Kurtz, of Sausalito!"

Lawrence hugged me in congratulations, followed immediately by Wolf and Eddie. Against even my own expectations I was going to be in the posedown as well!

Finally the winner of the master's class was announced, and the lineup for the posedown was set. It was Josh, the hunky seventeen year old, Eddie, the shredded lightweight, Wolf, the beautiful middleweight, Me, the huge heavyweight, and Brad Wilbur, the really bulked up 47 year old masters winner. To put it politely, the shit was about to hit the fan!

In a posedown any of the competitors was allowed to do as many poses as possible in a three minute period. Stepping in front of another contestant was allowed, as was almost any other tactic to call attention to your body. It could really get frantic on stage for those fateful three minutes.

The five of us stepped to the center of the stage as the other contestants collected their trophies and headed backstage to the locker room.

Finally, the announcer told the crowd that the posedown was about to start. The house lights dimmed, the spotlights on the stage came up, the music started, and we went into the posedown!

Each of us started to hit as many poses as possible as quickly as we could. I stepped to the front and did a double bicep, then Josh jumped in front of me and did a full acrobatic split while showing off his back. Eddie and Wolf seemed to be in a competition between themselves to show off their backs, while Brad was trying to upstage me by showing off his hugely sculpted thighs and calves. It was utter chaos and the crowd was loving it! They were standing, cheering as we jockeyed for stage position. When the announcer called; "Thirty seconds", Wolf surprised me by stepping in front of everyone, doing a full rear bicep pose, then reaching up and pulling the hair clip off of the bun of hair on his neck. The crowd went nuts when his mane of black hair dropped down over his shoulders and his chest.

Wolf spun in an amazingly acrobatic dance move, tossed his head so his hair flipped back, dropped to one knee in front of all of us, and did a classic double arm bicep pose just as the announcer called; "Time!"

The five of us stood together, our chests heaving and the sweat running down our bodies with the effort of the last three frantic minutes. We all hugged together on stage as the crowd applauded, then settled down to await the judges rulings. I had actually forgotten what a real rush doing a posedown could be. The knowledge that you were trying to show off your body while the other contestants were doing the same thing at the same time was exciting enough, but the occasional contact between your body and the sculpted, hot muscles of the other guys was a real turn on as well.

Finally the announcer stepped back up to the mike.

"Let's hear it for all our contestants. No matter who wins tonight, they're all winners in my book. Do you agree?"

The crowd stood up and cheered their approval.

"All right. Here are the judges final decisions. In fifth place... Brad Wilbur!"

The crowd applauded as he collected his trophy. I had suspected he would finish in fifth since, while he was bulked, he didn't have really good definition to his body.

"In fourth place... Josh Perez!"

This was an amazingly good showing for a seventeen year old guy in his first contest ever. I had the feeling that he could go on to join the pro ranks if he worked at it.

Then I realized that it was down to Eddie, Wolf and me!

We held our breaths as the announcer stepped back to the mike.

"In third place... Eddie Wong!"

Wolf and I both hugged Eddie tightly as the crowd cheered. This was also Eddie's first contest, and to take third overall was great.

The announcer stepped back to the mike after Eddie was given his trophy.

"I understand that our last two contestants are actually a couple, in a relationship. The is really going to make their lives interesting, don't you think?"

There were cheers and laughter from the audience, along with a few scattered catcalls. If someone was having a problem with Wolf and I being gay, well, fuck em!

The announcer joked; "What, are you surprised that there might be a gay guy or two in a bodybuilding contest in San Francisco? I'd be more surprised if there were any straight guys here tonight!" The crowd laughed, cheered and applauded.

The announcer said; "I think I'm just gonna cut to the chase here. You two step up and give our audience one more look at you, then I'll just call the winner. Sound fair to you?"

Wolf and I just nodded and stepped up and each did a double bicep shot and then a most muscular chest, the crowd's favorite poses. Then we hugged each other in front of several hundred screaming, cheering bodybuilding fans!

Finally, the announcer stepped between us and said; "All right. Here's the moment you have all been waiting for. The winner of this year's Winter Amateur Classic is ..."

Chapter 13

Consequences

I stood in the dungeon feeling the solid wood of the St. Andrews cross pressing against my back and legs, a feeling I hadn't felt for a while, but I had never totally forgotten. My wrists and ankles were bound to the ends of the cross by the thick leather restraints, holding my naked body tightly spread-eagled and exposed.

My sensations were limited to only what I could feel and smell as my head was covered by my tight leather hood, eliminating my sight, blocking my hearing, and preventing me from speaking. The scent of used leather filled my nose with a pungent, but also erotic smell.

The impossible had happened; Wolf had beaten me in the bodybuilding contest! It was almost unheard of for a middleweight bodybuilder to beat a heavyweight in the final posedown, but that's what happened. Wolf had only beaten me by a very few points in the final judging, but he had beaten me nonetheless. Now I had to make good on my bet by serving as his slave for a full month!

As I stood spread-eagled on the cross, I remembered back just a couple of hours to what had happened after the results of the contest were announced.

The announcer said; "All right. Here's the moment you have all been waiting for. The winner of this year's Amateur Winter Classic is…Carlos Greywolf!!"

Wolf howled triumphantly and threw both arms in the air, jumping a good foot straight up in celebration of his victory.

The crowd went nuts as we hugged on stage again. I was so proud of Wolf. He had won!

Then I blanched slightly when realized that I had lost my bet to him. Wolf had just grinned his crooked smile and said; "I hope you're ready for some pain!"

The guys in the locker room all applauded and congratulated Wolf and I when we finally walked backstage. Wolf had gone out to the front of the stage and had done some more posing with his trophies while dozens of fans were shooting pictures. He was in heaven. I knew Wolf was a real exhibitionist, so he was really in his element.

When we saw the final score sheets, it came out that Wolf and I were virtually tied for points before the final posedown. Wolf's posing and showmanship must have made all the difference in the final tally. To put it simply, Wolf out posed me!

When we ran into Danny and Eddie backstage, we all hugged each other tightly before Danny, always the smart-ass, said; "Well, well, well. So much for Mr. Perfect Eric!"

He said to with such a wide grin that I couldn't actually be mad at him. Besides, he was right. I realized that sometimes I came across as arrogant and ego driven, so this was going to be a real reality check! But, I couldn't let him get away with that crack Scot free.

"That's true. But, at least I had the balls to make my bet with Wolf. What did you bet with Eddie if he did good, huh?" I growled.

He grinned at me again as he said; "Wolf, Eddie, and I agreed that if you won, Eddie could be your slave for a week. But, if you lost, he gets to help your new master torture and torment you any way he wants. Good enough of a bet for you?"

I just turned and looked open mouthed at Wolf. He just gave me a sheepish grin and shrugged before kissing me again.

I couldn't help it then and just started laughing.

"Why, you sneaky little so-and-so!" I grinned at him.

"See if I ever trust you again! Especially around this character!" I said pointing at Danny. At that, all four of us just broke up laughing.

It took us about an hour or so before we could head back home. On the way, I asked Wolf about our bet, and when did he want me to start serving as his slave.

Wolf just turned and grinned at me. "There's no time like the present, I guess. You can start as soon as we get home." Then he leaned over and kissed my cheek.

All I could do once we were home was to strip at his order, kneel in front of him and wait silently while Wolf buckled a plain black slave collar around my throat.

He led me down into the torture chamber, spread-eagling me on the cross with the thick leather restraints on my wrists and ankles. After I was secured to the cross, Wolf placed the hood over my head. Just before inserting the gag in the mouth hole of the hood and lacing the hood tight, he asked me; "What do you want me to do to you, slave?"

I could only answer one way. "Master Carlos, I want you to torture me! I lost and I deserve to be punished! Please, Sir. Torture me!"

He pushed the leather gag into my mouth and laced the hood tightly around my head. I felt his strong fingers begin to stroke down my chest and begin to twist my nipples. I began to twist on the cross as the erotic feelings in my tits began to slowly morph into pain as the play with my nips became more and more intense.

I was moaning and grunting into the gag filling my mouth as the nipple torture continued. Wolf, or rather "Master Carlos" now, was pulling on my nipple rings hard enough by now to stretch my flesh to the limit. I could feel the sweat flowing down my stretched body as I had to endure actually being tortured for real for the first time in over five years! Wolf and I had played at my being tortured by him lots of times, but he had never actually tied me up and worked me over. Even so, I knew that Master Carlos knew enough that I felt totally confident in his abilities. I knew he wouldn't actually injure me.

Suddenly the twisting and pulling on my nipples ceased. The relief was almost as much of a torture as the pain itself! I wondered what was going to happen next. My question was answered when I felt Master Carlos' hot mouth on my right nipple.

I groaned into the gag again at the feel of his tongue caressing the tender, sore flesh of my tit. The hot mouth sucking on my nipple felt so good, but the pleasure was balanced by the frustration I felt at not being able to stroke my hands up and down Master Carlos' back. I struggled against the restraints as the feeling of frustration grew and grew until I thought I would scream! God, now I knew what Wolf felt when I teased and tormented him. I had often said that mental torture could be as effective as physical torture, and now I was experiencing just how true that was!

My master's sucking and worshipping of my tits went on for what felt like hours, even though I knew it was just a few more minutes. Suddenly I felt his body pressing against me, and heard; "Don't go anywhere, slave" through the hood.

For the next few minutes I endured the feeling of absolutely nothing. It was almost impossible to explain how, but even spread-eagled on the cross and hooded, I could tell that there was no one else in the dungeon with me. I had to assume that Master Carlos had gone upstairs to change, or something.

I was still musing quietly to myself when I was startled by the sudden feel of a pair of hands stroking down the sides of my torso. Master Carlos had managed to walk back up right in front of me without my even knowing that he was there. Damn, he was good!

I felt his hands begin to unlace the hood from around my head. I blinked at the sudden light in my eyes when the hood was pulled off.

My new master stood in front of me. I moaned softly at the sight of him. Master Carlos was wearing just his chaps and his highly polished combat boots. He had his red bandanna rolled and tied around his head, with his jet black hair flowing down over his bronze shoulders and chest. He looked incredible. His skin was glistening with beads of sweat that were trickling down his torso, leaving tiny trails. Every muscle in his pumped, sculpted torso stood out in sharp definition under his skin. The deep golden bronze of his body contrasted with the shiny black leather he wore.

His thick brown nipples, surrounded with the reddish marks of his brandings stood out on his pecs. As I watched, Master Carlos began to gently stroke a fingertip over his own nipples. As they got harder and harder, his cock was swelling and growing right along with them, until he actually had three erections!

"I've waited so long to see you like this, Eric. Stretched out and helpless. All of those huge muscles just waiting for me to use anyway I want. Oh yeah!" Master Carlos almost moaned as he reached out his hands and began to feel and stroke my entire physique. My own cock was so hard it was almost sore! God, I was so incredibly turned on!

Finally, I couldn't help myself, and I groaned; "Oh God. Please Sir, torture me. Please, Master Carlos, hurt me, Sir. Please! I want to suffer for you, Sir. Please torture me!"

Master Carlos moaned with lust as he clamped his mouth down on mine, kissing me savagely. As our tongues explored each others mouths, his hands slid up my chest and began twisting my nipples again. I moaned into his mouth as the pain began to spread throughout my pecs from the two tender points of swollen, hard flesh.

Suddenly, without any warning, Master Carlos pulled back from my mouth, bent down and began to bite my left nipple! I screamed in pain and shock from the blast of pain from my tit.

"OH FUCK! OH SHIT! YESSS! HURT ME, DAMMIT!" I screamed! I really meant it, too. I really wanted to be tortured! For the first time since Mike died, I was lusting for some serious pain.

Master Carlos stood up in front of me and slapped me hard across my face!

"You want pain, slave? I'll give you pain, boy! That's what you get for not calling me Sir!" he snarled.

I gasped in a combination of pain and mild shock. I never knew Carlos to be this aggressive before. It was somewhat disconcerting. I had seen first time tops lose control in a scene, but I hoped that wasn't happening to Carlos.

Turning to the shelves that held my toys, he picked up the biting double row nipple clamps! Turning back to me, I saw a gleam in his eyes I had never seen before. His face twisted into an expression of raw lust as Master Carlos fastened the clamps on my tits. As the teeth bit into the flesh above and below my nipple rings I threw my head back and screamed!

"OH-MY-GOD!! OH FUCK, THOSE HURT, SIR!!" It took every bit of my strength to keep from calling out "Red-light," our control word. I had never experienced pain like this, even when I had gotten my nipples pierced years ago, since I had never had any reason to try the nipple clamps on myself.

All I could do was to stand there helpless while the searing pain in my nipples peaked and then miraculously started to fade slightly. I was gasping for air and twisting on the cross, while Master Carlos watched me, slowly stroking his thick cock. I was shocked to realize that my cock was rock hard and streaming, as well.

Finally, he wasn't able to resist any longer, and Master Carlos dropped to his knees and sucked my thick shaft deeply into his throat. I thought that I would go totally nuts with lust at the feel of his hot mouth surrounding my cock. The pleasure of having my cock worked by an expert cocksucker was balanced by the still searing pain in both nipples and my inability to move a muscle, except to writhe and twist in agony on the cross.

God, this was frustrating! The sweat was pouring down my body as I strained and struggled in a futile effort to tear my arms loose from the restraints.

Within another few minutes, I knew I was on the verge of cumming, I grunted and groaned as the feeling grew in my balls, until I couldn't hold out any longer, and shot a huge load of sperm into the hot mouth working on my cock.

I threw back my head and shrieked as I came. 'OH SHIT! OH SHIT! OH MY GOD!"

Master Carlos kept on sucking my cock until my balls were totally drained of their huge load of sperm. Then he suddenly stood up and clamped his mouth over mine. I instantly knew what was coming next. I was going to have to swallow my own sperm!

Master Carlos opened his mouth and I immediately tasted my cum dripping into my mouth. I swallowed my load, enjoying the taste, but also noticing the difference from the way Carlos' sperm tasted.

Finally Master Carlos broke off the kiss. Stepping back, he began to jack his own cock with one hand while he started to slowly pull on the chain between my nipple clamps with the other. I groaned loudly and began to writhe in sheer agony at the renewed burning, searing pain in both of my tits and pecs.

"Oh yeah, slave. Show me those muscles. Struggle for me, slave. I wanna see you sweat, boy. Come on, muscleman, flex for me." He moaned while jacking his cock harder and faster while tugging on my tit clamps to continue my nipple torture.

The pain was ripping through my nipples, causing me to twist and strain on the cross in a futile effort to escape the agony.

Suddenly Master Carlos stopped pulling on my nipples and practically lunged towards me, burying his face in my sweaty, straining, widely opened right armpit. I could feel him continuing to jack his cock even while he was frantically licking and sucking on my pit. His tongue was flicking into the depths of my armpit, licking up my sweat as fast as he could, moaning with lust the entire time.

Master Carlos pulled back, but just as suddenly, he buried his face in my other armpit, continuing to lick up my sweat. While he jacked his cock with his right hand, his left hand was sliding up and down my sweat glazed torso, wherever he could reach.

Within another minute or so, he started gasping and groaning loudly. Finally, Master Carlos stepped back from my body, twisted his own nipples almost savagely, and shot a thick load of cum across my abs. Some of his hot sperm started to drip down onto my cock. Master Carlos just moaned again and began to lick his own cum from my body, worshiping my helpless physique one muscle at a time. I flexed my abs as he licked them clean of his load, then I just groaned with pleasure as he licked my cock and balls clean.

When he finally stood up, I mentally steeled myself for what was about to happen. Master Carlos reached out and gently opened the clamps that were torturing my nipples.

"AAAAUUUGGGGHHH!" I shrieked at the incredible blast of raw pain that shot through my entire torso from my nipples! My God, this was pure, raw torture! I had forgotten just how sensitive those two knobs of thick flesh on a man's chest could be.

At that moment, I had to wonder how Wolf was able to endure the brutal tortures that I had inflicted on his nipples over the time I had known him. I knew that he was a natural masochist, but his ability to endure torture was never more evident to me then right now. Wolf would have screamed out his pain for sure, but he also would have been incredibly sexually aroused at the same time. I couldn't really think about sex while the agony was tearing through my chest. Master Carlos was gently rubbing my tits to keep them from bruising, but even the gentle touch of his fingertips was exquisitely painful.

Just when I thought that was finally going to have to scream out "RED-LIGHT", he stopped and stepped back from the cross. My chest was heaving. I actually had to swallow a couple of times to calm the nausea that was roiling in my gut. Finally, I felt my legs begin to quiver like they were rubber, then the strength finally went out of them. I slumped down, gasping at the pain as my widespread arms suddenly had to support the entire weight of my body.

Master Carlos immediately released the pivot on the support of the cross and rotated it to a horizontal position. Next he began to release me from my bondage. As soon as I was freed, he stepped to the small refrigerator in the next room and brought back a bottle of water.

"Here, just take a few sips." Master Carlos said, supporting my head. The cold water flowed down my throat. I had never tasted anything so good in my life!

My earlier fears about Carlos' ability to maintain his control as a top man began to ease somewhat as he gently supported my head as he waited for me to be able to sit up and slowly ease off of the cross. I knelt in front of my incredibly sexy new master and whispered; "Thank you for torturing me, Sir. May I serve you any other way, Sir?"

He smiled down at me and said; "My boots need a good cleaning, slave. You can start there." He was exaggerating for my benefit, of course. His boots gleamed with a high gloss, almost like two black mirrors. But, he is my master!

I bent down and began to lick Master Carlos' right boot. I began to remember more of the training I had received from Mike while licking Master Carlos' boots. The taste and feel of the leather on my tongue was a powerful reminder of my training.

I moaned softly as I began to lick and clean the boots in front of me. I actually began to pant with a growing sense of lust and desire to serve Master Carlos any way he ordered me to. I knew in the back of my mind that my servitude to Master Carlos was only temporary, but I couldn't help it. I wanted to serve this hot, masculine man! I was his slave, his property, his plaything, and I was slowly being consumed by my desire!

I continued my worshipping of my master's boots until he stepped back and gently lifted my head up until I was looking into his deep brown eyes.

"Thank you" he murmured.

"Yes, Sir. You're welcome, Sir. I would be honored to clean your boots anytime, Sir" I said softly.

"No, I mean thank you for trusting me enough to let me use you. I've never really been a top before, and this really means a lot, Eric. Thank you."

There was a glimmer in Master Carlos' eyes as he told me to stand up, before he wrapped his strong arms around my sweat soaked body.

"It's been a long day. What do you say we clean up before we go to bed, boy?" he grinned at me.

I smiled back and said; "Yes, Sir. My pleasure, Sir."

We headed up the stairs to the master bedroom on the second floor. I dutifully undressed my master, hanging his sweaty leathers out to dry properly. When Master Carlos was totally stripped, he reached up and unbuckled the slave collar from around my throat.

"O.K. Here's the deal. If it's all right with you, you only have to serve me as a total slave when I put your collar on. The rest of the time, we can just be lovers as usual. Will that arrangement be satisfactory, Eric?"

I wrapped my arms around is still sweaty, muscular body and looked down into his eyes.

"Whatever arrangement you want, I'll go along with. I lost, and I'm going to honor my bet with you. Your suggestion will be fine with me, champ." I smiled before kissing him deeply and passionately.

Carlos giggled when I called him "Champ".

"Wow, nobody's ever called me that before" he said.

"Well, you earned it!" And I meant it, too. I was so proud of what Carlos Greywolf had accomplished in the time we had been together. When we first met, he was on the verge of being homeless, and had to resort to hustling sex for money to just be able to eat. And now, less than two years later, he was a titled bodybuilding champion, in a stable, loving relationship with a man who loved him deeply, and had earned more than enough money to never have to work again. I knew that most of his money had come from me, but with the investments I had made with the money going into his portfolio, he was quite a bit richer than even I could have been able to pay him.

"There's only one thing. You're going to have to do all the cooking and cleaning for the next month." He said, grinning his crooked, slightly lopsided smile at me.

"O.K. Sir, if you think you can survive my cooking!" I chuckled.

"Well, I guess I'll just have to take my chances. I guess if you could survive eating your own food for the years before I started to cook for you, I should be able to choke down whatever you whip up." He laughed.

"Jeez, what a smart ass. Give a guy a little power and right away it goes to his head!" I groused. "Bitch, bitch, bitch. Sheesh! Choke it down? You've never had any problems swallowing anything else I've ever stuck in your mouth, so why are you worrying about it now?"

Carlos just looked at me and totally broke up laughing. I couldn't help it then and started laughing too. We finally fell on my bed still gasping with laughter, tears rolling down our faces. I guess the emotions of the contest, Carlos' victory and our session in the dungeon had finally caught up with both of us.

I was totally helpless with laughter. Every time I looked at Carlos, I was consumed by a fresh wave of hilarity while watching him laughing as hard as he could.

Finally we both started to calm down. My sides actually ached from laughing so hard.

I wrapped my arms around Carlos and hugged him tightly. We kissed deeply and passionately, our hands sliding up and down each others hard backs.

When we finally broke the kiss, Carlos said; "God, I love you, Eric."

"Believe me, the feeling is mutual, Carlos." I murmured. "Now there's something else I want to do."

I rolled Carlos over so he was lying on his back. I grasped his arms and stretched them out over his head. He smiled up at me, knowing what I wanted to do.

Carlos put his hands under his head and just closed his eyes.

He moaned with pleasure as I started to lick the sweat from the valley between his thick sculpted pecs. I ran my tongue gently over the dark bronze skin that covered his muscles. I thoroughly enjoyed the salty, spicy taste of my incredibly sexy lover's sweat as I lapped it from his body.

I worked my way from his chest down into Carlos' right armpit. He groaned in delight as I gently started to chew and nip at his skin. The feel of the muscles and tendons flexing and bulging under my tongue was almost too much for me to bear. I had to control myself, as I wanted to enjoy myself as long as possible. I ran my mouth down Carlos' right side, licking at each bulge of muscle, and every rib rippling under his skin.

He was moaning almost constantly as I gently worshipped every inch of his torso over the next hour or so. I licked his gleaming, bronze body from his earlobes all the way to his toes. I sucked each of his toes into my mouth one at a time, drawing a loud groan and a hissing; "OH FUUUUUCCCK!" from Carlos. Then he groaned even louder when I managed to open my mouth wide enough to get all his toes on his right foot into my mouth at the same time. He was actually writhing on the bed as I worshipped his feet. I had never really worked on Carlos' feet before, and I didn't know how he would react. He groaned again even louder then before when I sucked the toes on his left foot into my mouth.

When I finally was done worshipping his feet, Carlos was panting with lust. I looked up and saw that his chest was heaving while he was lying back with his eyes closed. I also saw that his thick, eight inch cock was absolutely rock hard with desire.

I gently slid up and licked the underside of the thick, throbbing shaft.

Carlos groaned; "Oh shit, yes!" as I gently tongued the shaft, feeling the veins that stood out on his cock.

Finally I slid the head of his cock into my mouth. Carlos moaned in pleasure as I began to slowly deep-throat the entire length of his cock. As I worked the cockhead deeper and deeper into my throat, I felt his body shift. His hands gently grasped the sides of my head as Carlos began to thrust his hips up and down, fucking my hot, sucking mouth.

I moaned deeply in my throat at the sight of Carlos' washboard abs flexing just inches from my face as he drove his cock in and out of my throat. I reached out and began to stroke the rippling muscles in front of me. The feel of his rock hard abs contracting and releasing under my hands was almost indescribably sexy.

His muscles were shining with a fresh coating of sweat, as he was really turned on. As he began to thrust his cock in and out of my mouth faster and faster, I reached up and began to play with his nipples.

Carlos hissed; "OH YESSS" as I started to twist his tits. Within another minute or so, he groaned as he held my head tightly. Carlos gasped and growled deeply in his throat as he filled my mouth with another load of his sperm. It wasn't as big as the load he had shot earlier in the dungeon, but it still tasted great!

I swallowed my lover's load of cum and then decided to tease him a bit. I ran my tongue over the sensitive head of his cock, flicking it back and forth, while Carlos groaned and writhed under me. I knew I could drive him nuts doing this.

Finally he squirmed out from under me, gasping in pleasurable agony.

"Damn, you know how much I hate that!" Carlos gasped.

I just grinned widely at him. "Oh, poor baby" I teased.

"Just wait until the next time you're spread out in the dungeon, about to be tortured. We'll see if you think 'poor baby' then!" He grumped.

"Promises, Promises" I said, echoing one of Carlos' favorite lines he liked to say to me, whenever I would mock threaten him with some horrific torture. He just looked at me for a second and started to giggle when I stuck out my tongue.

I slid up until I lying on top of his hard body. I looked down into his eyes, realizing that for once it didn't really matter who was the "master" and who was the "slave". I was just in love with this hot, sexy young man.

I whispered "I love you" just before I kissed my lover as deeply and as passionately as I had ever done. As we lay there, our tongues intertwined, I felt his strong hands sliding up and down my broad back.

We kissed for the better part of a minute before I finally pulled back from Carlos' face. He moaned with pleasure and lust when I just moved down a bit and lay my head on his solid pecs. We lay there a while, Carlos gently stroking my hair, while I listened to the rhythm of his heartbeat and the sounds of his breathing.

We just lay there until Carlos said; "I think we better hit the shower before we both fall asleep."

We walked into the master bathroom where I adjusted the multiple heads in the shower until we would both be surrounded by a spray of hot, steamy water.

Carlos and I both softly moaned in pleasure at the feel of the water coursing down our hard bodies. I always loved the sight of my lover in the shower with me, his body glistening, and his long black hair glued to his chest and back by the water.

We both gently washed each other's hard bodies, loving the feel of our hands sliding up and down each others skin. I groaned gently when Carlos began to gently rub my still tender nipples. He stroked them with his fingers while I just leaned back against the shower wall, moaning with pleasure at his touch.

I groaned even louder when I felt his hot mouth slowly surrounding the head of my swollen cock. He knelt in front of me, sucking my entire nine inches into his hot mouth while the warm water ran down our bodies. He knew how much I loved getting a hot, sexy blow job in the shower. There was something about the feel of the water and the hot, steamy air, combined with the sight of Carlos kneeling in front of me in the shower with his skin gleaming and his hair plastered to his back and shoulders that I was really turned on by.

This night was no exception. Within minutes, I was moaning loudly as Carlos' expert manipulation of my cock continued, until I couldn't hold back any longer, and I shot another thick, hot load of my cum into his sucking mouth. This time, he swallowed my load before standing back up and hugging me tightly.

"God, I love you." I whispered into his ear.

Carlos just kissed me again and said; "So do I, Eric, so do I."

I shampooed Carlos thick mane of hair before we both stepped out of the shower. After drying and brushing out his luxuriant head of hair, we headed back into the bedroom.

As we curled up together in my bed, both of us tired out by the day's exertions, I just held my lover's hard body against me.

As we both drifted off into sleep, I couldn't help but wonder what the next month held in store for us. Was Carlos going to make a good master? Could I endure being a slave, and being tortured for the next month? Only time would tell.

Chapter 14

Enslaved

Late the next morning I woke up when I felt Carlos stirring in the bed next to me. I leaned over him and kissed him gently. I looked over at the clock and saw that it was almost noon.

"Good morning, champ" I said softly.

He kissed me back and grinned; "Flattery will get you nowhere. You still have to make breakfast, boy. I feel like a ham and cheese omelet and some toast this morning."

I grinned back at him. "Funny, you don't look like an omelet. You just look like you always do in the morning. Really gross!" Then I stuck out my tongue.

I ducked as he swung a pillow and smacked me in the side of the head.

"Smart ass." Carlos growled, but with a gleam of humor in his eyes. "You'll pay for that. Come here."

I stepped to his side of the bed and knelt down. I knew what he was going to do. He picked up the collar and buckled it around my throat, signifying my return to slavery.

"Now let's see if you can keep a civil tongue in your head, boy. Go fix us breakfast. You have my order. Make the same for yourself."

"Yes, Sir." I answered dutifully. I knew I had to be serious when I was collared, as I would expect Wolf to behave properly when he was collared, as well. It was all part of our deal as a result of my losing my bet.

I slipped on a pair of gym shorts and walked down to the kitchen. It took me a bit to pull together the ingredients for our meal, but I kept at it and finally had two omelets and toast made up. As I was just finishing up, Master Carlos padded into the kitchen wearing sweat pants and a tee shirt. I set the table and served up his breakfast.

While he was eating, I knelt next to the table, just waiting for his next order. It was a real throwback to the days when I was being trained up as a slave by Mike. I realized that by the end of the month, I would have a renewed appreciation for what Wolf went through as my slave boy.

When he was done, Master Carlos allowed me to eat, then he ordered me to clean up the kitchen. While I was working, I thought about how well he seemed to be adapting to the role of a topman. Secretly I was pleased. Since he knew what was expected of him as a slave, I thought that it was important that he also understood the mindset of being a top, even if he wasn't the topman in a scene, or even in our relationship. Knowing what your partner was feeling is important in any relationship, but it was especially important in an S+M relationship, where trust and communication were vital.

When I was done in the kitchen, Master Carlos said; "Go out and get the paper, boy, and bring it to the living room."

I brought the Sunday paper in and knelt in front of my Master, who was sitting on the couch.

"Your paper, Sir." I said as I handed it to him.

He looked at me for a second with a smile before he simply said; "Footstool, slave."

I should have seen this coming. I had used Wolf as a footstool while I was refreshing his training recently, so it was only fair that Master Carlos would use me as one as well. I assumed the position on my hands and knees in front of my master, then moaned softly with pleasure as I felt his legs settle on my back.

As I knelt in front of my Master, I had time to think about our relationship, and how it had evolved and changed in the time we had been together.

He had entered my life as a young, eager, but untrained bottom boy who wanted to be trained as a pure slave. From that beginning, Wolf had evolved into a dedicated, loving and well trained slave. Now he was taking on the responsibility of being a topman. We both knew that it was just for a short time, but we also both wanted to see if he had the personality and the proper mindset to be a top. Even if he never served as a topman again, this would be a vital lesson in helping him understand where any master he had was coming from mentally.

I knelt in front of the couch with my Master's feet resting on my back for what felt like at least an hour or more. It was a bit boring, but at the same time it allowed me time to think without any other problems or responsibilities interrupting my train of thought. I was planning what I could do to help Master Carlos enjoy his time as a topman, and how I could serve him. I also trusted him implicitly to not do anything that could injure me while I was in the dungeon, even though I suspected that I was going to have to endure some real pain for the first time in several years.

Eventually, Master Carlos slid his feet off of my back and ordered me up.

"I know you need to see the paper to keep up with your business news, boy. You can read it after you've finished your chores for the day. Is that acceptable, boy?"

I bowed my head. "Yes, Sir. That will be fine. Thank you, Sir."

Master Carlos gave me a list of chores to attend to, including turning on the heat in both the sauna and the hot tub. I guessed that this meant that he was planning on using them later in the evening. I also had to straighten up the dungeon, and, I had the pleasurable task of helping to re-arrange the contents of the trophy case in the house to accommodate our latest awards. We had both won two trophies at the contest each, one for winning our respective weight classes, and our bigger trophies for winning first and second place overall. I was proud that the biggest trophy in the case now belonged to my lover.

When the trophies were in place, Master Carlos turned to me and smiled; "I still feel like celebrating, boy. I want you to go into the bathroom and clean out. When you're done, come to the master bedroom. You can read the paper later."

I merely nodded my head obediently and said; "Yes, Sir."

I knew what he wanted to do to me. I was going to be fucked by my hot, sexy lover.

He didn't get to fuck me very often, but we both enjoyed it when he did. When Wolf was serving as my slave, we both agreed that I could fuck him whenever I wanted to, but he really had to earn the right to fuck me. It wasn't that I didn't enjoy it, because I did, but I felt that it wasn't his place as a slave to fuck his master, unless I wanted him to, as a reward for exceptional service.

When I was done in the bathroom, I walked into the master bedroom to find Master Carlos waiting for me. I knelt in front of him, and waited for him to speak.

"O.K. boy, face down on the bed and spread out." He ordered with a gruff tone in his voice that was belied by the wide grin on his face.

I lay on the bed, and within a minute, I was spread-eagled, shackled to the corners of my four-poster with my padded leather restraints. To add to my serving as a slave, he next slipped my leather blindfold on my head, cutting off my vision totally.

As I felt the bed shift as Master Carlos climbed on to straddle my butt, I heard him moan softly, almost to himself; "God, what a beautiful back and ass. I love those muscles!"

I felt his strong hands begin to gently stroke down the length of my back. He started at my thick shoulders, worked his way over my spread back muscles, over my ribcage, stroking every ripple of my ribs and lats, and down to the base of my spine. Master Carlos moaned again softly, just before I felt him shift his position, followed by the feel of his mouth starting to nuzzle the back of my neck.

I groaned with pleasure at the feel of his warm lips gently kissing my neck, as he started to orally make love to my spread torso. The frustration I felt at not being able to watch my sexy lover was a real form of torture in itself. I just had to imagine what his hard, bronze body looked like, every muscle flexing as he moved.

I moaned at the feel of Master Carlos' hot mouth kissing and licking every inch of my thick, bulging shoulder muscles while his hands continued to explore my bound body. The feel of his hair lying on my skin as he worshipped my body was incredibly erotic. But the feel of his thick, rock hard cock sliding on my back, trapped between our bodies was even hotter. I knew that soon I was going to have to endure having that thick shaft driven into my ass.

Master Carlos slowly worked his way down my body, licking the light coat of sweat that I could feel on my skin. Just knowing that I was going to be fucked by my master was enough to get me totally excited, which caused me to start to sweat.

After what seemed to be hours of anticipation, I felt Master Carlos' hands on my ass. I moaned as I felt him spread my butt open, then groaned; "Oh, shit!" at the feel of his hot tongue starting to lick my exposed asshole.

I could do nothing but groan and writhe helplessly, bound spread-eagled on the bed, as my master licked my ass, forcing his face deeply between my ass cheeks. His hands were holding my butt wide open, his hot breath feeling like flames on my ass!

I groaned loudly as Master Carlos finally forced his tongue inside my tight asshole as far as he could. He was growling with sheer lust as he ate out my ass, tonguing my hole for a good five minutes or so. I was moaning and groaning constantly, my own lust compounded by the incredible frustration I was enduring at not being able to move.

God, this was torture! I wanted desperately to be able to reach back and hold my Master's head and stroke his hair as he worshipped my ass, but I couldn't! Damn, this was driving me crazy! I was struggling against the restraints holding me spread-eagled, but I couldn't get loose. I had trained Master Carlos too well!

Finally, he lifted his head from between my ass cheeks. I felt his weight shift on my back as he reached up to the headboard of the bed for the bottle of lube I kept there.

I moaned into the pillow under my head as I felt one, and then two of Master Carlos strong fingers begin to lube up my ass, slipping deeply into me. The incredibly erotic feeling lasted for a few minutes before I heard Carlos gasping out "Oh yeah" as he stroked his throbbing cock, coating it with lube.

I felt his weight on my back as he lay down on top of my wide spread body. The heat of his chest and abs on my back was totally a turn on.

Within seconds I felt the thick head of Master Carlos' cock begin to press against my asshole. We both groaned simultaneously as his cock slid into my ass, the plum shaped head stretching my sphincter.

"Oh fuck!" I gasped. "Give it to me, Sir. Fuck me, master. Fuck me. My ass is yours, Sir. Use it, please, Sir."

"Damn right your ass is mine, slave." Master Carlos growled. "Your whole muscleman body is mine to use, slave! I'm gonna enjoy using it for the next month, boy!"

I heard him begin to grunt and growl with pleasure as his cock slid deeper and deeper into my hole, until I felt Master Carlos' entire weight on my back, his cock driven it's entire eight inch length into my willing asshole. I moaned with lust as Master Carlos slowly and teasingly began to ever so slowly thrust in and out of me.

I moaned with almost overwhelming pleasure as my incredibly sexy master lay flat on my back and slid his hands under my spread arms and down under my pecs, to play with my nipples as he fucked me. I could feel every solid muscle of his torso flexing and bulging under his skin, which was rapidly becoming coated with a coating of hot sweat. He started to drive his cock into and out of my ass in a slowly increasing rhythm. Faster and faster the thick shaft plunged deeply into my hole, until I was moaning and whimpering constantly with an almost uncontrollable lust. Master Carlos was grunting and growling deeply in his throat as he pounded his cock into me.

Just when I was sure I was going to scream with desire, Master Carlos slowed his furious fucking of my ass as he lay on my sweat drenched back. I could feel his heart pounding in his chest and felt his hot breath on my neck.

"Damn, that's a good ass, boy!" He gasped into my ear. "I need to slow down. I want to enjoy that ass for a good long time, boy. Would you like that, boy?"

"Oh God, yes, Sir!" I groaned. "Fuck me as long as you want, Sir. I love it, Master. Please fuck me, Sir."

"Yeah, slave. Beg for it, boy. I wanna hear you beg like the dog you are, boy."

I just couldn't help it. I was desperate for my Master to fuck me. I wanted, no, I needed his cock driving deeper and deeper into my helpless ass!

"Fuck me, please, Master. Use me, Sir. I need it, Master. Please, Sir, Please fuck me as hard and as long as you want, Sir. Please!"

He growled into my ear; "You want it, boy? Well, you're gonna get it!"

With that, I felt Master Carlos plant his hands on my shoulders, lift his torso from my back, and begin to pile drive his swollen cock into my ass harder then I had ever been fucked before! He started to growl with each thrust of his hips, slamming his cock into me almost savagely. I felt the sweat dripping from his muscled body onto my back. I could only imagine what my Master's golden bronze body looked like, his muscles rippling and flexing under his glistening skin, while his jet black hair hung down on either side of his face and lay stuck to his thick shoulders and his broad back by his sweat.

Damn, I was going crazy with desire! I just wanted to be able to see Master Carlos while he was fucking me! I wanted to be able to see his magnificent body in action, but I couldn't! I was howling with lust by now, as Master Carlos pounded into me harder and harder, going faster and faster by the second.

He was groaning and grunting as he slammed his cock into my ass in a furious pace. I thought that he was going to keep fucking me until he shot into me within a minute or so more, but he surprised me by slowing down.

Master Carlos kept up his agonizingly teasing ass play for at least another ten or fifteen minutes or so, driving himself to the edge of cumming in my ass, then slowing down. He would lay on my spread back, our bodies slick with sweat and gently rock his hips back and fourth, sliding his swollen cock in and out of me with a slow rhythm that was driving me absolutely nuts with lust! I wanted him to fuck me as hard as he could, until he shot his load, but he was my master now, and I had to accede to his desires and wishes.

Finally, Master Carlos began to thrust into me harder and harder. His breath was hot on the back of my neck as he gasped for air while fucking me as hard as he could!

Just when I thought I might pass out from sheer desire, I felt Master Carlos pull back, shift his weight as he pulled his cock out of my thoroughly stretched hole, and begin to gasp; "Oh yeah, oh fuck yesss!"

He pumped his cock with his hand for just a few seconds before I heard him howl; "OH FUCK" and felt a huge stream of his hot cum splashing on my back, feeling almost as hot as molten lava in my mind.

I could do nothing but writhe in an agony of frustration, bound helplessly on the bed as I felt Master Carlos begin to lick his still hot load from my skin.

"Aw, shit!" I groaned again as his tongue slid across my sweat soaked back muscles. The feel of his tongue on my still quivering back was incredibly erotic. Master Carlos ran his tongue over every square inch of my back, licking up his cum as it mixed with our mingled sweat.

I could do nothing but groan with desire and an almost desperate sense of lust. I couldn't remember the last time that I was this turned on. It seemed as though I was slipping into an almost trancelike state, as though I was hypnotized by the feel of his hot, licking tongue on my skin. The almost delicate feel of his hair on my back just added to my euphoric state of mind.

Master Carlos' worshipping of my back continued for what seemed to be an eternity to my addled mind. I was in ecstasy the entire time, totally absorbed by the unbelievably sensuous feelings shooting through the hyper sensitive nerve endings on my body like jolts of electricity.

Finally, after what felt like hours of pleasure, Master Carlos flopped down on my back.

"Damn, that's a hot ass, boy!" He groaned into my ear.

By this time I was actually unable to say anything coherent. My brain was flooded with endorphins and I could only moan weakly.

We lay there silently, just recovering for a good ten minutes or so until Master Carlos finally rolled off of my back.

"Oh-My-God!" He groaned. "That was the best ass I've ever had!"

"Thank you, Sir." I moaned softly. My cock was so hard that it actually hurt, trapped between my abs and the bed.

Carlos slipped the blindfold from over my eyes, lifted his head, and smiled his crooked smile at me.

"We're not done yet, boy." He chuckled. "I'm not gonna make you suffer much more. You still need to get off, boy. And I've got just the way to get you off."

Master Carlos released me from my bondage on the bed and ordered me to follow him downstairs. When I stood up, my cock stood out in front of me, rock hard.

Carlos grinned at the sight. "We better get that thing off before it explodes, boy. It looks like it's ready to go off any second!"

He led me down into the dungeon and into the room where the sauna was located. Stopping only long enough to grab four short lengths of rope, we stepped into the stifling hot room. Master Carlos ordered me to lay down and stretch out full length on the upper bench along the back wall of the sauna. Within a couple of minutes he had me tied flat on my back with my hands and feet bound to the slats of the bench.

I could look down the length of my tautly bound torso, dripping with streams of sweat, gleaming in the dim red light of the sauna. Every rib and muscle rippled with my every breath and movement. My cock arced up over my washboard abs. The veins tracing the length of the swollen shaft pulsed gently in time with my heartbeat.

"God, that's beautiful." Moaned Master Carlos. His bronze physique was also gleaming with sweat. He stroked a hand down my chest, stopping to tweak my nipples, which caused my cock to jump and throb.

"Don't go away, boy. I'll be back in a few minutes." He grinned down at me.

"Yes, Sir. Thank you, Sir." I said.

Carlos turned and walked out of the sauna, leaving me bound, sweating in the intense heat. I looked at the dial of the thermometer mounted on the wall and saw that it was close to 200 degrees.

I could only wonder how long my master intended to torture me by forcing me to endure slowly roasting in the heat. The sweat was running down my forehead into my eyes, adding to my suffering. Within a very few minutes more I was gasping for air. The intense heat made taking a deep breath almost impossible.

Just when I thought that I couldn't take any more, the door opened and Master Carlos walked back in. His hair was hanging down loose around his shoulders, and his body immediately began to shine with sweat. My cock immediately started to swell again at the sight of his amazing body.

He walked over to where I was stretched out on the bench and, without a word, bent down and began to suck on my right nipple. I groaned at the feel of his mouth sucking and nibbling on my tit, and at the feel of his hair laying on my chest. His hands were gently stroking up and down my torso as his hot mouth worked back and forth across my chest, going from one nipple to the other. I knew that Carlos was in love with my muscles as much, if not more than I was in love with his incredible physique.

Master Carlos continued his nipple and muscle worship of my bound body for several more minutes. I was groaning with almost unbearable lust the entire time. He would chew on my tits, then work his mouth into my stretched, open armpits to lick the sweat running down my skin.

Finally he stood up next to the bench I was stretched out on. His entire body gleamed with sweat. He looked unbelievably sexy in the dim red light!

"I think you're ready, boy." He grinned at me.

With that, he climbed up on the bench and sat straddling my abs. Reaching behind his butt, he stroked my throbbing cock. Lifting himself up, he held my cock upright and slowly lowered himself down onto my dick. I groaned and Carlos gasped as my cock slipped inside his tight ass. He gently lowered himself until he was totally impaled on my nine inches.

"Oh fuck, that's great!" He groaned as he began to slowly ride up and down on my cock. I watched, totally mesmerized as Carlos began to stroke his own sweat-glazed muscles. I moaned in unbridled lust when he began to pull and twist his nipples and stroke his fingertips across his pecs and abs. His eyes were closed as he seemed to be lost in total ecstasy. Carlos was moaning softly to himself as he continued to make love to his own ripped, flexing muscles under his sweat streaked, bronze skin.

I moaned again louder when Carlos finally stopped his muscle worship, grinned down at me, and reached up to the overhead beam in the sauna. He slowly straightened out his legs on either side of my body.

"Watch this, boy." He growled, with a wicked grin.

I stared, amazed as he slowly started to pull his entire body weight up using his arms, like he was doing a wide grip pull-up in the gym! He held his legs straight out in front of his body, which caused his washboard abs to bulge, showing every cut of the muscles. His biceps bulged as Master Carlos began to slowly pull himself up and lower himself back down on my cock.

I panted with lust as I watched his incredible body flexing and straining as he rode up and down on my cock, using just the strength of his arms and shoulders to support his entire weight.

"Oh fuck, Sir. That's amazing. That is so hot!" I gasped.

Carlos' teeth were gritted and his eyes were closed as he concentrated on riding my swollen cock. He was grunting and gasping with the effort he was putting out in the intense heat of the sauna. His hair was stuck to his chest and shoulders by his sweat, as every muscle in his torso strained to the limit.

The spread of his lats behind his deep, straining armpits looked like Carlos had sprouted a pair of wings. The sweat was streaming down the sides of his torso, flowing over his rippling ribcage in solid streams.

The sight of the amazing body in front of me was one of the hottest things that I had ever seen. The feel of his tight ass riding up and down on my cock was unbelievably sensual, as well. I struggled against the ropes holding my hands bound to the bench. I desperately wanted to feel every rock hard, straining muscle of Carlos' body under my hands, but I couldn't! Dammit, this was frustrating!

The veins were popping out across Carlos' pecs and on his thick, rock hard biceps as he continued to ride my cock for another couple of minutes, until I gasped; "Oh fuck, Sir, I'm gonna cum, Sir. I'm gonna shoot!"

Master Carlos pulled himself up totally off of my cock and let his weight down across my legs. He leaned forward and took the head of my cock into his hot mouth just as I howled and shot a huge load of cum! He reached up and twisted my nipples savagely as I screamed in pleasure-pain while filling his mouth.

"OH SHIT-OH SHIT. FUCK, SIR. OH FUCK!" I shrieked as the pain ripped through my nipples, contrasting with the pure ecstasy of my orgasm. Master Carlos continued to twist and pull on my nipples until my orgasm was finally spent. My head started to swim as all I could hear was the sound of my own blood roaring in my ears. I vaguely felt Carlos body flop down across my torso, then I knew nothing else as blackness engulfed my entire being.

The next thing I felt was a cool cloth being wiped across my forehead. As I slowly became aware of my surroundings, I realized that I was lying on the small cot in the main room of the dungeon. Master Carlos was kneeling next to me, dabbing at my forehead. I saw a look of total relief on his face when I opened my eyes.

"Thank God. I was afraid that I had done something really wrong, Eric." He said. "You've been out for almost fifteen minutes. I thought that I was going to have to call 911 for help. I'm so sorry!"

He seemed to be on the verge of tears, so I smiled up at him and stroked his arm.

"It's o.k. I'm fine. I just need a drink of water." I reassured him.

He jumped up and got me a bottle of water from the fridge. I slowly sat up on the cot. Immediately my head started to spin again as I held on to Master Carlos' arm for support.

"Whoa, what a rush!" I said when my head finally cleared. I took a couple of swallows of the water and started to feel better. I smiled at Carlos who was sitting next to me on the cot, to let him know that I was all right.

"I'm just dehydrated, that's all. Being tied up in that heat for almost an hour will do that to you. And, I haven't shot a load like that in a long time. You are sooo fucking hot, Sir! That was the most amazing feat of strength that I've seen since I tied you between the horses at Chuck's ranch last summer! How did you come up with an idea like that, Sir?"

Master Carlos grinned. "I actually saw a video of a guy fucking himself with a dildo like that, so I thought that I'd give it a try. And, knock off the 'Sir'. You're not wearing your collar right now, Eric."

I felt my neck and realized that he was right. I hadn't even noticed.

He leaned against my shoulder for a while before he started to weep softly.

"What's the matter, Carlos?" I asked.

"God, Eric, I thought that I had hurt you, or worse. When you passed out, I tried to wake you up for a couple of minutes before I realized that I had to get you out of the heat. I thought that I was never going to be able to pick you up and carry you out of the sauna. I was so scared!"

I wrapped my arm around his shoulders and let him cry against my chest.

After he calmed down, I kissed his tear streaked face and said; "Everything's all right now. Turn off the sauna and the hot tub and we'll go upstairs and get a shower. That'll help me cool down and then you can lavish me with attention for the rest of the night."

Carlos looked at me for a second before he started to giggle with relief.

"Yeah, I guess you are all right. You're back to beeing your old pushy self. Me, me, me, it's all about me!"

I chuckled. "You better believe it, kiddo!"

We both started to laugh as we slowly made our way back up the stairs and out of the dungeon after Carlos had cut off the sauna and the hot tub. We wouldn't be needing them after all. I felt that sitting in the hot tub wouldn't be a really good idea after what had happened to me in the sauna!

After a long relaxing shower to cool my temperature back down to normal, and a couple of glasses of Gatorade to help with the dehydration, I felt a lot better.

Unfortunately, Carlos' self confidence had been badly shaken by the incident in the sauna. Despite my assurances that I was fine, that there were no problems and that I didn't blame him in any way for what had happened, he seemed to be on edge, constantly asking me if I felt all right.

Finally, when it was time for us to go to bed, I told him that I wanted him to sleep with me tonight. He relaxed a bit as I held him in bed. We talked about what had happened, and I told him that it was just a minor mistake, and that he should look at as a learning experience.

I said; "Hell, how many times have you passed out as a result of being tortured? I don't panic, I just make sure you're all right and wait for you to wake up."

Carlos smiled and said; " I guess you're right. I remember you telling someone that no one is born a topman, and no one is born a slave. I guess I just need a bit more experience as a top."

I assured him that I had pulled a lot bigger screw-ups while I was being trained as a top by Mike, but we had both survived. Carlos laughed, and finally seemed to relax before he kissed me and drifted off to sleep. I just hoped that this incident didn't have any long term effects on his ability to perform as an effective topman. Only time would tell!

Chapter 15

Strength

Over the next couple of days I tried to fulfill my duties as a slave to the best of my abilities. I thought that most of Master Carlos' uncertainties of his ability to be a topman had been for nothing, as he resumed his position as my master. I had to do all the cooking and house cleaning, as well as any other duties that my master ordered. Each night we would go down to the dungeon, where Master Carlos would try different ways of binding me before subjecting me to various tortures. He would try some of the tortures that I had subjected him to over the time that we had been together, such as cock flogging and sounding, electro torture of my nipples, and hot waxing my chest and abs while I was being stretched on the rack. Whatever the torture I had to endure, however, we would always end our session with Master Carlos' cock being driven deeply down my throat until he would fill my mouth with a hot load of his salty sweet cum! I guess that he thought that turnabout was fair play.

We also resumed our regular schedule of working out at the local gym, even though we both had decided that we didn't really want to try any more bodybuilding contests for a while.

Finally it came time for the one thing I was not really looking foreword to, our first visit to the Eagle with Carlos serving as my master. Even though most of our friends at the bar knew about our bet, I knew that I was going to have to endure a whole lot of razzing from them. However, I also knew that this was very important to Master Carlos, so I was prepared to accept whatever harassment our friends might throw my way. Besides, I knew that it would mostly be in the spirit of good-natured fun, and I liked to think that I was mature enough to accept whatever they did.

Also, I loved Master Carlos so much that wouldn't do anything to spoil this night for him! He had earned it over the last several months.

We both dressed for the bar, Master Carlos in his chaps over denims, his rubber tank top and his vest, along with his combat boots, while I was ordered to wear just my oldest pair of battered and torn denims and my engineer boots.

We both had our leather coats, but they would be checked at the bar, so I would be spending the time in the bar stripped to the waist, except for my collar and wrist restraints. I didn't have a problem with that, other than the fact that it was still rather cold, but I figured that master Carlos might want to have a bit of fun with me, considering how much he disliked the cold. Maybe it was my time to suffer a bit!

When we arrived at the bar in the Sky, I hopped out and held my master's door open for him. When he was out of the car, Master Carlos clipped the leash onto my slave collar before leading me into the bar. Once we had checked our coats, he locked my wrist restraints together in front of me and led me into the main room of the bar.

Almost immediately the comments started to fly!

Heads all over the bar turned when Joey, one of the bartenders on duty loudly announced; "Well, well, well. Look at this. How the mighty have fallen!"

Some of our other friends congratulated Carlos on his victory at the bodybuilding contest, before turning their attention to me. I heard comments like; "*Couldn't you find a better looking slave anywhere?* " and "*How well trained is that boy? He looks pretty undisciplined to me!* "

Master Carlos looked at me with a wide grin when he answered; "Well, he was the best I could find at such short notice. So far, he seems to be doing all right, but you never know!"

Our friends laughed when one of the guys said; "Hey look, he's blushing!" It was true, too. I could feel my face burning with good natured embarrassment. I remembered what it was like to be a slave from my time with Mike, so their comments didn't bother me all that much. I could tell that they weren't mean spirited, but just teasing.

I had to serve my master in the bar by running to get him any drinks that he wanted, and I also had to obey his orders, like any good slave would. I fetched more drinks for various men, and kissed more boots then I had done for years. I could tell that Master Carlos was enjoying the attention, so I did whatever I needed to do to add to his pleasure.

About an hour or so after we had gotten to the bar, I was surprised when Eddie, Danny's slave came walking into the Eagle by himself. Normally he never went out without his master. I was even more surprised to see that he was in full leather.

Master Carlos grinned down at where I was kneeling next to him and said; "Well, now the fun really starts." I wasn't so sure I liked the sound of that!

Eddie walked over to us and wrapped his arms around my master, giving him a deep, passionate kiss. He stepped back after breaking the kiss and asked; "Is your slave ready for tonight, stud?"

Master Carlos looked down at me with a grin that was positively satanic.

"I hope so. Of course, just to add to the fun, he has no idea what's going to happen tonight." Then his grin widened as he said to me; "Surprise! Remember that Danny said if Eddie did good in the contest he could help me use you any way we wanted? Well, tonight's your lucky night!"

I smiled a bit to myself when I realized that I was going to have to endure being tortured by two hot, horny musclemen tonight! I thought; "Threaten me with a good time!" as Wolf sometimes said.

As I knelt at the feet of the two musclemen, I asked; "Permission to speak, Sir?"

Master Carlos said; "Go ahead, boy."

I looked up at Eddie and said; "Where is Master Daniel tonight, Sir?"

Eddie grinned and said; "He had to go up to Sacramento to a regional sales manager's meeting. We both figured that this would be the perfect opportunity for me to help your master do whatever evil, twisted, and totally sick things that he wants to do to you!"

I just smiled up at both of my masters for the night and said; "Yes, Sirs. Whatever you want, Sirs." I then bent down and began to lick Master Carlos' boots right there in the middle of the front room of the Eagle. I smiled a bit even while continuing my boot worship when I heard comments like; *Damn, I never thought I'd see the day. Eric, licking someone else's boots."* And *"Well, whatta you know. Wolf's finally got that stud on his knees!"*

When I was done with Master Carlos' boots, without a word, I started in on Eddie's. I heard him moan lustfully when I started to lick his right boot. I thought: "What the hell. I'm gonna show these guys here that I can be as good a bottom as I am a top. Master Carlos is worth it!"

I stayed down on my knees licking Eddie's boots until both of them were clean. When I finally sat back up on my haunches, there were about ten or fifteen guys standing in a circle around us, just watching. Among them I saw our friends Joe and H.J., his boy.

Master Carlos grinned at them and said; "Hey guys, want to come along and help work over this slaveboy? I bet he can handle being used by four guys at the same time."

Joe grinned and said; "Sure. Anytime I have an opportunity to work on someone with a body like that, I'll take it!" With that, we all headed towards the door and towards our respective cars, only stopping to collect our coats from the checkroom.

When we arrived home, followed closely by Eddie in his Prius, and Joe and H.J. in their RAV4, I was ordered to prepare the dungeon and the sauna and hot tub for use. When I had finished with that task, Master Carlos instructed me to bring in my old Olympic weight bar and some of the weight plates from the storeroom where they were kept.

Finally we all gathered in the main room of the dungeon. Master Carlos instructed me to strip down to my boots and my collar. When I was undressed, I assisted him and Eddie in stripping down to just boots and chaps. Joe was helped by

H.J., until everyone was either in chaps and boots, or just boots.

Master Carlos stepped in front of me and growled; "Open up, slave!"

I immediately open my mouth and was rewarded by his fat cock sliding into my mouth, until the entire eight inches was down my throat. Master Carlos groaned with pleasure as he started to fuck my mouth. He moaned even louder when Eddie stepped behind him, wrapped his arms around his torso, and started to play with his thick, pumped tits.

I thought that Master Carlos was going to fuck my mouth until he came, but, to my surprise, he pulled his swollen dick out of my mouth after just a few minutes. He grinned down at me and said; "You have to wait for it, boy. You can have our loads only after you've earned them. Right, guys?"

To my surprise, Eddie, Joe and H.J. all said; "That's right."

I began to suspect that all of these guys being in the bar tonight was more than just a coincidence. Apparently, Master Carlos was a bit more devious than I had previously given him credit for!

Over the next hour or so, I took all the other guys cocks in either my mouth or ass, sometimes both at the same time. For one incredible scene, Master Carlos lay down flat on his back on one of my old weightlifting benches. He ordered me to sit on his cock until its full eight inches were impaled in my ass. Next, Eddie sat behind me and slowly leaned me forward until I was almost lying on Master Carlos' chest, with his cock still deeply in my ass. Eddie slowly began to slip his long, thin cock into my stretched hole, next to Master Carlos' thick shaft, until I had both cocks driven deeply into my ass at the same time! The feeling of the two cocks sliding in and out of my hole was incredible!

Master Carlos lifted his head up and kissed me deeply, while Eddie started to run his hands up and down my chest and abs. The heat of the two bodies pressed against me front and rear was making me sweat even more than usual. I slowly lifted myself up until my arms were straight, one hand on either side of Master Carlos' head, grasping the edges of the bench.

His hands began to run up and down my arms, feeling my thick triceps and biceps, and tracing the veins under my skin. At the same time, I could feel every muscle in Eddie's torso flexing against my back as his hands cupped my pecs and played with my nipples.

The sensations running through my body were amazing! The feel of two cocks in my ass, and four hands stroking and feeling my muscles was almost more than I could bear.

Then, to add to my pleasure, Joe stepped in front of me and growled; "Open up, boy."

When I opened my mouth, he drove his solid eight inches deeply into my throat with one swift thrust. His hands grasped my head as he began to fuck my mouth, while Master Carlos and Eddie increased the intensity of their ass fucking.

This was the first time I could ever remember having three cocks in me at the same time! I could see H.J.'s hands sliding up and down his master's torso while Joe fucked my mouth.

The triple fucking lasted almost ten minutes, with the guys alternately speeding up and slowing down the intensity and speed of their fucking, to keep from cumming. All of us were gasping for air and groaning with sheer pleasure. Everyone's bodies were dripping with sweat in the warmth of the dungeon, and from the sheer intensity of the scene.

Finally, Master Carlos announced; "That's enough for now, guys. I have another plan for this slave to get off. We're gonna see just how strong all those big muscles of his really are!"

Joe reluctantly pulled his cock out of my mouth while Eddie slowly backed his cock out of my ass. I groaned at the feeling of the long cock sliding out next to Master Carlos' thick dick. Finally, my master ordered me to stand up, sliding his cock out of me. I groaned again as I stood up and helped Master Carlos up. He looked amazing, with his bronze physique streaming with sweat, and his hair glued to his shoulders. Joe and Eddie looked almost as hot, their bodies gleaming and their skin contrasting with the gleaming black of their leather chaps and boots.

We took a few minutes to recover before Master Carlos ordered me to bring the weight bar and the plates into the center of the floor. Next, he told me to put a 25 pound plate on either end of the bar. When I had done this, I knelt on the floor next to the bar and awaited my master's next order.

With a positively evil grin, he said; "O.K. slave, do a full shoulder press and hold the weight straight over your head. Hold it there until I tell you that you can put it down. If you let it down before I tell you to, well, I guess we'll just have to see what kind of punishment you need."

I stood up, grasped the weight and did a classic clean and jerk maneuver to get the weight over my head. I could press more weight than this, but I had never tried to hold it there for any length of time.

When I had the weight over my head, Master Carlos said something softly to Eddie and H.J.. I groaned when the two boys stepped up to me and bent down to start sucking on my nipples. I realized what Master Carlos was going to do to me. I was going to have to hold the weight over my head while everyone else teased and tormented my body. How fiendish!

All I could do was close my eyes and concentrate on holding up the weight, while trying to ignore the feel of the two hot mouths sucking and chewing on my hard tits, and the four hands stroking and feeling my already quivering muscles. I groaned even louder when Joe knelt behind me and started to eat out my ass. His breath was hot, but when his tongue started to flicker across my hole, I thought that I was going to drop the weight for a second.

I couldn't help it, and growled "Oh shit!" when Master Carlos knelt in front of me and started to lick the length of my cock, and suck on my balls.

The next few minutes were sheer agony. It seemed that the weight was growing heavier and heavier by the second. At the same time, I desperately wanted to drop the weight and use my hands to stroke and feel the hot muscles of all the guys that were making love to various parts of my body, but I couldn't!

Master Carlos was sucking on my cock, his head pumping back and forth on my shaft, while Eddie and H.J. alternated between sucking my nipples, and licking and tonguing out my stretched, straining armpits. Then they started running their tongues down my sides and licking up the streams of sweat running down my ribcage.

Joe had his face buried between my ass cheeks, his tongue sliding across and sometimes into my asshole.

The pleasure torture lasted a good ten minutes or so, before Master Carlos pulled back from my cock, just before I felt sure I was going to cum in his mouth, with or without his permission. He told the other guys to back off, leaving me standing in the center of the dungeon floor, muscles shaking and sweat pouring down my entire physique as I strained to hold the weight straight-armed over my head.

Master Carlos smiled evilly and said; "That looks too easy. Eddie, Joe, you guys grab another 25 each and add them to the bar."

I almost screamed in agony when the guys reached up with the plates and slid them onto the bar over my head! God, that was another 50 pounds! I felt my arms start to buckle under the strain, before Master Carlos stepped in front of me and growled; "I didn't say you could lower the weight, slave. Hold it up, boy!"

I could barely grunt "Yes, Sir" as I forced my arms straight again.

Master Carlos looked at Joe and said; "O.K., now it's your turn. Have fun!"

Joe smiled wickedly at me as he stepped to my toy shelves and picked up one of my lightweight floggers. I groaned in anticipation, then gasped in pain when he laid the tails of the cat across my chest. He started out lightly, but gradually increased the intensity of his flogging.

In less than a minute or so, I couldn't keep quiet any more, and began to shriek at each hit of the tails across my chest and ribcage. It felt like my skin was on fire as the pain grew and grew with each passing second. This was pure torture!

Joe had a look of concentration on his face as he whipped my chest, mixed with a look of pure sadistic delight. It was almost scary to see. Also, his cock was rock hard, so I knew that he was really turned on by torturing me.

As I stood there enduring my torture, Eddie had wrapped his arms around Master Carlos' body and was kissing him deeply. I knew that Eddie really was hot for Carlos, so it seemed that he was taking full advantage of the opportunity to make love to Master Carlos' muscles.

Joe finally seemed to be finished flogging me, but my relief was short-lived when he stepped behind me and began to flog my rock hard, quivering back and shoulder muscles. To add to my already considerable suffering, H.J. stepped back in front of me and began to chew on my nipples again!

The combination of sensations was almost overpowering. Every impact of the flogger on my back felt like the skin was being ripped off of my screaming muscles. The feel of H.J.'s mouth chewing and biting my nipples felt like my tits were being held in the flames of a couple of candles. And, being forced to watch Eddie making passionate love to my master while I was helpless to do anything was almost too much to bear.

Within a couple of minutes more I just started to sob. I couldn't help it, and the tears just started to flow down my face. Still, I was determined to endure the torture as long as I physically could.

Thankfully, within another couple of minutes, Master Carlos told Joe that I had endured enough flogging for one night.

Then he grinned at me and said; "Now it's time for your final test of strength. Keep that weight up there, no matter what, boy!"

I grunted; "Yes, Sir."

Master Carlos dropped to his knees and took my hard cock into his mouth. He started to pump it in and out, while reaching up and beginning to squeeze and twist my already sore nipples. I started to gasp with the feel of his hot mouth sucking my cock, and the incredible strain of trying to hold the 130 pounds over my head.

Within a minute or so, I started to holler as the strain in my shoulder muscles reached unbearable levels, even as I felt my cock explode with a huge orgasm, filling Master Carlos' mouth with my cum!

I barely kept my knees from buckling with the intensity of my orgasm, while desperately trying to hold the weight steady over my head, knowing the consequences if I dropped it on my kneeling lover.

Finally, Master Carlos stood up in front of me and said; "Great load, boy. Now you can put the weight down."

I actually screamed with relief when I lowered the weight bar down to my chest, and then muscled it down to the floor, barely keeping it from dropping. When it was down, I could only sag down to my knees, totally exhausted from my torture.

Master Carlos knelt down in front of me and wrapped his arms around me, as I always did when I was finished with a heavy torture session on him. There seemed to be a haunted look in his eyes as he hugged me.

"Are you all right?" he whispered as he held me.

"Yes, Sir. I'm fine, Sir." I whispered back.

Master Carlos just held me for a few more minutes before he stood up. Looking down at me, he announced; "I guess it's time to give this slave his reward for his feat of strength."

He stepped over to the toy shelves and picked up the behind-the-back bondage straps and collar. Within minutes, I was kneeling in the center of the dungeon floor with the collar strapped tightly around my neck with my arms pulled painfully up behind my back.

Master Carlos started to stroke his hands over my still welted back and shoulder muscles, while murmuring almost to himself; "Oh yeah, that's what I want to see."

He turned to the other guys watching me and said; "Now it's time for his reward. I want each of you guys to fuck his mouth! I want all of you to cum in his mouth. I want to see this slave sucking up all those loads of cum! Joe, I want you and your boy to go first, since you're our guests."

He bent down and whispered in my ear; "Don't worry. Joe and H.J. showed me their latest HIV tests, and they're both negative. Eddie is as well, so it's safe to take their loads."

I whispered; "Thank you, Sir."

Master Carlos stood up and said; "Just to give him something else to think about while he's sucking your cocks, let's try these."

With that, he hung a two pound lead weight from each of my nipple rings!

I started to scream at the intense pain ripping through my entire body from my tortured nipples, but my scream was muffled as H.J. stuffed his solid cock deeply into my throat and began to fuck my mouth. Joe stood next to his boy, watching him.

Then Joe moved behind me and grasped my head tightly between his hands as his boy's cock slid in and out of my mouth. H.J. started to gasp and groan as he raped my mouth, growling; "Oh yeah, that's a hot cocksucker!"

It only took a few minutes before he threw his head back and howled as he filled my mouth with his load.

As soon as H.J. had pulled his now softening cock from my mouth, Joe stepped in front of me.

"I've been waiting for this" he growled, as his hard cock slid between my lips. I looked up at his solidly muscled, lean torso, streaming with sweat with his hair stuck to his face and shoulders. The hard washboard of his abs began to ripple in front of my eyes as Joe grasped my head and started to thrust his cock all the way into my throat. He had a solid 8 inch dick that filled my mouth.

Ever since I had seen Joe for the first time, I had wanted to have sex with him, but this wasn't exactly what I had in mind!

He continued to thrust in and out of my mouth, grunting and gasping with the effort and the pleasure. When I looked up again, H.J. had stepped behind his master and was now playing with Joe's hard, reddish brown nipples.

Within a minute or so, he growled; "Take it, slave!" as his cock exploded with a huge load of hot, salty cum in my mouth. He held my head in his firm grasp until the last drop of his sperm had been pumped out of his cock, for the second load I had to swallow.

He finally released me as he stepped back and slid his cock out of my mouth.

"Good mouth, boy" he growled. Looking at Master Carlos, he said; "That's a hot slave you've got here. Take care of him."

Master Carlos smiled and replied; "Thanks. I'll do my best."

Next it was Eddie's turn. He looked down at me as he stepped in front of me, every muscle of his ripped, hard body rippling under his gleaming, golden brown skin. His cock wasn't as thick as Joe's or H.J.'s, but it was every bit as long and hard.

His eyes were gleaming with a look of mischief as he said; "Open up, slave."

When I opened my mouth, Eddie thrust the entire length of his shaft into my mouth, almost causing me to gag when his cockhead hit the back of my throat. He moaned with pleasure as he began to slowly face fuck me. His amazing eight-pack abs were flexing only inches in front of my face, but I couldn't get my hands free to feel the hard muscles, which only added to the feelings of frustration and helplessness of being a bound slave.

I heard Joe murmur "Man, what a body" just before he started to stroke his fingers up and down Eddie's torso. Eddie moaned with pleasure when Joe bent down and began to suck on his right nipple. Almost immediately, H.J. started to do the same on Eddie's left tit. Eddie's hands were holding my head still as he slowly started driving his cock deeper and deeper into my waiting mouth. He was panting with a combination of pleasure as his nipples were worshipped by two hot mouths while his cock was fucking my mouth, and effort as he fucked my mouth faster and faster until, with a howl of pleasure, he shot a huge load of sperm deeply into my mouth, filling my mouth with the third load of cum within ten minutes or so.

Eddie thrust his cock deeply into my mouth until the cum finally stopped shooting from his cockhead. With a gasp, he finally pulled his still hard cock from my mouth, then playfully slapped my face with his long dick.

At last, it was Master Carlos' turn. He stepped in front of me, every muscle of his bronzed torso rippling as well. All the other guys were really hot looking, but none of them were as purely sexy as my lover. I looked up into his brown eyes, and he looked down at me, smiling slightly.

His hair was hanging down over his chest and shoulders, glued there by his sweat. His sculpted physique shone in the lights of the dungeon. I moaned with pure lust before I bent and began to lick his boots. Every movement of my body caused the weights hanging from my nipple rings to swing, increasing the torture I had to endure, but I didn't care. I was totally consumed by the desire to please my master!

After cleaning both of my master's boots, I straightened back up and opened my mouth. I moaned with delight as I felt Master Carlos' thick shaft slowly sliding deeply into my mouth, before starting to pump in and out slowly, almost teasingly. I could only close my eyes and surrender to my lust when Master Carlos grasped both sides of my head in his strong hands and began to fuck my mouth faster and faster.

"Fuck that slave's mouth!" I heard Joe growl. "Give it to him!"

Master Carlos started to growl deeply in his throat. That sound usually meant that he was about ready to shoot a huge load of cum. I was almost frantic in my desire to run my hands up and down his rippling, flexing washboard abs, and play with his nipples and his sculpted pecs, but I couldn't! I was too tightly bound to be able to do anything other than kneel helplessly in front of my master while he threw back his head and, with a deep-throated howl, filled my mouth with his load of sperm. The cum kept shooting out of Master Carlos' cock in jet after jet, until he had shot at least eight hot streams of cum into my mouth. I swallowed my master's load as quickly as I could, for the fourth load I had swallowed within twenty minutes.

After what seemed to be an eternity of Master Carlos filling my mouth with his hot sperm, and me swallowing as fast as I could, he finally pulled his cock out of my mouth.

"Oh fuck, that was great, boy." He groaned.

Turning to the other guys, he said; "Well, has he earned a rest?"

They all nodded and murmured their agreement. Master Carlos knelt down in front of me and ever so gently removed the weights that were still painfully torturing my nipples. I gasped with relief as the pain in my nipples eased as the weight was removed.

"Thank you, Sir." I moaned.

Master Carlos helped me to my feet before wrapping his arms around me and kissing me deeply while holding me. I reveled in the feel of his strong arms holding me, and in the feel of his solid, muscular chest pressed against mine. Our sweat-soaked bodies slid against each other as he released my arms from their bondage and took off the collar.

Master Carlos whispered in my ear; "Are you sure you're all right?"

I smiled down into his eyes and said; "Yes sir, I'm fine. Thank you for asking."

When he finally let me go, I helped him and Eddie slip out of their chaps and boots, while H.J. helped Joe undress.

Joe, Eddie and H.J. headed into the sauna, while Carlos and I headed out to the hot tub after a quick rinse off in the shower.

We both hurried across the outside pool deck in the chill of the night air. I gasped with a combination of pain and pleasure when I stepped into the steaming water. I enjoyed the warmth, but the water felt like acid on my tender, flogged skin and my sensitive nipples.

It took a minute or so before I adjusted to the heat, then I could start to relax. I moved into my favorite spot in a corner of the hot tub, where I had a great view down the hill from my property, overlooking the bay, and the lights of the city spread out beyond.

Carlos slipped into his regular spot in front of me and leaned back against my chest. He sighed with pleasure as I wrapped my arms around his hard body and just held him.

We sat for a while, just enjoying the view before Carlos turned to look at me.

"Eric, there's something I need to tell you, but I'm afraid that you might get really mad at me" he said, with a rather forlorn look on his face.

"Do you remember what I told you the first day that we met in the bar? I said that you never need to be afraid to tell me anything. Other that you telling me that you want to leave me, I can't think of anything that you could tell me that would make me mad at you." I said gently.

"Oh God, no. It's not anything like that at all, Sir" Carlos said with a shocked look on his face.

I was wondering what possibly could have Carlos so upset that he was nervous about telling me. We had never had any secrets from each other in all the time we had been together, other than my not telling Carlos what I had gotten him for Christmas.

He looked like he was going to say something when the door out of the dungeon opened up and Eddie, Joe, and H.J. stepped out and headed for the hot tub.

Carlos whispered in my ear; "I'll tell you later" before greeting the guys as they all stepped into the hot water.

The rest of the evening was a lot of fun, with all of us soaking for a while before heading back inside. Joe and H.J. had to leave, but Eddie was free to spend the night.

The three of us went upstairs to the master bedroom, where I had the pleasure of having a hot, muscular man lying on either side of me in my bed while they alternated sucking on my nipples for a while before we all enjoyed a three way mutual cocksucking and muscle worship session. Everyone got to suck everyone else's cock at least two or three times, before I finally shot another load, this time deeply into Eddie's mouth, while Eddie came in Carlos' mouth, and Carlos filled my mouth with another hot load of man cum.

As we finally drifted off to sleep, my last thought was "What was bothering Carlos so much?"

Chapter 16

Truth

The next morning I woke to the wonderful feeling of two hot men curled up next to me, one on either side, still sleeping soundly. I just lay in the bed for a while, listening to the sound of their breathing and enjoying the warmth of their bodies against my skin.

As I lay there, I began to try to figure out what was bothering Carlos so much that he couldn't even tell me what it was. I thought back over the last few weeks to try to remember if I had done something to offend him, or hurt his feelings, but I couldn't think of anything.

In another ten minutes or so, first Eddie and then Carlos finally began to stir. I felt the light touch of their hands slowly beginning to run over my body. Eddie lifted his head and kissed me before saying; "Good morning, Sir. Did you sleep well?"

I smiled at him and said; "Sure did. How about you?"

He lay his head down on my chest and murmured; "Me too. Last night was great." He then started to gently suck on my right nipple. When I moaned with pleasure, Carlos lifted his head and growled; "What's going on here?" in a seemingly offended, but totally fake tone of voice. "What do you think you're doing to my lover, boy?"

Eddie just lifted his head and grinned; "Well, someone's got to take care of this hot muscleman. If you won't do it, I guess it's up to me." With that, he bent his head back down and continued to suck on my tit.

Carlos' eyes flew open wide at his friend's tone, but I could see the laughter in his eyes from Eddie's needling.

Carlos grumped; "You need someone to show you how to do that the right way, boy. Let a pro show you."

With that, he lowered his head down and started to suck on my left nipple.

I gasped out; "Don't fight, boys. There's plenty to go around" before I just lay back and surrendered to the incredible feelings of two hot mouths sucking on my nipples, while four strong hands stroked and caressed my muscles.

Their mutual muscle worship session soon evolved into a contest between the two boys to see who could pleasure my body the most thoroughly. Every time Eddie would kiss, lick or caress a muscle on his side of my body, Carlos would respond by trying to do it better. Needless to say, I was thoroughly enjoying their attention!

Within a few more minutes, all three of us were gleaming with sweat, while I was moaning constantly from the incredible feelings of pleasure flooding through my entire body from the two hot men making love to my muscles, from the lobes of my ears, to the soles of my feet. It seemed that Carlos and Eddie were determined to not miss a square inch of my body!

It took only another ten minutes or so before I felt the familiar tightening in my balls that meant that I was about to shoot another thick load of cum.

"Whoever wants my load, get your face down there" I gasped.

Immediately, both Carlos and Eddie started to lick the head of my swollen, throbbing cock. Within seconds, I threw back my head and howled as a huge load of sperm flooded out of my cock. Both boys took turns gulping down a portion of my load. I groaned with pure pleasure at the feel of two hot tongues caressing the now incredibly sensitive head of my cock.

When my load was finally spent, I flopped back on the bed, my chest heaving.

"Damn, that felt good!" I groaned.

Carlos smiled. "It tasted pretty good, too."

Eddie nodded his agreement before slyly saying to Carlos; "I wonder if your load would taste as good."

Carlos grinned back with his lopsided smile; "It's funny, but I was just thinking the same thing about you. Let's find out."

For the next few minutes, I was treated to the erotic show of the two young, hot, hard bodied muscle boys making passionate love to each other's sculpted physiques. Wolf's long black hair contrasted with Eddie's now blonde and black Mohawk. Wolf was somewhat bulkier than Eddie, but both boys had amazingly ripped and shredded physiques. They both licked and stroked each others ripped, gleaming muscles and deep-throated each others cocks until almost simultaneously, both of them shot equally thick, creamy loads of sperm into each other's mouths. They both moaned and growled with pleasure while swallowing the hot man juice filling their mouths.

Finally, both hot boys lay back down on the bed on either side of me again. I could feel the still racing heartbeats of both muscle boys as they wrapped their arms around me, and each other in a tight group hug of sweaty, glistening muscles.

Carlos just moaned; "Damn!"

Eddie laughed softly and said; "I totally agree!"

I chuckled softly as the two boys lay their heads on my chest.

We just lay there for another ten minutes or so while we all recovered from our session of hot three-way sex. As we lay there, I thought again of how lucky I was to have such a hot, sexy man as my lover, and how lucky I was to have such a good group of friends in the city, as well.

I finally said; "I don't know about you two lazybones, but I need some breakfast."

Both boys chuckled their agreement.

Eddie said; "If you guys don't mind, could I make it? I love to cook, and I'd like to do it to help thank you for such a great night."

I looked at Carlos and gave him a wink. "Do you think we can trust his cooking, boy?"

Carlos grinned and said; "I'll risk it if you will, Sir."

Eddie momentarily flushed at our teasing before starting to laugh. "Hey, I haven't poisoned Master Danny in over a week now."

"Well, that's good enough for me." I grinned.

We all laughed before rolling out of bed and heading for the shower in the master bath. I had remodeled the shower so it was big enough for three or even four people to fit into at the same time, with multiple shower heads at various angles. The three of us enjoyed the feel of a hot, steamy shower while all of us lathered up each other's bodies from head to toe. When we were finally done, Eddie headed downstairs while I finished brushing out Carlos' luxuriant mane of hair.

By the time I was done, Eddie called up that breakfast was ready. We went downstairs to find that he had made a stack of pancakes and sausage.

We all enjoyed breakfast, and when we were done, Eddie announced that he had to head back home since Danny was due back in town later this afternoon.

"Will we see you tonight, guys?" he asked before he left.

Carlos looked at me and then nodded. "I hope so. We're planning on going out to the Eagle, so I figure we'll see you there."

We both gave Eddie a hug before he left to head home.

Now that Carlos and I were alone, I hoped that we could discuss what it was that was bothering him. However, when I asked him about it, his answer surprised me.

"Do you mind if I wait until tonight to tell you? I don't mean any disrespect or anything like that, but I really feel that I need to wait until we're out in public to answer you. Please don't be offended, Sir, but I really want to wait."

He seemed to almost be begging me. This was such a change from Carlos' usual demeanor that I was temped to demand that he tell me what was on his mind right now! But, when I looked into his eyes, the look of almost desperate pleading was so great that I just didn't have the heart.

"O.K. You can wait until tonight" I told him, giving him a hug.

His look of relief was palpable.

"But, it better be worth all this mystery, boy." I added with a grin, to let him know that I wasn't really mad at him, just intensely curious.

"Don't worry, Sir. I think you will like what I have to tell you." He grinned.

I didn't occur to me until later that Carlos had started to call me "Sir" again. Looking back on it later, maybe he was unconsciously trying to give me a hint of what was on his mind.

The rest of the day passed uneventfully. I did my usual work on my computer, checking on the business in Indiana. I was still sore from the intense torture that I had endured the night before, so I wasn't in the mood to do much of anything strenuous today.

We went downstairs where Carlos straightened up the dungeon and put the weights back in the storage room, while I just puttered around rearranging some things on my toy shelves. When we were done, we both went out and soaked for a while in the hot tub.

I moaned with pleasure at the feel of the hot water bubbling and swirling around my back and shoulder muscles. I was still hurting from the effort of having to hold the heavy weight over my head while being flogged and sucked off, so the hot water was a blessing.

When we had soaked for a while, Carlos asked if I would like a gentle massage.

"Are you kidding? I'd love it!" I smiled.

He unfolded the massage table and said; "Your pleasure awaits, Sir. Hop on."

I lay down on the table and was rewarded with an hour or so of the most gentle, yet sensuous massage that I had been given in quite some time! Carlos' hands were warm, strong yet incredibly tender as they worked on my battered back and shoulders.

I moaned in sheer bliss as he gently rubbed away the soreness from Joe's expert flogging and the effort of holding the barbell over my head for longer than I had ever done before.

I was so relaxed by the time Carlos was done with my back that I could barely sit up. Carlos actually had to help me up the stairs to the shower. I took a quick rinse off and announced to Carlos that I was going to take a nap until it was time to go out.

"That's a good idea, Sir. I have the feeling it might be a long night." He smiled at me. "I've got a few chores I need to do while you're sleeping. I'll make sure you're up in time to go out."

I lay down in my bed and almost immediately fell soundly asleep. I didn't know anything until I felt Carlos gently kiss me and heard him say; "It's about time to go out, Sir. Would you like a snack before we go out?"

"Sure, I'm starved." I was rather hungry, since I hadn't eaten a thing since breakfast. When I had finished the sandwich Carlos had made for me, he asked if there was anything else I wanted.

"Thanks, but I'm fine. I better get dressed. I'm dying to hear what's on your mind."

When I went to the closet to get my leathers, I was surprised to see that one of the chores Carlos had done was to polish both pairs of our boots until they shone like onyx mirrors. He normally kept them shone, but this time he had outdone himself.

We dressed in our leathers, me in my chaps over tight, faded denims, my vest with no shirt under it, and my leather bike jacket. Carlos wore his leather pants and his bar vest, also with no shirt, and a leather headband to keep his long hair out of his eyes. I always thought that he was incredibly sexy looking in leather, and he had often said the same thing about me.

We used my car and drove into the city and down to the Eagle, off of Folsom St.

When we arrived, I waited for Carlos to put the collar on me, as part of his winning our bet. However he surprised me by just strapping the collar around his right boot. He also surprised me by asking me to move my keys back to the left side, the dominant side, of my belt.

We walked into the bar, where I checked my bike jacket at the coat room, then went out to one of the tables in the outdoor courtyard where we usually met our regular group of friends.

Danny and Eddie were there already, as were Joe and H.J., along with several other couples that we were friends with.

"Hey, guys" called out Danny, when we walked up. "What's the big mystery? Eddie told me that there's something Wolf wants to tell everyone."

Apparently, he and Eddie had talked the previous night while I was asleep.

I was totally confused. "I really don't know what's going on."

I turned to my lover and said; "I think it's about time that you told us exactly what the hell's going on! No more waiting, no more dodging the question! Talk, boy!"

He sheepishly turned to me and said; "Yes, Sir."

Carlos turned to the group and said; "You all know about the bet that Master Eric and I made before our bodybuilding contest. As it turned out, I won. But, I feel that I couldn't have won without Master Eric's coaching and driving me to train harder than I had ever trained before. I feel that it was as much his victory as it was mine."

He took a deep breath before continuing; "Master Eric was honorable enough to fulfill his part of the bet, by serving as my slave. He was willing to allow me to use him as a slave in public, in front of all our friends, without worrying about his own reputation. As much as I enjoyed the sight of him in bondage and being used as a slave, I also knew that it was wrong. He is my master. I am his slave, and that's the way I feel that it needs to be."

Carlos turned to look at me with tears running down his face.

"Sir, would you think it wrong of me if I asked you to call off the rest of our bet? I wish to go back to being your slave. I'm not cut out to be a topman. I know that now. When you passed out in the sauna, I almost panicked. Also, watching you being tortured may have been exciting, but it also hurt me. Please, Master. This slave wishes to go back to serving you. Always, Sir."

With that, he dropped to his knees in front of me, and lowered his head in a posture of submission, waiting.

The rest of the guys watching us were totally silent as I contemplated the figure kneeling in front of me. He was the single sexiest man I had ever seen in my life. He was the perfect slave, as well.

I finally stepped up to him and growled; "You wish to serve me, slave? Prove it."

With that, he bent down and began licking my boots. As he worked on my boots, I realized that our relationship had come full circle. We were standing in front of the very same table where this young, incredibly sexy Amerindian-Latino boy had knelt in front of me to clean my boots for the first time almost two years earlier.

We had gone through quite a bit together since that first hot afternoon.

Wolf's slave training, his brutal torture at the ranch in the mountains capped by the branding of his nipples, our learning about each other's pasts, and even our friendly competition at the bodybuilding contest, all of these events seemed to have led up to this moment in the bar, the reaffirmation of our relationship.

I allowed him to lick my boots for a while before I ordered him back up onto his knees.

"Where's your collar, boy?" I snarled to him. "You can't be a slave without your collar to show the world exactly who you are. A boot licking, cock sucking, cum guzzling slave!"

Carlos smiled up into my eyes as he unbuckled the collar from around his right boot and held it out to me with both hands. I took the collar and held it out in front of him. He leaned in and kissed the inside of the collar, before reaching up and holding his hair out of the way. I wrapped the collar around his throat and buckled it tightly. Carlos moaned softly with pleasure when I reached into my pocket and pulled out the small padlock that I always kept there when it wasn't on the collar.

I slipped the lock through the stud on the collar and said; "Last chance to change your mind, boy. When I lock this, you are my slave forever."

He smiled up at me with the tears still streaming down his face, softly saying; "Do it, Master. Oh God, please, do it, Sir!"

Wolf moaned with pure pleasure when I snapped the lock closed then looked down into my slave's face.

"What's your name, boy?" I growled.

He smiled an almost beatific smile. "This slave's name is Wolf, Sir."

The guys surrounding us murmured their approval as my boy acknowledged my total mastery over him. It was as if the snapping of the padlock on his collar had thrown some internal switch in my boy, returning Wolf to the total slave that I had grown to love.

I gently said; "You asked me if I would think any less of you if you wanted to call off our bet. No, I won't. I would actually think less of you if you insisted on going forward with it even if you were unhappy with it. I told you on the first day that we met that you should always tell me the truth. But, even more importantly, you must always be true to yourself. Now, stand up, boy."

Wolf rose to his feet and stood in front of me. As I looked at him, I realized that I had never been prouder of him than I was at this moment. He had publicly confessed his own doubts about his abilities as a top without a thought as to what anyone other then I would think of him. I was also humbled to know that this man, Wolf, was so in love with me, just as I was with him, that he would go to these lengths to gain my approval.

I reached out and cupped my hand under his chin, as I had done many times before. This time, however, when I lifted his face up so he was looking into my eyes, I leaned in and kissed him deeply. I felt Wolf's arms slip up and wrap around my back. I grasped him back as our kiss continued, our bodies now pressed tightly together. The warmth of his bare chest flowed into my body.

We stood there, holding each other tightly, locked in our kiss for what seemed to be minutes before Danny, always the smart-ass, piped up; "Jeepers, why don't you two get a room?"

Wolf snorted a muffled laugh. But within seconds, we both pulled back from each other and started laughing out loud. We just couldn't help it.

I turned to Danny. "We have a perfectly good room to use. As a matter of fact, we have three rooms to use. If you don't watch it, you might find yourself a guest there. We have plenty of shackles."

Danny, along with all our other friends laughed at my mock threat before he turned serious.

"You know, that's a very special slave boy you have there, Eric. You need to do whatever you can to keep him."

I was a bit surprised to hear him talking like that. Usually Danny was quick with a joke or some offhanded remark, but he rarely spoke with the gravity that he was showing in his voice now.

I looked at Wolf and smiled.

"Believe me, I know how special he is. I've known it since the very first minute that I laid eyes on him. You should know. You were here."

Danny quietly said; "I remember. I asked if you thought that he might last longer than any of your other slave boys."

I grinned at the memory. "Yeah. I also said I was going to try my best to get him home that night to my dungeon to see how much he could take."

I looked at Wolf. "I never told you that, did I boy? I was hot for you from he very first instant I saw you. I know you said that you were sure I was supposed to be your master from the first time you saw me. Well, I knew you were supposed to be my slave the first time I saw you!"

I smiled at my slave. "It seems to have worked out pretty well, don't you think, boy?"

He smiled gently before dropping back to his knees. "Yes, Sir. This boy thinks that it worked out perfectly. Thank you, Master."

The rest of the evening was one of the most enjoyable nights that I had spent in the bar in quite some time. My friends and I were in a great mood, the crowd was active, and best of all, Wolf was attentive to my every need and desire.

I know that he was probably uncomfortable being outside with just his vest on above the waist, as it was still chilly at night, but he never said a word about being cold. Wolf just served me as a properly trained slave boy should serve his master.

I decided that it was time for him to get his ultimate marks as my slave. He had earned them by his actions, not just in the bar this night, but every minute of the time we had been together. While Wolf was going to the check room to get my coat I had a quick word with Joe. We agreed that he would come by later the next day for some fun, which would include Wolf getting his nipple piercings but H.J. was not going to be able to be there. He had to go to work.

Joe smiled; "I've wanted to work on those tits since the very first time that I met you guys. Those are the hottest nipples and pecs that I've ever seen."

About that time Wolf walked up with my coat. He dutifully helped me put it on before kneeling in front of me one more time and kissing my boots.

"Come on, boy. It's time to head home." I told him. "I'm in the mood for some fun tonight, and I hope you're up for it as well."

Wolf just smiled. "Always, Sir."

Our friends waved and called out their good nights as we left.

As we drove home, I thought about Wolf's words. I knew that after tomorrow we would be together. Always. The way we were meant to be.

We didn't say too much to each other on the way home. We really didn't need to say much. Wolf just leaned his head against my shoulder as I drove.

When we arrived home Wolf helped me undress and hung out our leathers to dry before being put away. We just crawled into my bed and held each other for a while, not speaking. I felt that we both knew that tonight was not going to be a time for a hard session in the dungeon, but rather we needed to spend a night just making gentle love to each other. We each explored every inch of each other's bodies before both of us pumped huge loads of cum into each others mouths during a hot 69 cocksucking session. When we were both sated, we lay on my bed, our sweat-soaked bodies pressed against each other, our arms holding each other tightly until we both drifted off to sleep. Late the next morning I awoke to an empty bed. As I was just about to head out of the bedroom looking for Wolf, he stepped into the bedroom carrying a tray.

"Good morning, Sir. I made breakfast for you. I hope you enjoy it." He smiled before setting the tray across my lap. I was a bit amused. It had been a while since Wolf had served me breakfast in bed.

Wolf knelt next to the bed while I ate, awaiting any orders that I might have for him. Apparently, he was totally serious about wanting to re-commit himself to serving as my slaveboy, not just as my lover. I was glad, because after this afternoon and evening, Wolf was going to be mine forever.

"That was very good, boy." I said when I was finished.

Wolf smiled. "Thank you, Sir. May I be permitted to give you dessert, Sir?"

I had a pretty good idea what he had in mind. "Go ahead, boy." I told him.

Wolf nodded his head obediently before he took the breakfast tray away, then crawled into bed between my legs. He moaned softly once before sucking my rapidly swelling cock deeply into his mouth. I leaned back against the pillows as my slave concentrated on his task. My hands ran over Wolf's head, stroking and caressing his thick black hair.

I groaned with pleasure at the feel of his hands beginning to run up and down my torso, feeling my hard muscles. Wolf's fingertips outlined each cut of my washboard abs, felt every ripple of my ribcage, and finally began to play with my solidly engorged nipples.

All the while, his head bobbed up and down as he sucked and orally worshiped my thick fully erect cock. His lips molded themselves to every ridge and vein bulging on my shaft, while his hot tongue flickered up and down the entire length of my cock. I groaned again when he started to rapidly flick his tongue back and forth across the incredibly sensitive head of my dick.

I barely had time to grunt; "Here it comes, boy" before I filled his mouth with another load of my hot sperm. Wolf growled deeply in his throat as he swallowed my cum.

When he finally pulled his head back from my now softening cock, all I could do was groan; "God, that was great. Thank you, boy."

Wolf grinned; "My pleasure, Sir. May I have permission to finish, Sir?"

I knew what he wanted to do. "Go ahead, boy."

He slid up my body until he was sitting on my abs and started to stroke his own hard cock. As he jacked his shaft, I reached out and began to twist and torment his nipples. Wolf gasped and growled as my fingers stretched and pulled his tits, until with a grunt

and a labored; "Oh shit!" he shot a thick stream of cum across my pecs. Wolf kept pumping his cock, and I kept twisting his nipples until his sperm finally finished shooting from his dick.

Wolf leaned forward and began to lick his still hot load from my chest. I groaned at the feel of his tongue sliding sensuously across my sweaty skin. The feel of his silky hair caressing my body was unbelievably erotic, as well.

As Wolf worshipped my muscles while cleaning his cum from my skin, I thought about how incredibly lucky I was to have him in my life.

Wolf had publicly stated his desire to remain my slave forever, so today he was going to receive his final signs of his slavery, his nipple rings. I was proud to still have the rings that had been set in my tits by my master so I felt that Wolf had finally earned his as well.

Wolf finally finished his tongue cleaning of my chest. When he sat back upright he gave me one of the broadest smiles I had seen from him in quite a while.

"Thank you, Sir. This slave hopes you enjoyed your dessert."

I pulled Wolf down so he was lying on my chest before kissing him deeply.

"I sure did, boy. But if I was getting dessert, how come you were the only one eating anything?"

Wolf started to giggle. "Gee, I never thought about that, Sir."

I growled threateningly; "I guess I'll just have to teach you to think things out before you start making promises you don't intend to keep. Dessert, my ass!"

Wolf gave me a wide-eyed, innocent look. "I didn't know you wanted your dessert in your ass. If you had told me, I could have put it there."

I looked at him for a second before I totally broke up. Within seconds I was howling with laughter. Every time I would look into his face, with his put-on innocent expression, I would break up even more. It was a few minutes of total loonyness. Before I could finally calm down, Wolf was laughing as hard as I was.

"Oh you're gonna pay for that one, boy" I gasped when I could finally speak. "I may just have to torture you for two or three more hours!" Of course, we both knew that my threatening Wolf with torture was rather like threatening a starving man with a banquet!

Wolf just gave me his loveable slightly lopsided grin. "That's another reason I love you so much. You know what I like."

"Damn right, boy. And you better learn what I like, as well!"

Of course we both knew that he had been my slave long enough that he could practically read my mind. That's why it was so much fun to try to surprise him, like I was planning to do this afternoon when Joe showed up

"Did you eat yet, boy?" I asked him.

Wolf grinned again. "Just a couple of loads of protein, Sir."

I groaned; "God, all the hot slave boys in the city, and I had to get stuck with a smart ass! What did I do to deserve this? Oy!"

Wolf giggled; "You're just lucky, I guess!"

I looked up into his eyes and told him; "Go have a light meal, boy." I gave him an evil smile as I added; "I have some plans for you today, slave."

Wolf said; "Yes, Sir. Thank you, Sir!" as he took the breakfast tray and headed downstairs.

As he busied himself in the kitchen, I gave Joe a call and set up the time for him to come over to do Wolf's piercings. I could tell Joe was excited about the opportunity to work on Wolf's thick, pumped nipples, and I had to admit that I was anticipating seeing him struggling against his bondage as his tits were pierced and ringed with thick stainless steel rings signifying his total and permanent slavery.

Chapter 17

Rings

Wolf and I got dressed in jeans and tee shirts and just hung out for a while in the house. I read the paper while Wolf attended to his normal chores such as the dishes and a bit of light housekeeping. I suspected he was really curious about what I had planned for him, but he was well trained enough that he knew better than to ask. Wolf knew that he would find out what was on my mind when the time was right.

Finally, at about six in the evening the doorbell rang. I ordered Wolf to answer it. It was Joe, carrying a small satchel about the size of a doctor's bag. After greeting him, we headed downstairs to the dungeon. When we got there, I told Joe he could set the bag down on the small table in the corner.

I turned to Wolf who was standing in the middle of the dungeon. "Strip" was all I said.

He immediately began to take off his clothes, starting with his boots. When he was totally naked, I ordered him to kneel in front of the two of us as I took off my own shirt.

I looked down into his eyes and said; "Boy, tonight is going to be a special night. You proved to me last night just how extraordinary of a slave you are."

I knelt down in front of him on the floor as Joe stepped back to give us some privacy.

"You proved your loyalty last night when you admitted your feelings about being my top. I didn't have any problems with serving you, but you had to be true to yourself. That took guts, especially telling me in front of everyone else. For being so honest and truthful, as well as being just incredibly sexy," I grinned at him; "you are going to be rewarded today."

I wrapped my arms around his hot, hard muscled back and pulled my slave to my chest, kissing him deeply. His hands began to slide up and down by back, feeling my muscles as our tongues probed deeply into each others mouths. Finally I broke the kiss, pulling back from my lover.

Wolf whispered; "I love you so much, Sir. I love you more than anything else in the world, Master" as tears ran down his face.

I rose to my feet and told Wolf to stand as well. When he did, I was amused to see that his cock was already totally erect, in anticipation of whatever was coming up.

I led him over to the bondage table, which I rotated to its almost vertical position.

"On, boy" was all I needed to say.

Wolf immediately stepped onto the short lip on the bottom of the table and leaned back. I knelt down and began to use the leather straps to bind my willing slave to the table.

Within minutes he was secured by thick leather restraints on his ankles, knees, waist, biceps, wrists and throat. I had fastened him down with his arms just slightly spread out from his sides, so that when Joe pierced his nipples, the rings would be even from side to side. As usual, when Wolf was put into bondage, his cock got even harder than usual. The veins were bulging out the entire length of his thick, swollen shaft, and the head of his cock was almost purple.

I motioned for Joe to come and stand next to me in front of my helplessly bound slave boy. I wanted him to be able to help me tease and torment Wolf before we got down to the serious business of getting Wolf's nipple piercings done.

Wolf moaned with pleasure when I started to gently stroke my fingers over his solidly muscled torso. I loved the feel of his warm, silk-smooth skin. I traced every muscle on his chest and abs with my fingertips. Wolf closed his eyes, surrendering to the soft, sensual feel of my hands making gentle love to his body before his upcoming torture.

I reached up and started to stroke his thick, raven black hair, murmuring softly in his ear; "I want you to know I love you, boy. I love you like I've never loved anyone before in my life."

"Thank you, Sir." He whispered.

I bent down and began to suck on Wolf's hard right nipple. He gasped with pleasure, then groaned louder when Joe leaned in and took Wolf's left nipple into his mouth.

"Aw, fuck that feels good, Sir. I mean, Sirs. Damn!" Wolf moaned. He then began whimpering and whining in total ecstasy as we both started to nibble and chew on his hot, thick nipples.

I had originally planned on subjecting Wolf to a long session of brutal nipple torture before having his tits pierced, but this seemed to be so much more fun. Joe and I worked on Wolf's thick nipples with just our mouths for a good ten minutes or so, while we stroked and felt his helpless, bound body with our hands. During our nipple worship session, Joe stepped back and stripped off his shirt before leaning back in and starting to work on Wolf's nipple again.

Finally Joe and I stepped back from Wolf's body. Wolf gasped; "Thank you, Sirs" as we stood in front of him.

I turned to Joe and said; "Do you think he's ready?"

Joe grinned. "As ready as anyone I've ever seen. I know I'm ready to work on those tits. I've been waiting for this ever since the first time I saw Wolf with his shirt off."

He pulled the small table over in front of the bondage table, as I went to sit on my chair so I could watch Wolf getting his piercings.

Joe set out his equipment, which included several wrapped piercing needles, several sets of stainless steel rings, a bottle of antiseptic, and sterile rubber gloves. He put on the gloves and used a small towel to dry Wolf's chest. Wolf just lay his head back on the table, his eyes closed as he awaited the pain he was going to have to endure.

Joe turned to me and said; "Would you like to pick out which rings you want me to use?

I don't know what size you'd like."

I stepped up to the table, where we spent a couple of minutes holding various size rings against Wolf's chest to see which ones would look the best. When I had chosen the pair I thought looked the nicest, Joe put them into a small bowl, to which he then added some of the antiseptic to sterilize the rings. While the rings were sitting in the bowl, Joe cleaned Wolf's chest again with the towel, then wiped his nipples with the antiseptic.

Finally, Joe pulled one of the rings out of the bowl and set it on a sterile gauze pad. Pulling on a pair of surgical gloves, Joe picked up the slightly curved piercing needle and a pair of forceps. Grasping Wolf's left nipple with the forceps, he pulled it taut. Wolf moaned in a combination of pain and pleasure, mixed with no small amount of anticipation.

Joe placed the needle against Wolf's nipple. Taking a small block of Styrofoam and holding it on the other side of the hard tit, Joe began to push the thick, hollow piercing needle through Wolf's tit!

Wolf clenched his teeth, his thick biceps flexing and straining against the restraints, the rope-like veins standing out on his muscles, groaning loudly as the razor-sharp metal slid through his nipple, cutting out a core of flesh before coming out the other side. Holding the block of foam with the piercing needle stuck into it, Joe picked up the ring. He held one of the openings in the ring against the end of the needle and pushed the ring through the hole. I could see that Wolf was trying to keep from crying out at the excruciating pain ripping through his chest.

Finally the ring was fully pushed through Wolf's nipple. Joe carefully wiped the ring off with some antiseptic on a piece of gauze, then slipped the captive ball into place between the ends of the ring. It looked beautiful, the shiny metal contrasting with the golden bronze color of Wolf's chest and complimenting the reddish color of his brandings around each tit.

Joe quickly placed a pad of gauze over the nipple as the blood started to trickle down Wolf's chest. He expertly taped it into position before leaning in and softly asking Wolf; "Are you all right? Do you want me to do the other right away, or do you want to wait a few minutes?"

Wolf opened his now bloodshot eyes, grinned weakly, and said; "That felt great! Can you do the other one right now?"

I chuckled softly. "I told you he really loves pain. Maybe we ought to put a ring through the head of his cock while we're at it!"

Joe grinned. "I'd love to, but I didn't bring the right piercing needles or rings for doing a Prince Albert. Maybe next time."

Wolf moaned, apparently both turned on and scared at the thought of a sharp steel needle sliding through his cock, followed by a thick steel ring.

I shook my head. "No, I was just kidding. I don't think he needs a P.A. right now. I think his cock is too pretty just the way it is."

Joe smiled at me. "You're right. That's a hot dick. I hope you'll let me suck it when I'm done. Then, I hope you'll let me suck yours as well, Eric."

"Deal" I grinned at Joe.

He smiled before turning back to Wolf. Joe repeated the procedure, setting the other ring in Wolf's right nipple. This time, when the needle was coring through Wolf's tit, he started to growl deeply in his chest before finally shrieking in pain.

Wolf continued to howl and scream until Joe finished setting the ball in the ring. When Joe wiped the ring off and fastened the gauze to my slave's chest, Wolf moaned loudly before finally relaxing and laying his head back on the table. Throughout the entire procedure, however, his cock hadn't softened a bit, so I knew he was really turned on by the pain.

I stood over my boy and stroked his face with my fingertips. "Are you O.K. boy?"

He opened his eyes and smiled at me. "Oh God, yes, Sir. Thank you, Sir. Thank you for my rings, Sir. I've waited so long for them, Sir."

"Well, you've earned them, boy." I smiled back down into his eyes.

I turned to Joe. "It looks like he's ready for you to finish."

Joe grinned at me before turning to Wolf. He gently stroked his fingertips up and down the length of Wolf's throbbing, swollen cock. The head of his cock was almost purple, it was so engorged. The length of the shaft was covered with veins, pulsing with the beating of Wolf's heart.

Joe moaned; "Oh yeah" as he leaned in and slid the thick head of my bound slave's cock into his mouth.

Wolf moaned softly as Joe's head began bobbing back and forth as he slid the thick cock in and out of his mouth. It seemed as though the burning agony in his nipples was beginning to be replaced with growing feelings of pleasure as Joe expertly worked Wolf's cock with his mouth and tongue. Joe gently began to stroke his hands over the sweat-streaked, rippling skin of Wolf's washboard abs, tracing each of the thick, solid ridges of muscle with his fingertips before working his hands down to

Wolf's solidly sculpted thighs.

Wolf was moaning louder and louder as Joe's blowjob continued. Joe's hands explored Wolf's hard physique as he sucked the fat cock filling his mouth. Finally Wolf began to growl and grunt deeply in his throat as his orgasm neared.

Within another minute or so, he gasped and groaned; "Oh, Fuck" as he filled Joe's mouth with his hot load of cum.

Joe coughed a couple of times, but still managed to swallow every drop of the load in his mouth. Wolf moaned louder as Joe continued to flick his tongue across the now sensitive head of his cock. Finally Joe pulled his head back, allowing Wolf's now softening cock to slip out of his mouth.

"Damn, that was good. That's one fine cock that boy of yours has, Eric. And he shoots a real tasty load, too." Joe grinned.

I smiled as I slowly stripped off my boots and dropped my denims. "If you like his, I think you'll like mine, as well. Come on over here."

Joe's face split in a wide smile as he stripped off his boots and jeans as well. I sat back in my master's chair as Joe dropped to his knees in front of me. I leaned back as he slowly ran his tongue up and down the entire length of my nine inch cock.

Wolf moaned lustfully from the bondage table as he was forced to watch me get my blowjob from Joe. I reached out and began to stroke Joe's thick brown shoulder length hair as he started to suck my cock. He had a wonderfully hot mouth. I couldn't help but moan softly at the feel of the head of my cock hitting the back of Joe's throat, and at the feel of his short goatee brushing against my nuts. He gagged slightly before shifting his position and slipping my shaft all the way into his throat.

I groaned out loud when his hands began to explore my body, feeling every muscle under my gleaming skin.

I gasped "Oh yeah, man" when Joe began to gently twist my nipples and pull on my rings. He began to work his mouth up and down the length of my cock faster and faster. Finally I couldn't hold off any longer. I grasped his head tightly and started to thrust my cock in and out. Joe's hands began to work my tits harder and harder, until I threw back my head and pumped a huge load of my sperm deeply into Joe's hot, waiting mouth.

"Oh fuck, oh fuck. Swallow that load, man. Take it! Take that cum!" I growled while the sperm kept shooting out of my cock. Joe was moaning and swallowing my load, even while he was still twisting my horny nipples!

Finally I let his head go. Joe pulled back from my cock, gasping for air.

"Don't move, please!" He panted. Joe stood up between my legs and began to pump his own hard cock furiously with one hand while twisting his own tits with the other.

I loved watching the play of his muscles under his tanned, sweat streaked skin. The veins were standing out on his biceps, and the washboard of his abs was rippling with each labored breath. Joe stood in front of me, his eyes closed, his head thrown back, grunting and groaning with the effort, even while twisting and pulling harder and harder on his hot nipples.

"AW FUCK!" he howled when his cock erupted with a huge load of cum which sprayed all over my chest and abs. Some of his sperm even dripped onto my softening cock as well.

Joe growled; "God, you've got the hottest body I've ever seen, Eric. Wolf and Eddie are both hot, but you're a fucking wet dream muscle god! I want to make love to every one of those muscles!" just before he leaned in and began to lick up the cum and sweat that was coating my torso.

I could hear Wolf moaning with lust as he was forced to watch another man making love to my body. I knew he was always turned on watching someone else worshiping my muscles, but he also suffered enormous frustration when he was bound and couldn't do anything but watch.

When Joe had licked all the cum from my pecs and abs, I leaned back slightly in my chair and put my hands behind my head. Joe whispered; "Oh yeah" again before burying his face in my left armpit. I groaned at the feel of his tongue licking the sweat out of my open pit. I loved having a hot, horny man making love to my armpits. Wolf enjoyed trying to clean all the sweat out of my pits even when we were sitting in the sauna.

Joe worked his way across my chest, sucking on my hard nipples and playing with my rings with his teeth before repeating his armpit worship on my right side.

I was enjoying watching Wolf. He was staring at the hot scene in front of him, the sweat streaking down his body, his cock rock hard, even though he had cum just a few minutes before. He was literally whimpering with lust, since he was so turned on. I knew he was desperate to jack his cock while he watched Joe worship my muscles, but he couldn't, since he was so securely bound.

Finally Joe stood up in front of me. "God, you two are the hottest couple I've ever seen." He said, looking from Wolf to me. "I'd love to stay and keep on making love to the two of you, but I need to get home. H.J. is going to get home from work soon, and he's going to get a surprise. I'm probably going to have to spend the next couple of hours fucking him since you guys have me so hot!"

I grinned at him. "Come on back whenever you want. We can have a torture contest between your boy and mine or, if you'd like, I could just spend an hour or two fucking that hot ass of yours!"

Joe smiled. "You're on. We'll arrange a time to come over, and then we'll see what happens."

He packed up his equipment and dressed while I was releasing Wolf from his bondage. When Wolf was free, he knelt in front of Joe and I.

"I want to thank you both. This afternoon has been so special for me. Sir, thank you for arranging for me to finally get my rings! I've waited so long to have my nipples pierced. I promise that I will always remember what these rings signify. I am your slave, and I always will be your slave. Thank you, Sir."

At that, Wolf leaned down and kissed my feet. When he straightened back up, he turned, still on his knees, and faced Joe.

"Thank you, Master Joe for doing my piercings. I will take care of them, and honor them."

Wolf then kissed Joe's boots.

Joe smiled. "Those are about the nicest nipples I've ever done. It was my pleasure. I guess I'd better get going. I suppose you two are going to want to be alone for a while."

I grinned knowingly at Wolf. "My thoughts exactly. We'll see you around."

Once Joe had left, I gathered Wolf into my arms and just held his hot, hard, muscular body close to me. I could feel him shaking slightly. I suspected it wasn't from the pain, as Wolf had endured much more intense tortures for far longer, but that his shaking was probably from pure emotion.

My thoughts were confirmed seconds later when Wolf began to cry in my arms. I felt his tears begin to drop onto my chest as he sobbed.

"That's O.K. boy, let it out" I softly whispered in his ear.

Wolf cried in my arms for a good five minutes or so before he finally began to calm down. I just continued to hold his body against me as his breathing finally slowed down and began to even out.

Wolf lifted his head from my chest and gave me his familiar lopsided smile that I loved so much.

"Thank you, Sir. I hope you don't think I'm being silly or anything, but now I feel like my life is complete."

I smiled down into his eyes. "I don't think you're being silly at all. I remember how much I loved it when Mike gave me my rings, so I think I kinda know how you're feeling, boy."

The tears started to run down Wolf's face again. "It's not just the rings, Sir, although I understand what they represent. I really mean that I feel like my life is now complete. I finally have everything I could ever want in my life. I have the greatest lover and master a boy could ever hope for. I live in a beautiful home. I have great friends in the city. And, I feel like I have a purpose in life. To serve you, Sir. I mean, what more could anyone want?"

I could feel the tears start to well up in my eyes and run down my face as I actually started to choke up. I couldn't say a word. I just held my lover in my arms as we both began to softly cry. We held each other for another five minutes or so, not speaking, just holding each other naked in the middle of my dungeon.

Finally I felt like I had to say something.

"I feel the same way. I was really lost when my parents were killed in the plane crash. Mike may have saved me from myself, but then I lost him as well. Now I have you, boy. I don't know if I've ever told you this, but I feel that you have completed me, as well. Money and possessions are all well and good, but if you don't have anyone to share them with, well, all the expensive toys in the world are just so much clutter. I love you Carlos Greywolf, and I always will. I just hope I never lose you."

Wolf didn't respond for a few moments, then he lifted his head from where it was resting on my chest. His eyes twinkled with mischief as he said; "Well, in that case, I guess I'd better hang around for a while longer. How does the rest of my life sound to you, Sir?"

I grinned down into his smiling face.

"That sounds just fine, boy. But, if you're going to be a smart-ass, I just might have to start to torture you again, as soon as your nipples are healed."

"Yeah, yeah. Promises, promises!"

I feigned a shocked look as I gave Wolf a dope-slap on the back of his head.

"That just earned you about three or four more hours of some of the most painful tortures and punishments that I can dream up, boy." I growled at my handsome, grinning slave.

I actually was glad to see that his natural sense of humor was re-asserting itself.

We both started to chuckle and then laugh, both of us getting a relief from the serious feelings that we were working through. Wolf and I both would sometimes cry after a scene, or sometimes we would be consumed by helpless laughter. Either way, the emotional release felt great.

When we had finally calmed down, we headed back upstairs, carrying our clothes. I told Wolf to just relax for a while as I made the two of us a light dinner.

Later that night Wolf and I dressed in baggy sweats and t-shirts and sat on the couch in the living room watching the flames dancing in the fireplace. As we sat there, my arms wrapped around my lover's hard body, a feeling of real peace settled over me like a warm blanket. Wolf was leaning back against my chest with his head resting on my shoulder. I couldn't remember when I had ever felt such a sense of belonging. I gave a sigh of contentment when I realized that I had everything I could want in the world.

Wolf finally sat up and looked at me.

"A dollar for your thoughts, Sir."

"A dollar? I thought it was a penny."

He grinned. "Inflation. What can I say?"

I chuckled. "I was just thinking about what we need to plan on doing later this year after your nipples are healed. I think I mentioned that I need to go back east to Indy to check up on some business with my company. I thought that on the way there, we might make it into a road trip and do some sightseeing and get in some bicycle trips along the way. How would you like to go to Moab in Utah and ride the slick rock trails there? Or we could go to Glenwood canyon in Colorado and ride the bike trail along the highway. What do you think, boy? Come August, we might even try riding in the RAGBRAI in Iowa "

The RAGBRAI was a bike ride across the entire state of Iowa from Nebraska to Illinois.

Wolf grinned. "I'd love it, Sir. I've read about some of those places in the bicycling magazines, but I've never had the chance to go to any of them. It sounds great. Besides, I've always thought that you look so sexy in bike gear. Muscles and spandex, what a combination!"

Wolf and I both loved to ride our bikes. We had a selection of both road bikes and mountain bikes that we both rode extensively. I thought that Wolf was the sexiest man I had ever seen on a bike, especially when we rode stripped to the waist. He looked so hot with every muscle rippling under his golden bronze skin, gleaming with sweat, and his hair flowing down his back from under his bike helmet.

I laughed. "You aren't so bad in skin tight spandex either, stud. But first, you have to let those nipples of yours heal up so I can get used to torturing a pair of tits with rings in them. How about electricity running through your rings, boy, or imagine the feeling of your rings slowly getting hotter and hotter in your nipples from candle flames! I can't wait to watch you struggling and flexing those big muscles of yours. And, I really love to hear you screaming in pain as you're being tortured. How would you like that, boy?"

Wolf moaned softly. "I can hardly wait, Sir."

I grinned at him. "I thought that you'd say something like that."

With that, I leaned forward and kissed my lover. He moaned softly as I stroked my hand down the back of his head, feeling his thick, luxuriant mane of hair flowing down across his shoulders. I felt his hands begin to run up and down my back. Wolf's tongue began to probe the inside of my mouth.

We stood up together as I slowly slid my hands down his thick back muscles, lower and lower, until I was cupping the twin globes of my slave boy lover's ass. Wolf moaned into my mouth as I began to gently knead the hard muscles of his butt.

"Let's go upstairs, boy" I said as I broke our kiss.

We slowly climbed the stairs to the second floor and walked into my bedroom. I walked over to the bay windows that overlooked the slope of the wooded hills running down towards Sausalito and the expanse of San Francisco bay, with the lights of the city twinkling in the distance. Opening the French doors leading onto the balcony outside, we stepped out.

I wrapped my arms around Wolf again as we leaned against the balcony railing and took in the view.

"It's beautiful, Sir." Wolf murmured. "I've always loved this view. It looks like the whole city is waiting for us."

"More than the city, boy" I said. "The whole world is waiting for us. Once you get healed up, how about you and me go on out into that world and see what's out there? We can plan our road trip back east, and then we'll see where else we want to go. We could go to Alaska. Or, how about Australia? Anywhere you want to go, we can go."

Wolf turned to me, his eyes brimming with tears.

"Wherever we go, it'll be fine with me, just as long as I'm with you, Sir. Alaska, Australia, hell, we could even go to a great sounding camping outing for gays in rural Kentucky that I heard about on the Internet. When I'm with you, Sir, I'm happy, no matter where we are."

We stood silently for a while watching the lights of the city. As we stood there, I thought about this man and all that he meant to me. I knew now that I couldn't see living my life without him by my side. Not only was the world waiting for us, but the future was waiting, as well. He had evolved from merely a sexy boy in a bar that I wanted to get into my dungeon into a major part of my life, and my true soul mate.

"I think we need to go inside now, boy. I'm starting to get chilly."

When we stepped back inside, Wolf turned to me, his familiar lopsided grin on his face.

"Feeling a bit cold, Sir?" He grinned. "I think I know the way to warm you up."

He led me over to my bed and dropped to his knees in front of me.

"I love you, Eric Kurtz, and I always will. I love you as my lover, my master, and my friend." He whispered as a single tear ran down his cheek.

Wolf, my lover, my slave, and my friend, bent down and began to kiss my feet.

About the Author

Alan Weyant

Alan Weyant grew up on the west coast of Florida. After graduating from high school, he served stints in both the U.S. Merchant Marine, and the U.S. Navy.

He lived in the Tampa Bay area before relocating to his current home, on 5 rural acres of wooded riverfront property in southern Kentucky, next door to his lover's 14 acres. Alan has been active in both the leather community, as a lifetime associate member of The Adventurers leather club of Florida, and in the bear community, as a former member of The Growlers of Tampa Bay.

He is an over-the-road long distance truck driver. His interests include weightlifting, reading science fiction, plus he is an avid bicyclist, carrying his bike with him in his truck, allowing him to ride wherever he finds himself in the country.

Alan Weyant is also the author of *The Wolf Chronicles*.

Available at TheNazcaPlainsCorp.com, Amazon.com, or check your local bookstore.